DMITRY DORNICHEV

THE COMING OF GOD OF DEATH

BOOK THREE

MAGIC DOME BOOKS

ALSO BY DMITRY DORNICHEV:

A Shelter in Spacetime
A LitRPG Apocalypse Series:

A Potato A Day Keeps Monsters Away
Berlin, Here I Come!
Fantastic Freaks and Where to Hire Them
Between Two Worlds
Sleep is for Chumps!
War of the Smartasses
The Rocky Road to Success
Father of Nations
Globalization

The Village
A LitRPG Progression Fantasy Series
(with Alexey Kovtunov):

Rabbits: Keep Out!
Goblins: Keep Out!
Orcs: Keep Out!
Lizardfolk: Keep Out!
Sentinels: Keep Out!

We Are Legion
A RealRPG Action Adventure Series
(with Evgeny Fox):

Books 1-4

TABLE OF CONTENTS:

CHAPTER 1

The Academy
Morning
Gauss and the sisters

THE MORNING HAD BEEN ROUGH and deeply embarrassing for the girls. They trailed behind me, their faces burning with shame. As for me, I strutted forward proudly, my massive belly jutting out, large enough to hold a small piglet, as I headed toward my building.

People openly stared. One girl got so distracted that she tripped and fell. For the record, I wasn't wearing a jacket or a proper shirt — just an oversized, stretched-out sweater. With a belly like mine, nothing else fit.

That said, my stomach had shrunk significantly overnight. The parasite had done its job well, though even it had limits — or so it claimed.

"Pocket patriarch, are you pregnant? Is it a boy or a girl?" came a mocking laugh. I spotted my classmate, Killian Deming, a vile grin on his face.

"A cake," I said with a satisfied smile, patting my stomach. "And I have no regrets."

Killian froze, no doubt trying to imagine just how much cake it would take to grow a belly like mine in a single day. I wasn't about to ruin his psyche — or anyone else's — so I kept walking. People continued to gawk. Even the professors stopped whatever they were doing just to stare. I was practically a star.

"Alex? How... how is this possible?" Basel stood in the corridor of my classroom building, staring at me in disbelief.

"It was delicious," I replied, brushing past him.

Basel trailed behind me, though it took him a moment to recover from his shock. My classmates reacted much the same way, and I faced a new issue: with a belly this size, I couldn't sprawl across my desk for a nap.

"Well, well! What an honor — you're actually awake in my class, Mr. Scully!" exclaimed the teacher as he entered the room.

"Yes, and today I'll answer all your questions," I said with a smile, though my tone carried a subtle threat.

"Is that so? Then come to the board and draw the Gol rune for us."

That was a mistake. I rose slowly and made my way to the board at a snail's pace. With a belly like this, speed wasn't an option. The teacher's eyes practically popped out of his head.

Once at the board, I began drawing the rune painfully slowly. I explained each line, each curve, and every single symbol in exhaustive detail. I even threw in plenty of irrelevant commentary, sharing the musings of various rune masters and my own random thoughts.

"Enough! Sit down. Good job. You get an A," the teacher growled through clenched teeth. He looked at the clock — one-third of the lesson had already passed. Forced to speed up, he struggled to keep up with his syllabus.

The second lesson played out similarly. Another teacher marveled at my wakefulness but didn't dare call on me or ask a question. I had to seize the opportunity myself to showcase how brilliant (and insufferable) I was.

Thus, the first half of the day dragged on. Hopefully, this would teach them not to penalize me for napping in class.

At lunch, our team gathered in the cafeteria as usual. Even though I wasn't hungry, I still had to join them — our next practical assignment was coming up soon.

"I want that too," Anna said as she arrived, seeing me. The rest of us were already seated.

"What do you mean?" Polina asked, confused.

"Whatever he ate — since he still hasn't gotten rid of that belly," Anna replied, gesturing at me.

"Unfortunately, we're both too weak for that," I said, shaking my head. "I barely survived yesterday, and next time, I might not be so lucky."

"What are you even talking about?" Polina blinked in confusion.

"I get it," Anna said as she sat beside me.

"What do you mean, you get it? What's there to get? Explain!" Polina demanded, looking utterly lost.

"Only those destined to be together by fate can understand," Anna declared solemnly. She began stroking my belly. "So smooth and firm! I bet my belly will be like this when I'm pregnant."

Polina looked like she was about to faint. Basel had to rush off and grab her a cold soda, which quickly revived her. We then turned to discussing our next assignment.

The entire team would use teleportation to reach the site, paying for it in cash. The Academy would handle any loot we recovered, and we'd just received points for clearing the previous gate.

"I can't bring even half my equipment," Anna sighed.

"Well, they did gear you up like you were heading to war," Basel laughed.

"Want me to share my points?" I offered. All three of them stared at me in surprise. "What? I don't need anything but my sword."

The truth was, I'd give all my points to my sisters, assuming I had enough. I also needed to check out the pile of artifacts I'd collected last week.

"No, thanks. I'm sure I have plenty of gear I don't actually need. I'll sort it out with my dad,"

Anna replied, smiling.

"By the way," Basel began, "Gloria has another concert tomorrow. How about we go after the Academy? My treat."

"I liked her singing. I'm in," I said. Why not? Her music was pleasant enough.

Polina, naturally, would go wherever Basel went, and Anna would stick to me like glue. She wasn't a fan of that kind of music, but the thought of spending even a day apart from me was unthinkable. It didn't bother me anymore, maybe I'd just gotten used to it.

In any case, everyone agreed. After discussing a few more details, they dug into their meals while I couldn't eat anything. Watching them eat was pure torture.

Then a senior student approached our table. He was of average height, slightly thin, with dark hair and bags under his eyes.

"Sorry to interrupt, but could we talk?" He was looking at me. Since I wasn't eating anyway, I figured, why not?

"Take a seat," I said, gesturing to the table. It was built for four, so he pulled up a chair and joined us.

"I won't waste your time. My family needs help with a curse," he said, his calm demeanor cracking slightly at the word "curse."

"How strong?"

"The church couldn't handle it. They said we'd need priests from the capital, but there's a five-year waitlist," he replied, grimacing. It was clear how overworked the church was; the sheer number of unclean entities was staggering.

"After classes today then."

"Wait, today? Seriously? That's amazing!"

The guy, whose name turned out to be Anton, quickly explained where we needed to go. I declined his offer to give us a ride. Naturally, Anna volunteered to come with me. And I'd collected some information about the guy and his family.

They were middle-class and had a decent business. The Emperor had honored them with various rewards for their military achievements, but it wasn't anything out of the ordinary. What was important — it didn't look like they were bought to lure and kill me.

By the end of the school day, I had thoroughly annoyed my classmates while gradually shrinking my belly — a sight that continued to baffle them. For most people, it was unnatural, but not everyone had a parasite consuming them from the inside.

When the day was over, the sisters went home, and Anna and I waited for our reinforced convoy.

"You look good," I said to the kikimora when she and Zhanna showed up. She wore a tailored black suit that fit her perfectly and large black sunglasses. Her hair had been cut halfway, which suited her surprisingly well.

"Yes, Kiki is a real beauty," Zhanna chimed in. She had clearly enjoyed dressing up my guardian.

"Kiki?" I raised an eyebrow at my assistant.

"Well, calling me Kikimora doesn't seem fitting..."

"Fair enough," I nodded. "Kiki it is, unless you want to pick a different name."

"Kiki suits me fine, Master," she replied. Her gaze briefly shifted to Anna. To Zhanna, it looked like she was sizing her up, but in reality, she was eyeing the poltergeist nearby. She was licking her lips at the same time, which startled the poltergeist badly.

We soon set off. The kikimora would stay behind to guard Zhanna, as would the raven. If needed, the bird could come to my aid.

The Vecher estate was a large, well-guarded property. However, the greenery around it was withered and rotting, clearly drained by the curse. The houseplants were dried-out husks, and even the grand tree in the main hall looked like it had been attacked by the curse.

It seemed the curse had really done a number on the estate, because everything outside it was normal. The leaves had turned yellow because it was autumn, the grass remained green, and it even looked like it intended to keep growing through the winter, thanks to the abundance of mana in the air.

Anna and I got out of our cars and walked to the porch, where Anton was already waiting for us.

"Thanks for coming." Relief flickered on his face, but his reaction was sluggish, almost lifeless. Honestly, it looked like Anton might collapse and fall asleep on the spot. And I couldn't blame him — I had barely slept myself that day.

"As you might've noticed," he began, "this curse is draining the life force out of everything living. And no, it's not just about the house — it's on the entire family." He sighed as he led us inside.

The servants looked exhausted, and every indoor plant had long since withered, leaving only dry, brittle stems in their pots. Even the once-lush tree in the center of the spacious hall had withered into something grotesque, resembling the twisted, malicious vegetation found in cursed lands.

"I can see that. This is quite the curse you've got here..." I muttered. "I won't ask how you managed to get yourselves into this mess. Just bring me two chairs, and I'll get started."

"Chairs? That's it? What about holy water? We've got plenty. Salt? Silver dust?"

"All of that's useless against a curse — it's an artificial magical entity." I shook my head and looked up at the ceiling. It was covered in a writhing black mass, resembling thousands of tangled snakes. Naturally, only Anna and I could see it.

"What about us? The curse is tied to our family, isn't it? Maybe we need to be submerged in holy water? I can gather everyone..."

I groaned and stepped closer to him, placing my palm over his left eye. For good measure, I expelled a lurking poltergeist from the mansion — it had been subtle, but I didn't want it drawing attention.

"Here's your curse," I said dryly. "It's not inside you — it's just following you around." With a small surge of divine energy, I forced Anton to see what we saw. He fell backward, landing hard and turning ghostly pale as his gaze locked on the writhing mass on the ceiling. "Now, get me two chairs and make sure no one comes in here unless they want the curse to kill them. It will defend itself."

"U-understood!"

Anton bolted, and soon the servants returned with two comfortable chairs before disappearing from sight. Just before I began, I noticed several security cameras positioned around the room.

Of course, there had to be cameras. We had some, too, back at our place. But cameras didn't bother me — I was about to light this place up.

Taking Anna's hand, I asked her to close her eyes. Raising my other hand, I summoned an intense, brilliant light that flooded the room.

And no, I wasn't distracted by hormones or anything trivial. I had been working on myself — meditating to calm my body and optimize its physical processes. "Calming Meditation" was an underrated technique, and I was surprised that modern mages rarely practiced it.

It steadied my mind, enhanced my body, and left me in peak condition — perfect for channeling my magic at full power. I even infused a touch of DE to add a little extra effect.

THE COMING OF GOD OF DEATH

*   *   *

The Estate's panic room
At the same time
The entire Vecher family

"Damn it!" cursed the Vecher patriarch, sitting in front of a screen. His entire family hissed and murmured in frustration as the bright light blazed from the monitors. But then, the light began to dim, and it was all because of...

"What is that?! It's horrifying!" cried Anton's mother, a frail and pale woman with thinning hair.

"That's it! I've seen it before! The curse!" Anton shouted, pointing at the screen.

Black, elongated shapes like enormous worms descended from the ceiling and slithered toward the couple in the center of the hall. Yet they couldn't get close, instead attempting to encase them in a cocoon-like structure.

"It won't kill them, right? Winters would destroy us if it did," the patriarch said in horror, watching the scene unfold.

Anna and Alex were no longer visible beneath the writhing mass, and the cocoon grew larger and larger. Soon, even the tree in the hall, near where they sat, was engulfed by the creatures.

"I think he knows what he's doing. He can see it all clearly," Anton tried to reassure his father and the rest of the family, his faith in Scully unshaken.

"The cameras! Check the external cameras!" someone shouted. It was Anton's older sister. The family scrambled to another monitor, and there...

"My God..."

The entire courtyard was crawling with the monstrous creatures. The guards, now discovering the abominations coiled around them, tried desperately to shake them off, but their efforts were futile. The creatures weren't physical.

Still, they eventually released the guards on their own, slithering toward the mansion instead. They passed through walls and doors with ease. Gunfire, predictably, had no effect. Neither did magic.

Meanwhile, in the hall, the cocoon of writhing entities had grown so massive that it occupied half the room. And it kept growing and growing...

* * *

Somewhere
Anna and Gauss

I stood on scorched black ground, surrounded by fountains of lava and bright stars overhead. Despite the chaos, it was undeniably beautiful.

"Alex..." Anna tugged at my arm, her voice uncertain. She looked oddly small and fragile, which was unusual for her. She was dressed in a rocker T-shirt and short leather shorts, holding a broken piece of a guitar in her hand.

"The curse can't harm us physically," I explained with a calm smile, noticing the blush spreading across her cheeks. It seemed she was awestruck by my true form.

Since we were here as our souls, it made sense that I appeared as Gauss, not Alexander. Our poltergeist flitted around us, still a shapeless black blot. It too had once been just an ordinary curse.

"So, we have to defeat the curse with our souls?" Anna asked, examining her "weapon." She swung the broken guitar experimentally, and the poltergeist fused with it, strengthening it.

"Yes. And I suspect it will try to exploit our fears," I said. Anna's nightmares were sure to manifest, but I wouldn't have brought her here if I wasn't confident she could handle it. Still...

"Perfect," she murmured, her face twisting into a maniacal grin. It was unsettling, even to me. That crazed smile...

Anna waited eagerly for the monsters to appear. She didn't have to wait long. Small green creatures with stubby legs and massive jaws, each about three feet tall, began crawling out of the lava, surrounding us.

Soul injuries are fatal, so we needed to be cautious. Or at least, that was the plan.

"Dieeee!" Anna screamed, charging at the horde. Her guitar suddenly became whole, only to shatter again moments later as she smashed it against the skull of one of the creatures.

The monster's head caved in, spilling blood, bones, and brains onto the ground. That guitar packed a punch.

Anna laughed — a wild, unhinged sound that made the green creatures hesitate. A moment later, her guitar crushed another skull, then re-formed in her hands.

Meanwhile, I covered her, wielding a black spear to pierce the monsters. They were slow, and as long as I avoided being surrounded, they posed little threat, but their numbers kept growing.

"You'll die… You'll die here… They'll catch you, torment you, and devour you…" a voice whispered from nowhere.

"Gauss, they want to torment you!" Anna cackled, but her joke almost cost her dearly. One of the creatures leapt high into the air toward her, but I managed to yank her back just in time.

"They can jump?! You filthy—" she screamed, unleashing a torrent of curses as she charged back into the fray. Her guitar swung in a wide arc, knocking down five creatures at once. Another swing from above cracked open a skull.

I stayed close, pulling her back whenever the monsters got too close, and impaled several with my spear.

"You're too jumpy!" I shouted as twenty of the creatures leapt at me simultaneously. A large, spiked shield appeared in my hand, and they slammed against it, forcing me back several feet. Embarrassing. I'd need to upgrade my altar to fix this.

My spear continued cutting through the horde, but the onslaught didn't stop. Anna needed constant rescuing, but eventually, the creatures stopped coming. This was only the beginning. A warm-up.

"So... beautiful... I want her..." came a rasping voice.

A monstrous figure emerged from the lava, its grotesque, shapeless head dominated by a horrific gaping maw. It stood over six feet tall, brandishing a massive club. Anna, was already running toward it, laughing madly.

The creature swung its club, but Anna dodged effortlessly and smashed her guitar into its groin, which was barely protected by a tattered rag. The monster's eyes bulged comically before it crumpled to its knees. A swift kick from Anna sent it tumbling back into the lava.

We'd found their weak spot. But I couldn't avoid the club at every attack, and my shield absorbed the blows as we dispatched the remaining monsters.

The larger creatures were slower to emerge from the lava, but their numbers were far fewer. Knowing how to kill them made the battle manageable, and we cut through a hundred of them without much trouble.

"You'll die... This is only the beginning..." the curse's voice threatened once more. And it wasn't lying. Suddenly, the sky began raining monsters — hundreds of them, in all shapes and sizes, ready to attack.

Anna's guitar, infused with the poltergeist, dissolved into black smoke and reformed as monstrous creatures identical to those surrounding us, but darker.

"Raaaargh!" the black monsters roared, while Anna's eyes burned with fiery determination.

"Make them suffer!" she commanded. Her creatures — two dozen in all — charged at the larger horde.

They wouldn't last long, but that didn't matter. I raised my arms, summoning my own forces.

"My souls! I call upon you to atone for your sins and find peace!"

Ghostly figures began materializing around me. Anna watched them curiously, unsure of their purpose, until I infused them with divine energy. The specters transformed instantly, donning black armor and wielding massive two-handed swords. Even I was clad in the same armor now.

"Kill!" I ordered. My hundred and fifty spectral knights charged into battle, Anna joining them gleefully. Her madness only grew as she found herself in black armor too.

A monstrous, twenty-foot-tall beast roared as it lumbered toward us, but Anna flanked it, and with a horrifying scream, stabbed her sword into its most vulnerable spot. The beast collapsed, and Anna finished it off with a single strike.

"Go for the kill! Give them a reckoning!" she shouted, laughing maniacally.

Our army fought relentlessly under divine protection, and I carved through enemies with single, devastating strikes. Yet, no matter how many we killed, more appeared.

"Why... why am I feeling happiness? This is

wrong... wrong..." the curse's voice cried out, trembling with disbelief.

"We've only just begun!" Anna yelled, leaping toward three of her poltergeist's creatures to give them some truly disturbing orders. Whatever she said was so horrifying that even I — and my spectral knights — had to look away.

Anna was unleashing her full fury, and I didn't mind. This was why I'd brought her here: to exorcise her demons and leave her nightmares behind.

"How... why... impossible..." the curse stammered, its forces weakening as we pressed on.

The poltergeist's army grew thirty creatures strong. It seemed the weaker the curse became, the more powerful Anna's poltergeist grew.

"Why aren't you afraid? This can't be..."

"It's time," I said with a grin, raising my hands toward the sky. "Come down here and face us yourself!"

Black tendrils shot from my palms, piercing the heavens and dragging down an enormous, writhing black worm.

As the creature hit the ground, the remaining monsters vanished — save for the ones Anna and her poltergeist had captured.

"Well, hello there," I said, crouching in front of the worm. It was barely two feet long now, squirming and squealing helplessly. I grabbed it with both hands and tore it apart, absorbing its essence.

The power surged through me — hundreds, then thousands of units of divine energy. My body pulsed with strength as the curse was reduced to nothing more than nourishment.

When it was over, darkness fell, and the next moment, Anna and I were back at the tree where we'd started.

"Ugh... and I was just getting into it," she muttered, looking at me. If I were an ordinary man, I might have recoiled in terror.

But with the cameras still watching, I had no time to waste. Acting decisively, I leaned in and kissed her. Her face shifted from wild madness to pure shock and confusion. Then she tried to use tongue. What the hell?! That's gross! Unsanitary! And how was she so strong?! "Damn it, poltergeist — stop helping her!"

CHAPTER 2

"I DON'T KNOW HOW to thank you," The patriarch of the Vecher family looked utterly drained, but it was as if he had found a second wind.

"Money," I grumbled, still in a foul mood. Anna, meanwhile, was practically glowing with joy.

"It was incredibly difficult. I lost count of how many times we were on the brink of death," Anna added.

"I didn't know the Winters were skilled at banishing curses," the patriarch said, his gaze lingering on her.

"I think you're well aware of our rich history with curses," she replied with a sweet smile that sent chills down the spines of everyone nearby.

"Yes... I do seem to recall something like that."

"In six more months, that entity would've become a poltergeist of such strength that much of the city would have been devastated. Not that you'd have lived to see it," I said, fixing him with a sharp look. "One more thing. Does the phrase, 'Suffer, Vecher, suffer as I did!' mean anything to you?"

The patriarch's face contorted in anger, his veins bulging with barely restrained fury.

"I see that it does. If necessary, I can draft an official report documenting this evidence."

"I'd appreciate that," he hissed through gritted teeth.

"My assistant will bring it to you this evening. You can also finalize the payment details with her. As for us, we need some rest," I said, shaking my head and groaning as I grabbed the dazed Anna by the hand and led her outside. I paused briefly. "I recommend eating plenty of high-ranked monster meat and using a mana diffuser. It'll speed up your recovery."

With that, we left.

At the gate, Zhanna and Kiki were waiting with the Winters combat convoy, who looked rather shell-shocked. Then again, a lot of people were in shock today. It's not every day you witness a curse, especially one so strong. And realizing it's been feeding on you the entire time, while you were powerless to stop it? That's truly terrifying.

Anna headed home, while I returned to my own place. On the way, I gave Zhanna instructions: the payment I wanted, as well as a request to assess the family's assets. Who knows? Maybe they didn't have enough liquid funds. I also decided to allocate a portion of the reward to Anna — her contribution had been significant.

Now for the bad news... Almost half of my summoned ghosts had redeemed themselves during the battle and passed on, significantly reducing my intake of divine energy.

But it didn't matter anymore. Despite the massive expenditures, my balance had reached 1,700 units. That meant I could finally upgrade my altar!

When I got home, instead of sitting down for dinner, I went straight to the basement where my altar was located. The sisters had tried to follow me, and judging by the subtle signs, they'd even attempted to sneak into the basement a few times. Those curious pests were probably starting to suspect something. To throw them off, I grabbed a few books, pretending I wanted some quiet reading time. If they didn't believe me, so be it.

Soon, I was seated in front of my altar. My belly had returned to normal, or rather, it was completely gone, replaced by a smooth, toned stomach. I began releasing my energy, channeling it into the altar. I noticed the energy flowed much more efficiently now. Maybe it was due to my sixth rank, or perhaps my improved physical condition. Likely both.

But why was it drawing so much energy? My altar wasn't complete before, which is why it only measured two inches... I wondered if I had enough energy for this, but hoped that I did.

I continued, and the obelisk in the center of the altar began to grow. Two inches... three...

three and a half... It kept rising. The first level was finally complete, and warmth spread through my body, signaling that I'd grown slightly stronger. But this was just the beginning.

Now the surrounding towers began to shift, moving slightly apart to make room for a ninth tower that appeared.

The towers stretched up to six inches, while the obelisk... Oh, now this was impressive! It reached eight inches. Much better than the pathetic two inches it started with. I thought at this rate, the third level might hit twelve inches or even sixteen! With an altar like this, I could hold my own among young goddesses.

"What... why..." came a weak groan from the parasite. It seemed the surge in my strength was too much for it to handle. I infused it with a few units of divine energy, and it sighed in relief. "Thanks..."

"Hang in there. I'll try to ascend in rank as quickly as I can."

Energy balance: 171
Souls repository: 90/390
Places in hell: 18/39
Number of guards: 2/4

Gains
Believers: 6,3
Souls: 9
Hell: 9
Altars: 40

Expenditure
Guards: -12
Servants: -29,1
Seals: -4
Fortress: -10

Total: 9,2

I needed to head into the gates for more divine energy immediately, or I might not survive a confrontation with a powerful enemy... But dinner... "Wait, I've got an idea! Ha, this is brilliant!"

* * *

Sometime later
Somewhere outside the city
Near the gates that had merged with a massive boulder, transforming into a dungeon
Gauss surrounded by a group of bewildered soldiers.

"Sir, this is an S-rank dungeon. Are you sure you want to go in there alone — with them? And... sausage?" The SCU officer looked at me as though I were a dwarf painting a dragon's egg while singing folk songs.

What could I say? I hadn't eaten dinner. I carried a backpack full of food on my back, a sword at my waist, and two sausages in hand. One was Polish-style, and the other wasn't sausage at all — just a thick cut of ham. Following me were Zhanna and my kikimora, armed with a B-rank spear and shield.

Why bring Zhanna? Because someone would need to clean up the kikimora after the fight — fix her makeup, tidy her hair, and so on. Oh, and I had the raven with me. The bird was napping on my backpack for now, though that wouldn't last long.

"This sausage is delicious. I just didn't get to eat dinner. Is that a problem?" I asked the soldier, puzzled.

"No... but the women—"

"They'll be fine." I signed the paperwork, ignored his grumbling, and stepped through the gates. The women followed close behind.

We found ourselves in a mountain ravine. Great. More mountains.

"The enemy is lying in ambush," the kikimora announced immediately, sniffing the air. At the same time, she began undressing, carefully folding her clothes as Zhanna assisted her — no point in ruining the outfit during a fight.

"Another cow," grumbled the raven, who had woken up on my backpack. He glanced at the kikimora's C-cup — still in a bra — then turned away, trying to go back to sleep. That didn't last long.

I grabbed the bird by the leg and yanked it toward me.

"Abuse! Caw! Injustice! Caw!"

"Were you about to sleep?" I asked.

"Maybe... Caw."

"Go scout. There's an ambush up ahead." I tossed it into the air, and it flapped its wings, reluctantly taking off.

"This is an S-rank dungeon! What if they kill me?!"

"Then you'll become a zombie raven," I said with a shrug, flashing a grin. "Or return to the underworld."

"Caw!"

The bird took off immediately, and I resumed eating as the kikimora finished undressing. She was ready for the bloodbath.

Our enemies were monstrous gorilla-like creatures. They were slightly less intelligent than goblins but knew how to use simple weapons and ambush tactics. The kikimora found this out firsthand almost immediately.

We had barely walked 300 feet into the ravine when twenty of the gray, gorilla-like monsters attacked her. Each was about six feet tall, with powerful arms, short legs, and sturdy bodies topped with menacing faces. They threw stones at my guardian, choosing a spot for their ambush where climbing the cliffs was nearly impossible.

But not for the kikimora. Extending her claws, she climbed with ease, while the raven above called out, "Caw!" A moment later, fireballs struck the gorillas' backs. Unfortunately, the creatures had strong barriers.

"Ug-oo!" one of the gorillas bellowed as stones were hurled at the raven. The projectiles came so fast that the bird barely managed to dodge, using magic to aid itself.

Bad move. The kikimora reached the top, and the first gorilla didn't even have time to react before she tore into it, claws ripping at its barrier with relentless ferocity. I fed her energy to make breaking the barrier easier, and soon the creature collapsed, lifeless. Then it stood up again.

With the altar's second level, I'd learned to re-animate puppets through my guardians. The gorilla puppet immediately turned on its former comrades, and chaos broke out.

While the gorillas had barriers, my puppet felt no pain. Not long after, the raven swooped down, dropping a spear into the hands of the most intact puppet. Things went much smoother after that.

Too bad the bird couldn't carry the shield. It claimed it couldn't even carry the spear — but it managed, didn't it? Soon, my puppets cleared out the left side of the ravine and charged the right.

Afterward, we took a break. The kikimora needed to recover from her wounds. She had taken a lot of hits, mostly from thrown stones. While she rested, I practiced magic on Zhanna and absorbed crystals to increase my rank.

We resumed the cleanup shortly after, spending nearly an hour navigating ambush after ambush. No wonder no one had cleared this shard in three attempts. It was easy to see why it had developed into a dungeon — few wanted to risk their lives here, and stronger adventurers didn't want to waste time on a "measly S-rank."

The ravine, however, was just the appetizer.

The main course? A gorilla settlement. The creatures lived in mountain caves, making the entire mountainside look like a giant anthill. I'll spare you the details — there weren't any stronger gorillas, though that would've made sense. There were just a lot of them.

At this point, I could control ten puppets, though with full concentration, I could stretch that to fifteen. Finding a cozy cave with a fire and some animal pelts, I settled in with Zhanna. One puppet stood guard while the others continued fighting.

When necessary, I released damaged puppets, and the kikimora raised new ones. That's how we cleared the settlement and eventually reached the gorilla boss.

I had to intervene, though. The boss was too strong and might have killed the kikimora. How would I explain to the SCU that three of us went in but only two came out, only for the kikimora to show up alive during another shard cleanup?

In the end, I didn't bother guessing the god's name. After destroying the core, I felt a wave of pure mana flood my body. I also heard the parasite's satisfied groan — it had siphoned off a portion of the mana my body couldn't absorb. Was that portion big or small? Hard to say, but he seemed a little too happy about it.

The artifact I received was a long, elegant elven bow. I had no idea what was the connection between mountain gorillas and forest elves. Maybe one of the elven gods had an unusual hobby. Either way, there was no way I'd guess the god's name.

Tarey'El's Bow
Rank: _S_
Description: The bow of the renowned elven hunter Tarey'El, famed for slaying countless powerful monsters and enemies of the tribe. When infused with mana, it can conjure both a quiver and arrows — standard or enchanted. The use of crystals is highly recommended.

"Not bad. I could sell it to the elves. Though they probably have something better. Maybe I'll give it to my zombies instead."

All in all, I was satisfied. Despite the expenses, I had earned nine hundred units of divine energy in a single run! It had taken a lot of time, though — it was probably nighttime already. Tomorrow, I'd catch up on sleep... during class, of course.

I had forty S-rank crystals in my pocket, along with a few E-rank ones I hadn't finished absorbing. Zhanna practically glowed from all the light magic I'd infused into her — she looked like she might turn into a firefly at any moment.

"Master, I found a small gold vein," the kikimora announced, holding up a chunk of gold ore.

"That's fantastic news! Too bad I don't have my own miners. Half of it will go to the SCU for extraction and sale. Ugh..."

My mood plummeted, so once everyone gathered, we headed for the exit. My appearance puzzled everyone waiting for us — I didn't have a scratch on me, and neither did my assistants. I also held a bow in my hand.

"There's gold ore in there," I said, further confusing the SCU officer who rushed up to us. I handed him a chunk of ore weighing about two pounds.

That's when the real circus began. Suddenly, anything could ask for was given to us — drinks, snacks, and even a place to relax while we signed over the mining rights to the SCU. As I mentioned earlier, they'd take half the profits.

We didn't get home until late at night, but it was worth it. Afterward, I slept deeply, which seamlessly turned into napping on my desk at school. By lunchtime, I had only just managed to catch up on sleep. Even then, my eyes were slits, threatening to close entirely and drag me back into the realm of dreams.

What happened after that was a blur, but now I was on the fifteenth floor of the city's main hotel — the tallest building in the entire east! It had a whopping sixteen floors. In the west, buildings reached the heavens, but not here. The higher the structure, the more likely it was to attract sky-dwelling monsters.

We were in the luxurious restaurant's lobby, waiting for something.

"Alex? Are you okay? You look lost," Polina asked, studying me.

"No, I'm fine," I said, shaking my head. I wasn't about to admit I'd only just woken up.

Looking around quickly, I saw Anna standing off to the side, chatting with some guy. I wondered if I should curse him. Then decided against it — he hadn't done anything serious enough... Wait, why was I even thinking this?

"And here comes Basel!" Polina interrupted my thoughts, drawing my attention to the big guy entering with a tall, slender woman wearing a name tag that read "Inna, Manager."

"Sorry for the wait," she said with a smile. "The issue has been resolved. Please allow me to escort you to your table."

Anna joined us then, waving to the guy she'd been talking to as he headed toward the elevator. "Call me tonight! I want to hear how grandma's doing!" she said cheerfully.

"Who was that?" I asked.

"I told you — my cousin..." She trailed off, a sly grin spreading across her face. "Wait, are you jealous?"

"No. Just curious. Polina's the jealous one," I said, noticing Polina shooting daggers at Inna-the manager, who was practically glued to Basel.

"She shouldn't be jealous — she should hit that painted hussy with a stick!"

Anna fixed her gaze on Polina, and I noticed the poltergeist heading for the manager. Thankfully, it didn't harm her. All it did was undo her bra under her white blouse with the plunging neckline.

Flustered, Inna asked a waitress to take us to our table and excused herself. Polina sighed in relief, and we soon reached a table by a large, reinforced window.

From there, you could see almost the entire city. I spotted my factory — intact, with no fires, smoke, or explosions. Everything was quiet and peaceful. Perfect.

Honestly, I had expected trouble. Maybe another Forester would challenge me to a duel or something worse. But no, we ate peacefully, chatting about trivial nonsense.

"Is it true that monsters were seen near the Vecher mansion yesterday?" Polina asked suddenly.

"That was a curse. I just forced it to manifest physically," I replied after chewing a piece of snake meat.

"Wow!"

"Rumors travel fast," Anna remarked.

"Well, it's the aristocrats," Polina giggled, glancing at her not-quite-boyfriend Basel.

Before long, the person Basel had been waiting for appeared. Gloria stepped onto the stage, scanning the room before her eyes landed on us. Basel assumed the look was meant for him, but it was clear she was relieved to see me. I simply smiled and returned to my food.

The concert went on for two hours and was exceptional. The food was good, though not particularly exciting. I didn't bother getting Gloria's autograph, but Basel, of course, did. As we finished eating and prepared to head home, Anna caught me off guard.

"Alex, there's the governor's reception on Saturday. If I show up without a date, everyone will pester me — trying to 'win me over' or propose 'favorable' marriage arrangements to my father."

"Oh, I'm going too!" Polina said eagerly, turning to Basel with an expectant look that practically screamed "refusal is not an option."

"Sorry, I can't go to events like that. What if someone recognizes me?" Basel said with a guilty expression, skillfully dodging the situation. Polina looked crestfallen.

"Then I won't go either," she said firmly.

As for me, I really didn't want to go. I'd rather spend the time dealing with gates. However, receptions like this were important — I might even find new clients. So I agreed. And if I found my enemies there? Well, I wouldn't hesitate to use divine energy on them.

CHAPTER 3

FRIDAY DISRUPTED OUR PLANS. It turned out there weren't enough teleporters, but too many teams. Plus, it wasn't clear when a teleporter would become available — if it would be an hour or five.

And since we dared to aim for a D-rank gate, and considering our tendency to collect trophies, our team was placed last on the list.

"Who wants to answer the question?" the teacher asked, carefully surveying our group of six. Yes, six. The others had either already cleared their gates and were at home or in the hospital, or were still clearing theirs. "No one?"

For the record, I was raising my hand, but the woman pretended I was invisible. Grouch. Meanwhile, Basel sat looking preoccupied, deep in thought, quietly staring at yesterday's photos of Gloria.

In short, it was boring. I had slept so much that I reached that dreadful state where I didn't feel sleepy at all. I had to listen to a lecture on material I knew by heart — better than the teacher herself.

Suddenly, the door opened, and our advisor entered.

"Excuse me, Maria, I need to take two of your students," he said, looking as half-dead as always. Pale, with dark circles under his eyes and the stare of a dead fish.

"Of course. One's daydreaming, and the other just woke up," she said with a smile. The advisor gave me a strange look. Why me? Basel was the one daydreaming. We grabbed our things and hurried after the advisor. He was clearly in a rush.

"Is there a problem?" Basel asked, noticing the tension in the man's demeanor.

"There are signs of a Wave near our gate. We need to get in, clear it, and leave quickly, or the soldiers guarding it are guaranteed to die."

"And if we don't make it in time?"

"Then we'll stay inside the gate until reinforcements arrive," the advisor sighed and groaned. "These damn bureaucrats would rather risk soldiers' lives than fail to carry out the Emperor's orders. It would hurt their careers! Bastards!"

We stopped to pick up Polina and Anna. Basel had already messaged both of them, and they were packed and ready to go. So we quickly moved to prepare and gear up.

Half an hour later, we stepped onto the teleportation platform, which looked like a metallic disc inscribed with magical runes. Numerous crystals were embedded around its edges. The platform was connected to a control terminal by a cable, and three mages stood by to create and stabilize the gate.

Frankly, it was impressive. The mages of the past would be "smoking on the sidelines," as they say these days. Teleportation here had reached an industrial level.

We stepped onto the platform, were scanned for artifacts and spells that could interfere with teleportation, and then disappeared in a flash of light, arriving on the other side. But we were too late.

"Damn it! We called ahead! Told you not to teleport! Recon messed up — they were off by ten hours!" shouted an SCU officer running up to us. He didn't look well, and it was clear why.

We were on a small hill with two large trees that, under the influence of the gate between them, had nearly fused into one and were on the verge of becoming a dungeon.

The hill was fortified. There were minefields and metal shields, nine pieces of heavy military equipment, machine gun nests, empty rocket tubes, and an anti-aircraft gun glowing red-hot as it ceaselessly fired into the swarms of creatures in the sky. But the sky wasn't the real problem.

The hill was surrounded. Trees in the forest were being crushed under the feet of creatures, some larger than elephants, creating clearings and enormous trails. If I wasn't mistaken, the creatures were coming from the south. We were near the city of Chita. And in the direction of the city, there was now a massive column of deathly smoke rising. The city's residents would not survive the Wave.

As for the soldiers around us, it was obvious. They would all die — every last one of them. They knew it, too. But, surprisingly, they continued to fight bravely, hoping to thin the horde so the city could defend itself more easily. Noble warriors.

"Scully! What are you standing there for?! Into the gate, everyone into the gate!" shouted the advisor.

He decided to hide the soldiers inside the gate, which was a good idea, since they could carry ammunition and supplies inside. But most of the soldiers remained behind cover, holding off the swarms. Only weaker creatures were attacking for now, as they were faster than their larger counterparts, and the soldiers were holding on for now.

"I'll cover you," I said, summoning Fireflies in my hands.

"Don't take unnecessary risks!"

The advisor ran toward the gate to help keep it open. It was clear it was taking a toll on him. As far as I could tell, Anna and the others were already inside, clearing out the D-rank area near the gate. Hopefully, they would manage. SCU equipment was nearly useless in such spaces, as technomagic worked poorly there.

"Scully! What's your plan? They said you could

help," said the commander of the 200-strong unit as he ran up to me.

"When the time comes, I'll unleash a light so bright it will temporarily blind everything alive around the hill," I said, releasing another Firefly. There were already nine hovering above the hill, and I began making a new one.

"Excellent! Our equipment has flashbang protection. I'll let you know when to activate them. Thank you!"

With that, we came to an agreement. Quietly, I absorbed the crystals I had brought just in case and continued charging the Fireflies, holding off their activation. It seemed I had just invented a new spell. I'd call it Flash Burst. Or maybe it already existed? I'd have to check later. In short, instead of glowing continuously, the Firefly would explode with light. Like a magical flashbang.

I continued working and watched the soldiers. Meanwhile, the monsters in the sky started hunting the Fireflies. I had to keep running to distract them, but at least it drew their attention. And the anti-aircraft team had time to haul their gun into the gate.

Currently, spider-like creatures were attacking the hill. They were about the size of boars and fast, but their chitin was weak, so they were easy to kill. The spiders occasionally spat acid and webs, but the soldiers — experienced as they were — quickly neutralized both with sprays.

But the "easy ride" didn't last. Soon, about forty larger creatures the size of rhinos charged at us from the southeast.

"Scully! On my count — five!" the commander shouted and began the countdown.

At that moment, the soldiers threw everything they had — rockets, grenades, mines, even detonating ammunition — before rushing toward the gate as a group. The hill was shrouded in smoke, covering the soldiers' retreat. But it only lasted a few seconds.

"Now!"

Hearing the commander's shout, I detonated twelve Fireflies. The sound nearly deafened me! So many creatures howling at once created a true sound bomb. And, judging by reports from the SCU, some even died from it, which was great news.

The soldiers poured into the gate, surprisingly orderly. Soon, only the advisor and I remained. He seemed slightly stunned by both the sound and the light.

"Scully! Scully! Into the gate! Quick!" he shouted, but... Could I? Half a million souls doomed to death and suffering couldn't leave me indifferent. Let's just say I was doing this for selfish reasons.

Before the advisor could finish, I shoved him into the gate and forced it to lock. And so, it was just me against the horde. My trusty sword and my ever-reliable ring at my side.

"Do spiders know how to use machine guns?" I thought, running toward the cover. Fallen monsters began to rise to their feet, and I had a couple of seconds. "Obviously, they do!"

Indeed, after raising about ten spiders, I directed a few toward the three APCs where the machine guns hadn't been removed. It was difficult, of course, but the powerful guns with magical ammunition started tearing through both large and small monsters. It didn't stop the advance, but I managed to take down some larger beasts. Two hyena-hippos the size of cows, for instance.

My spiders helped me descend the hill slightly and fight my way toward the monsters to raise them. But the creatures suddenly lost their enthusiasm. The hill didn't interest them anymore.

Still, it was on the way to the city. Most of the monsters decided to simply bypass the hill, while only a small stream (about a hundred creatures) rushed toward it. Likely because of the spider gunners shooting at the creatures.

"Hello, Zhanna," I said, calling her on the phone while protected by my puppets. The monsters hadn't figured out what was happening yet, and my hippo-beasts were confidently holding back the wave. As for the spiders, they were venomous and utterly disgusting creatures. Everyone avoided them, and those who didn't screamed after being bitten. Unfortunately, their venom reserves quickly ran out.

"Master! Are you all right? There's panic in Chita — isn't it right around where you are? The Wave!" She sounded far more panicked than the city's residents. It was nice to know someone cared about me and worried, but now wasn't the time!

"I'm fine. I have an idea, but I need Kiki."

"She's at home, with me! And… she's already undressing."

"Got it, thanks." Ending the call, I summoned the skeleton guardian. I thought I really should give him a name.

Emerging from the black goo, the warrior immediately stood up and straightened. The magical fire in his eyes burned even brighter when he saw the hordes of monsters.

"This will be… a glorious battle…"

"Behind us are half a million lives, and I want to save them. So we'll have to give it everything we've got," I said, patting the big guy on the shoulder and feeding him generously with my power.

The skeleton suddenly turned sharply and looked at the giant column of deathly smoke.

"Return me… please… to the afterlife… for a while… I beg you…" The skeleton turned to me, and I felt reluctant. He had already cost me six units of energy, and I spent ten more on his reinforcement. Still, I fulfilled his request, trusting he had a good reason. Then I dismissed him and summoned the kikimora.

"I'll kill you!" she roared, snarling as she charged at a six-armed baboon harassing my hyena-hippos.

The machine guns worked well until they ran out of ammunition. At that point, my small group was pushed back toward the cover, while below us, a whole sea of monsters bypassed the hill, heading toward the city.

The kikimora took down the six-armed creature, and as soon as it died, it came back to life as a puppet. I had to deactivate one of the spiders to make room, but it was already empty with no venom left.

I was actively cutting through the poisoned creatures, focusing on strange rats the size of wolves. They had trunks and tusks for some reason. Anyone I deemed useful, I turned into a puppet but didn't raise.

"Master... Souls... The monster-zombies... agree. To atone for their sins... to save lives... they beg," I heard the thoughts of my skeleton. Why not? I had been considering something more energy-intensive, but this might work. Not zombies, though — possessed puppets!

Zombies were costly, requiring significant energy for upkeep and restoration. Puppets, however, were much simpler. The souls wouldn't have to merge with the bodies, but they would make controlling them much easier. Essentially, I'd shift part of my workload onto the souls, allowing me to raise more puppets.

I could almost cackle out loud: "Mwahahaha!" A proper villain's laugh... and why not?

"Rise, fallen beasts! Terrors of humanity, it's your time to protect it! Mwahahaha! Rise, my army!"

I spread my arms wide and began releasing black energy containing the souls that wanted to help. Ten... twenty... thirty-five... forty-seven... seventy exactly! The dead started to rise, then fell.

Right, they were not human bodies. No problem; they'd adjust. Let them jump around and walk a bit first.

And they did, hopping and stumbling. Some slipped and rolled down the hill, right under the hooves and feet of the herd bypassing it.

A couple of seconds later, the souls left the broken puppets, and I had to find them new hosts. Luckily, fresh bodies kept arriving and dying. Nosy rats, swarms of spiders, strange monkeys, shot-down giant birds, a twenty-meter-long snake-centipede, and countless other monstrosities born from the gods' twisted imagination. Now they were my army — with the skeleton at the helm. And it was time to attack!

The air filled with howls, roars, hisses, and growls as my puppets charged down the hill, straight into the monster horde. I followed, repeatedly using Flash Burst. And munching on crystals. Mmm, mana with a hint of heartburn.

Leaping onto the back of the snake-centipede, I cut down every creature I could reach. Nearby, a herd of sheep-fish on long, thin legs ran by. Each beast was the size of a massive boar. We hit them from the side as they bypassed the hill.

My snake plowed into the flow of creatures, knocking over a dozen at once. It didn't stop there, barreling toward a larger beast about the size of a small elephant.

The sheep-fish slammed into the snake-centipede blocking their path. Some leaped over it, but my army appeared behind them, forcing the flow of monsters to stop.

The creatures behind them pushed forward, creating pressure on us. Some tried to bypass this new battlefield entirely. Others decided to go through the hill. Their orders were clear, and they were determined to carry them out. If I could find the monster commanding this Wave and kill it, the creatures would likely return to their territories, or start killing each other. After all, a monster is a monster's monster.

Reaching the leading sheep-fish, the snake bit into its side and started coiling around it. I climbed onto the beast's massive body and slashed at it with my sword. Once it was dead, I immediately raised it and placed a soul inside. Around me, the battle raged on. The vengeful spirits, driven by their desire to save the city and find redemption, used every advantage of their puppet bodies. Bite off a head? No problem! The head could still bite and devour the enemy from the inside. The same applied to severed limbs.

I made sure to release broken puppets and transfer their souls into fresh bodies. Before long, nearly my entire army had been replaced with sheep-fish. Meanwhile, the kikimora, the snake, and I relentlessly hunted down the leaders. They were no harder to control than the smaller creatures but far more effective in battle.

BOOK THREE

* * *

Chita suburbs
Defense perimeter
A few hours later

Artillery, cannons, mortars, and even combat aircraft were in action. The once wheat-covered fields surrounding the city were completely charred and riddled with countless craters. Yet the monsters kept coming.

They pressed and pressed against the defenders, forcing them to abandon the first line of defense and fall back to the second. Behind them lay the city walls, walls that were not designed to withstand such power.

"Damn it! Where's our reinforcement from Blaga?!" cursed the Emperor's governor, the ruler of this city, stationed at the temporary defense headquarters right on the front line.

He was covered head to toe in the blood of the creatures, as were the five patriarchs of the city's strongest families. Every aristocrat was required to stand in defense, and anyone who refused would be declared a traitor and executed. Only children and, under certain conditions, women were exempt from this duty.

The headquarters was a large tent equipped with mana diffusers, laptops, and even a coffee machine.

"Recon screwed up, which means reinforcements will be delayed," said an elderly patriarch with resignation. He was a powerful mage, but what good was power when there was no mana left? For now, he focused on restoring his reserves.

"We'll hold! Don't panic!" declared a red-haired giant with cracked skin. It wasn't the result of a bad curse but an intentional mutation caused by fire mana to enhance his control over it.

"We're going to die... we're all going to die, and there's nowhere to evacuate," groaned another patriarch as two healers worked to reattach his severed arm.

"Don't give up!" said the governor. "We haven't lost yet. Wait for reinforcements!"

"Governor!" An officer burst into the tent, looking stunned. "The Oak family is requesting support — they've lost two-thirds of their guard and half of their members!"

"Where the hell am I supposed to pull support from?! Tell them to hold on!"

"Understood," the officer replied and ran off, leaving the governor to groan in frustration.

"We will survive, got it?! I order you to win, and I don't give a damn how you do it!" he roared at the patriarchs.

The red-haired giant burst into laughter. "Understood, Governor," he said, grabbing his massive sword.

He stepped out of the tent and surveyed the scarred land filled with thousands of mangled corpses. "The smell of blood and burning flesh! Just how I like it. Wait! Hey, you panicky old-timers, why are the monsters running?"

"Did a woodpecker confuse you with a tree and peck your brain out? What nonsense are you—" The governor stormed out of the tent, his mouth falling open.

The monsters really were scattering. Some had even started fighting each other. Chaos erupted on the battlefield and spread to the defensive line. Soldiers and mages, commoners and aristocrats alike, shouted in joy. They had done it! They had defended their homes, their wives, and their children.

But it was too early to celebrate, and everyone knew it. There were wounded everywhere, countless in number, and there were still stragglers and aggressive creatures that would continue to threaten the city. In short, there was a ton of work ahead. Still, the people were so inspired that they would tear apart any monster that dared approach. And none of them knew what was happening not too far south, on a standalone hill.

CHAPTER 4

The hill
Sometime later
The advisor

THE VEIL INSIDE THE ARCH leading to the shard shimmered, and suddenly a man clad in black armor appeared. He carefully peeked out, wary that his head might get bitten off, but nothing of the sort happened. What he saw was far from what he expected.

"What happened here?" The young man, 27 years old, looked around and fully stepped out of the gate. Behind him, Anna emerged like a worried slug, but she quickly broke into a smile.

"This is horrifying..." Polina whispered. "What kind of nightmare happened here? It's hell on earth..."

The girl stared in horror at the site where the

SCU soldiers' camp once stood. Now, it was a bloody mess of mangled metal, remnants of what had once been military vehicles.

The hill was piled high with the bodies of various monsters, but this was just a drop in the ocean, compared to what was around the hill.

"This is a massacre. How could something like this happen?" the advisor said, utterly bewildered.

The forest around the hill was obliterated, covered with the countless monster corpses.

"I hear something! Chewing!" Polina exclaimed, and Anna immediately bolted toward the sound.

"Wait! What if it's monsters?!" the advisor called out, running after her. But it wasn't monsters. It was me. I was hungry, very, very hungry.

"Oh, you're out already? Want some food?" I asked, holding up a half-eaten leg of some creature. I had no idea who it originally belonged to; I'd just picked it up off the ground and roasted it. Hunger doesn't wait. Conveniently, there was a fire — well, technically, the remains of some creature still burning in someone's flames. I'd just tossed on some extra "firewood" to keep it going. Luckily, there was no shortage of "firewood" scattered around.

"We've already eaten, thanks," Anna said, approaching me and examining me carefully. I wasn't exactly unharmed, but my arms and legs were still attached.

My clothes, however, were mostly gone. All that was left was reduced to rags, but my underwear and a pair of knitted socks were protected by my divine power and alright. Those socks were indestructible and had been gifted to me without deducting any academic points, unlike my sword. They'd saved me more than once.

"What happened here?" the advisor asked. He wasn't the only one confused. People were emerging from the gate, stunned. The soldiers immediately began making satellite phone calls. It didn't take the good news long to travel.

"The city survived! The Wave was repelled!" the SCU commander announced. His words sparked an emotional explosion among the soldiers, making it noisy and difficult to talk. So I kept eating.

The meat was a bit tough and stringy, with hardly any fat. It reeked of smoke. But I wasn't picky — calories were urgently needed!

I wasn't about to recount the whole ordeal. I had used my army to thin out the monsters in the Wave, and then the creature that was behind it all showed up. It was a massive beast, the size of a mansion, with what seemed to be an indestructible barrier. It spat acid and healed any damage by consuming other monsters.

I didn't know its rank, but even a thousand B-rank monsters couldn't take it down. They attacked in groups of seventy, barely enough to break the barrier. As for physical damage, there was no question — it healed any wound with ease.

So we killed it another way — from the inside. Not through its mouth, though... The monster's stomach contained such corrosive acid that anything entering it dissolved within seconds — alive or not.

It was a risky plan. While my army distracted the monster, a diversion team of snakes, bugs, worms, and other similar creatures prepared. Meanwhile, I stored up mana and energy in my cursed ring. Just before it overloaded and exploded, I cast a diarrhea curse on the beast. That's when the interesting stuff began.

The giant monster's body opened a new exit, which for some became an entrance. Battling the monstrous pressure that sprayed processed fertilizer hundreds of yards around, the diversion team slipped inside the beast.

The next hour was grueling. The monster figured out where the attack was coming from and noticed me. The worse it felt, the angrier it became. The horde of monsters, along with the giant itself, did everything they could to destroy me. They came very close to succeeding, as my divine energy was nearly depleted.

Thankfully, the monster fell first. Then something I didn't expect happened. The change in fate for half a million people unleashed such an eruption of energy that I felt I could leap straight to the fifth level. But my body could only handle a one-time "payment" of five thousand energy units. If it had been transferred gradually, I might have been able to absorb any amount.

Still, even with that, I almost "kicked the bucket," as minotaur says. Or was it centaurs? Never mind. The point is, I suffered greatly and deserved a cake. And I wanted a honey cake.

"Scully!" the advisor screamed. Apparently, he'd been talking while I was lost in thought.

"Oh, right. I used an ancient and very expensive artifact. Always carry it with me. That's how I killed the main monster," I lied with a straight face. No way was I going to admit I raised an army of possessed puppets that infiltrated the monster and devoured it from the inside.

"Y-you? So it was you who caused the monsters to flee and retreat to the wasteland," said the SCU commander.

"What kind of artifact was it, and why wasn't it detected?" the advisor asked.

"It would be strange if something that powerful — and unfortunately single-use — could be detected," I shrugged and bit into the roasted meat. I offered some to Anna, who took a bite but wrinkled her nose in disgust. Not a fan, apparently.

"I carried it for self-defense. You know how many enemies I have. I should mention that I'm now defenseless if some powerful guy comes after me."

"I see..."

"SCU will find it difficult to express our gratitude, but we will try." The SCU commander extended his hand, which I shook, though I had no strength left in my fingers.

"By the way, how was the shard? Was it tough?" I asked Basel, who looked deep in thought. My question snapped him back to reality.

"Not really. Anna went berserk and started

cutting down those hyenas. We had to join in. Thankfully, the monsters weren't too strong, and they were terrified of Polina's fog."

"Good job." I nodded. "Too bad I didn't participate — I'll probably get a failing grade."

"Technically, yes," The advisor grimaced, wondering what to put in his report.

"This guy recently closed a C-rank gate with two beautiful ladies, and you're talking about some D-rank," the SCU commander said, shaking his head as he walked away.

Why did he have to say that? Not only did Anna emit a chilling aura, but the others also stared at me as if I were a male dragon that had inexplicably laid an egg.

"What? I'm just strong," I shrugged and winced — my muscles hurt.

The next hour was spent resting. Meanwhile, the soldiers hauled their gear out of the gate, surveyed the hill, and cleared away the twisted remains of what used to be APCs. They also began clearing the area of corpses, preparing for helicopter arrivals.

The teleportation disk had been dismantled and packed away, so it was faster to wait for the helicopters. And with night approaching, the hidden monsters would soon emerge. I was certain there were plenty of them left — after all, the Wave wasn't destroyed, just scattered. This place would turn into a feast before long.

Fortunately, the helicopters didn't take long to arrive, though they all looked pretty battered. I only hoped they wouldn't crash.

And another thing — I didn't get a single believer! Outrageous. I suppose people need to know I exist to believe in me? But if that happens, Reyna will also find out... nothing but complications.

Some time later, we boarded the massive SCU helicopters and headed to the city. The land outside it was nothing but scorched earth and endless monster corpses. There was also plenty of mangled military hardware, too. The city's defenders had suffered significant losses. Thankfully, the city itself was mostly intact. Only a few flying creatures had breached its defenses, and the damage was relatively minimal.

The city was noisy and packed with people celebrating their survival. Meanwhile, my underworld was almost out of souls. I'd need to return to this city and visit its cemetery. I wouldn't touch the souls in Blaga for now — they might be needed for zombie workers. But I could use other cities to fill up.

That was for later, though. For now, we landed in the city, where a car was waiting to take us to the teleportation center. After half an hour of preparation, we teleported back to the Academy.

I was immediately whisked away by medics. After being examined and healed, I changed clothes and prepared to go home. My phone had been partially destroyed, so I couldn't call Ivan. Thankfully, Anna gave me a ride home with her military convoy.

"I wish I could stay and hear what really happened," Anna sighed wistfully. But she had to go home — Winters was furious, and Polina and Basel had been getting calls nonstop during our flight to Chita.

"I'll tell you tomorrow at the reception."

"Oh, right, the reception..." She grimaced, clearly not a fan of such events, but then managed a smile. "Deal."

After saying goodbye, she drove off, and I went inside, only to be immediately ambushed.

"Alex!"

"Y-you're choking me..." I croaked, trapped in Tatiana's "chest lock." Her physical strength was off the charts because she was a Combat Mage [Level 30–39]. If only she went into the gates, she'd make a fortune for the family. Why was she staying at home?

Barely escaping a ridiculous death, I quickly stepped aside. What if the redheads standing nearby decided to join in? I'd had enough hugs for one day. The last ones nearly broke my bones.

"We were all so worried about you," Lena said, standing there in a light blue nightgown.

"The news showed such horrors," she added.

"The Academy administration told us you went into the gates, but we were still worried," Katie chimed in. She was also in a nightgown but had thrown on a sweater.

Tatiana, however, was dressed in a formal gown. Apparently, she wasn't planning on going to bed, likely preparing for tomorrow's reception.

"Well, as you can see, everything's fine," I

smiled at them. "Now I just need to get myself cleaned up and eat something. By the way, are you going to the governor's reception?"

"The reception? Can we go?" Katie's eyes lit up, and after I nodded, she turned to her sister. "There's so little time left! We need to pick out outfits!"

The girls dashed off, leaving me bewildered — the dinner wasn't until tomorrow evening.

"So, you're going too? I thought you'd be busy as usual," Tatiana said.

"Anna asked me to. Plus, I'll try to find new clients with problems involving dark curses."

"Got it, good idea. I think I can help you with that," she nodded thoughtfully before leaving. And finally, I could relax.

But I didn't make it to dinner. I laid down "just for a minute" and immediately passed out, still fully dressed.

* * *

Somewhere in the city
Luxurious but small office
George Talster

A tall and rather plump man sat in an oversized chair, staring at a massive wall-mounted TV. Suddenly, his phone rang.

"I'm listening... Yes, Constantine, everything is on track. I'm paying close attention," the man said, instantly adopting a serious tone as he activated the call recording function — a rare move for him.

"So, Scully claims he used some kind of an ancient artifact of unprecedented power to destroy the monster leading the Wave? Any evidence?"

"Only his word. The monster doesn't show any external damage. But everything around... ahem..."

"Speak!"

"Well, the whole place is... uh... covered in excrement. The stench is overwhelming. Also, the guy had an F-rank ring listed under his belongings, but it was missing when we evacuated him."

"Could it be... that sneaky bastard! He disguised a high-rank artifact as a dud — that's how he... I understand. Thank you. The payment will be transferred within five minutes."

The person on the other end didn't respond, simply ending the call. The man quickly handled the payment, prioritizing monetary matters as always. Everything had to be done on time — that was his own rule.

"So, there really was a stash of artifacts... and such powerful ones at that," the man muttered as he completed his tasks, his temper slowly rising. "So, that's how he took down the elder Zverinksi. That mutt! We're moving too slowly. We need to speed up!"

Talster reached for his phone again, this time issuing a brief order, so curt it could hardly be called a conversation.

THE COMING OF GOD OF DEATH

* * *

Governor's residence
Evening, but since I just woke up — morning for me
Me and a bunch of women

"Alex, stop yawning, please — it's impolite! Or at least cover your mouth," Tatiana scolded. But I couldn't help it. I felt like a barrel of ale in a dwarf's hands — completely drained. My plan was to behave like an ancient elder: grumble, groan, and eat a ton. Though something seemed unnecessary in that list... probably the groaning.

We got out of the car and headed for the main entrance of the residence. I have to say, it was enormous! A true palace, and quite an exquisite one at that. Inside, it was even more extravagant. And let's not forget, all of this was likely bought with our taxes, wasn't it?

When the attendants at the door saw us, they announced our full names flawlessly, allowing the herald to inform the guests of our arrival. Only after this theatrical display were we permitted to enter. I didn't understand the point of this farse, it was a waste of time. But no, people do love feeding their egos.

The only ones worse than them are the high elves. Dwarves, on the other hand, are great folks. They don't know arrogance or vanity. Their kings could easily be mistaken for vagrants. You could brawl with some drunk who reeks to high heaven

5 6

in a dingy tavern, only to discover he's the ruler of the land.

Our arrival didn't interest anyone. We stepped into the spacious hall, which doubled as a banquet area, but no one even glanced in our direction.

The place was packed. How did this city even have so many aristocrats? There had to be at least five hundred people here, and more were arriving. The only saving grace was the delicious aroma of the food.

"Rr-rr-rrr!"

"All right, all right, hold on," I said, patting my ravenous stomach. Someone chuckled behind me.

"Alex, we're off to find some girls we know," the sisters said, clasping hands as they darted off.

"I'll head off too. Time to scout for some potential clients," Tatiana added before leaving me alone. And that was just fine.

I stepped into the center of the room and took a good look around. The people didn't interest me, so I focused on everything else. The banquet hall was divided into three sections. The first was the restaurant area, with tables, chairs, and buffets loaded with food. Guests could grab a plate, sit down, and enjoy a proper meal.

The second section was more informal, with high tables offering finger foods. People could grab a snack, chat, and move on. This part was the noisiest, filled with groups engaged in loud conversations, creating an irritating cacophony.

The third section housed the stage, a dance floor, and seating for relaxation. A live band played soft romantic tunes on the stage, with a middle-aged man singing. It was revolting.

After surveying the area, I, of course, headed for the buffet. Anna hadn't arrived yet, but she'd find me easily enough when she did.

By the way, there weren't many students here — probably because a lot of them were from out of town. I also didn't see anyone from smaller families like the Browns or the Krasnovs. Were they not invited? Was I even invited? Well, they wouldn't have let me in otherwise, right? But none of that mattered. Nothing mattered anymore...

"Wow!" That was all I could say when I saw it. I thought it might have been heaven.

Walking past the seafood buffet, then past the table with the meat dishes, I reached in to a massive table laden with every kind of cake imaginable.

There was even a magical cake made from ingredients harvested in fragments! It featured anti-gravity jelly, flaming chocolate, and animated gummy candies. Tiny gummy people fought each other with gummy swords, darting across the cake. Fallen and chopped-up gummies regenerated and jumped back into the fray. It was almost a shame to eat it... But of course, I'd eat it!

"Scully, you scoundrel! How dare you defile my daughter! I challenge you to a duel to the death!"

"Wait, what?"

CHAPTER 5

"STOP EATING ALREADY!" shouted a furious man in his forties. He was a bit overweight, with a face that somewhat resembled a rat — small, round eyes, a slightly oversized nose, and a prominent upper jaw.

"It's really tasty," I shrugged, continuing to savor the cake.

The little gummy warriors darted around on my plate, continuing their tiny battles and dodging my fork, trying to avoid being eaten. But they'd get their turn after I finished the amazing cake.

The layers were exquisite: a mix of flavors with a sponge that was moist yet light. It didn't sit like a brick in my stomach; instead, it made me crave more with every bite.

"You monster! After what you did to me, you're just sitting there eating so calmly!" cried the young woman dramatically, burying her face into her father's chest.

"Horrible, just horrible. You're a monster!" someone chimed in from the crowd.

A good thirty people had already gathered, watching the spectacle. More were bound to join. This father-daughter duo sure knew how to make a scene.

"He's really just eating..."

"What kind of cake is that? Looks interesting."

That last comment set off alarm bells in my head. These vultures were eyeing my cake! I had to act fast. Rising suddenly from my seat, I made the father and daughter jump back in surprise.

"Nooooo! He's going to kill me! Someone, help!" the girl shrieked.

"Who dares harm a lady?!" A gallant young man from the crowd burst forth. He was about twenty-five, tall, athletic, and annoyingly handsome.

"Him! He's going to kill me after what he did, after he defiled me!" the woman screamed, pointing at me.

"Mm-hmm?" I turned around, my face still smeared with cream, and resumed cutting another slice of cake, methodically piling pieces onto my plate.

Taking the whole cake would've been bad form, so I settled for half. I had so many flavors left to try, though.

"Idiots," muttered the knight-in-shining-armor type, glaring at the father-daughter pair before walking off in disgust.

"Scully! A duel! I'm challenging you!" the father insisted, clutching his crying daughter protectively. They stood behind me, clearly resolute.

"On my terms?" I grinned.

"Fine!" Fire lit up in their eyes.

"Then I choose a duel of cake-eating. Whoever eats the most wins!"

Silence fell. The spectators exchanged confused glances, and the "defiled" woman gaped at me, flabbergasted.

"No! That won't avenge my daughter's honor!"

"Alright, then how about this — whoever wins gets everything the loser owns? They hired you for this, didn't they?"

"No one hired me! Don't try to twist the truth and slander me! I have undeniable proof of your guilt!" the man roared, his voice trembling with indignation as the audience chuckled.

"Yeah, yeah, everyone says that at first. Then they're begging me to banish evil spirits for them. So, a duel?"

"A duel!"

The crowd immediately came alive, but it wasn't quite what I had in mind. They had moved the duel to the stage for some reason and then made us sign documents to officially confirm the rules.

"I declare the duel has begun! Bring out the cakes!" proclaimed none other than the Emperor's governor himself. He ruled the city and was supposed to arrive later, but apparently, he couldn't resist such an absurd spectacle and wrapped up his business early.

He stood before the rectangular table where I sat opposite my opponent. The governor was openly laughing at the sheer ridiculousness of it all. The audience was having a good laugh too. But they didn't know this was all part of my devious plan! I'd feast on all these cakes legally *and* win a prize for it.

"How's that little guy going to out-eat the fat one?" someone muttered from the crowd. Laughter erupted when Katie couldn't hold back her giggles, and Lena joined her. Anna, who had just arrived, stood there smiling. Only Tatiana was furious, her gaze practically shooting lightning bolts.

But I focused on the important part: they brought out a large tray with ten slices of different cakes. My mind was blown wide open — so many wonders in this world I'd never imagined! Ice cream fillings. Cakes made entirely of liquid. A cake shaped like a fish that wiggled and flapped its tail. And all of them were delicious!

However, there was one big problem. Watching us eat made everyone else crave cake too. Now the servants were rushing around, distributing slices to the spectators. They even set up tables so people could sit down. I could only hope they had enough left for the duel. If not, I'd be very upset!

Anyway, back to business. We both polished off the first round of cakes at the same time. It seemed I had a worthy opponent. He even smirked as if he'd already won. Yeah, we'd see about that.

The second round surprised me with a completely new selection of cakes. I was thrilled — these weren't available on the main tables, meaning they'd either just been delivered or were a special stash.

"The duelists are tied! Who will emerge victorious? And wow, now I really want some cake," the governor commented as he stood in front of our table. Of course, someone heard him, and soon he was handed a plate and a cup of tea, along with a small table. "Mmm, this strawberry-and-potato one is divine!"

Good taste! Maybe we could become friends. Or not, because now everyone wanted to try that cake, too.

Cheering and shouting broke out from the crowd. It seemed people were placing bets. Scratch that — they were definitely betting, with the governor's men organizing a full-on betting pool! Anna placed a bet on me. So did the sisters and Tatiana. But most of the crowd was betting on my opponent.

Unfortunately, I lost the second round. I was eating carefully, while my opponent just shoved the cakes into his mouth without chewing, relying on his sheer size. No matter — we weren't racing, it was all about quantity!

The third round featured simpler, much sweeter cakes. I wasn't happy about it — I don't like overly sweet things. My opponent, though, didn't care and kept inhaling the cakes like a conveyor belt. The parasite was working overtime, fueled by my energy, but my belly was starting to stick out.

Soon, they brought out the fourth round, then the fifth. By now, the entire audience had stuffed themselves full of cake, yet we kept going. My opponent soldiered on, though it was clear he was struggling. He forcefully shoved cake after cake into his mouth, drinking as little water as possible to avoid stretching his stomach. And, of course, standing up meant instant disqualification.

Time dragged on, and my opponent's face turned bright red. Pain and disgust etched across his features, he kept cramming cake into his mouth. Such disrespect for cake — it was horrifying.

I continued eating carefully and unhurriedly, washing it all down with hot tea. My stomach now rested on my knees, and my body was protesting, but it was nothing the parasite couldn't handle. Suddenly, my opponent began choking and then collapsed. He appeared to have died.

"The winner of the duel is Alexander Scully!" announced the governor, and the crowd erupted into applause. I had to stand up, and the audience gasped audibly upon seeing my bulging stomach.

"Honestly, this is the most unusual duel I've ever witnessed," the governor continued. "I'm amazed at how someone so small could eat so much!"

"Good metabolism," I said with a shrug and turned to the burly man approaching me. Broad-shouldered, nearly seven feet tall, and intimidating in appearance, he exuded authority.

"I see! Very well. I'll handle your reward personally, and we'll interrogate the girl about who ordered the smear campaign against your reputation."

"Thank you."

"No, thank *you* for the show!" he bellowed with laughter and gave my shoulder a hearty pat. I felt like a nail being hammered into wood.

Soon, I stepped off the stage and found something resembling a large sofa to sit on. The girls joined me, placing their hands on my distended stomach and using Warm Hands to ease my discomfort.

Meanwhile, the governor waited for the stage to be cleared before delivering his speech. The topic was a critical one — the emperor's decree regarding the Academy and the looming threat of a Wave.

Everyone had heard about Chita, and if not for a "coincidence" — clearly a veiled reference to me — the city would have suffered greatly. Though in truth, the city wasn't going to suffer, it was going to be annihilated.

But I digress. In summary, reconnaissance in the wildlands had reported a high likelihood of new Waves forming this year, likely targeting Blaga. The outlook was grim. Preparations for a potential defense were necessary. Additionally, expeditions into the wildlands were needed to cull the local monster populations and seal as many gates as possible.

This would help weaken any Wave. After all, it's called a Wave because, as it moves toward a city, it absorbs all the monsters in its path, growing larger and stronger.

Therefore, noble families were called upon to contribute to the collective effort, either by slaying a set number of monsters or aiding in other ways, such as donating money, artifacts, or crystals.

Should it even be said that the higher aristocratic families are expected to contribute more? It doesn't matter if the family lost a war, is in decline, or anything else. If the Emperor decrees it, then it must be done.

"So, what do we do now?" The girls looked at me, waiting for an answer.

"I hadn't even thought about the South... There are no people there and a ton of game!" I suddenly realized. "I'll go hunting tomorrow and work toward fulfilling the quota bit by bit. Although carrying all the proof — like heads — means I'll probably need a truck."

"Alex! It's incredibly dangerous out there!" protested Tatiana. "I'll go with you!"

"You'll just get in the way. Better protect the house. My enemies seem to be getting more active. What if they break in while I'm gone?"

"Fine." She bit her lip, but it was clear she understood. Leaving the house unprotected wasn't an option.

I, on the other hand, needed to start thinking seriously about the manor's security. But how? Zombies? Puppets? There's no way I was letting outsiders in. Something needed to be done. Enhancing the altar with "Fortress" was good, of course, but if the enemy was powerful or numerous, I'd risk exposing myself.

Then I thought about capturing and sealing poltergeists. The cost of maintaining seals would be hefty. But on the upside, they'd actively defend our home against any intruder. It was perfect. That's what I'd do. All that was left was to find some poltergeists.

"Alexander, may I join you?" A man I didn't recognize approached us.

"Go dance and have fun; I'm feeling better," I said to the girls. They nodded and left, but Anna immediately slid in beside me, clutching my hand. It didn't seem like she planned to let go anytime soon.

"Your mother told me you provide services against dark forces and the undead. I've also heard you saved the Vecher family from a deadly curse, not to mention helping the Winter family. Glad to see you're doing well, Anna," the man said, smiling warmly at her. She gave him a small nod, and he continued, "I've got a small problem with a shard. I'd really like it cleared so I can access it."

"Valuable resources?"

"Very. That's why I'd like to keep it confidential."

"No problem. Send me the details, and negotiate pricing with my assistant, Zhanna, or my family business manager, Ivan. I should be free on Wednesday."

"I'm acquainted with Ivan. Thank you," he said, shaking my hand before walking away.

"The undead must be pretty strong there if they can't handle it themselves," Anna noted.

"Likely malevolent spirits. If they're powerful enough, they can possess people. Ordinary workers would be easy prey."

"Hmm, yes, that makes sense. Will you take me with you?" she asked, looking at me. The stress of the reception weighed on her; her cold demeanor and the vice grip she had on my poor hand made that clear.

"If your father allows it."

"I'll talk to him tomorrow," she said, tightening her grip on my hand. We sat in silence, resting and digesting — both food and thoughts. I kept trying to master Purification magic, but it just wasn't coming to me.

Tatiana mingled among the patriarchs, keeping up connections. The sisters were laughing and chatting with girls their age, enjoying themselves. Anna's father was fully engrossed in business.

One person, however, stood out — a man who seemed to be searching for someone over the past two hours. Then he found his target. And to my surprise, it was me.

"Good evening, Alexander," he said, approaching. I stood to shake his hand. "Allow me to introduce myself — Theodor Alexy."

"Good evening, Theodor," I replied, noting his tall, stately figure, which attracted the attention of nearby women.

"Forgive me for disturbing your peace. I've been looking for you to express my gratitude," he said, suddenly bowing. "You saved my life after I was hit by a car that exploded."

"That was an attempt on my life," I noted.

"I know. As the victim, I had access to the investigation files. Unfortunately, the chances of the perpetrator being punished are slim. Nonetheless, you acted nobly, helping the injured regardless of their status."

"We're a family of healers — how could we not?"

"For that, I am sincerely grateful," he said, bowing again. "I'm not from here, came on business, and then... well, you know. As it happens, I'm here to buy goods. And by a stroke of luck, you own a furniture factory. I visited it and was impressed by the quality of your products. The wood you harvest is mana-rich, and the furniture made from it has excellent durability and craftsmanship. I'd like to arrange a supply contract."

"Let me discuss the details with the factory manager first, but I'm preliminarily on board."

"I've already given all my requirements to Maxim. He should be prepared for your visit."

"Even better," I said, pleasantly surprised. We shook hands, and I realized it was probably time for another visit to the cemetery. Expanding the company's workforce, so to speak.

Before long, Theodor left, and several other people approached me. Some inquired about healing; others were curious if I could lift a hypothetical curse. There were minor questions, but nothing substantial.

Overall, I was satisfied with the evening. When it ended, I headed home, and from there, to the cemetery. Anna wanted to come with me, but her father took her home.

I didn't linger at Cemetery #2, quickly setting up an alter and collecting a hundred souls — some of which were sent to Hell — and raised the undead. This time, I focused on factory workers and combatants since I had enough lumberjacks. With slightly lowered requirements for workers, I managed to raise thirty, who would train under Maxim and become capable employees. Already proven effective.

As for fighters, I raised nearly fifty. In total, I spent over a thousand DE, but it was necessary.

Maxim transported them to the factory. Zhanna and I headed to her place — not to stay the night, though she wouldn't have minded. I summoned the kikimora for her, checked on the raven, terrorized him a bit (lazy little pest), and finally went home to rest.

BOOK THREE

* * *

Scully Mansion
Late night
Strangers

One of the house's windows creaked open. Alarms, sensors, detection systems — all of it had been skillfully disabled. The mansion's security system was expertly hacked.

Four men in black clothing slipped into the building with practiced precision, quickly surveying their surroundings. They found themselves in the study of the family patriarch.

"There's a safe here, along with two hidden compartments," one of the four said, using sound and wind magic.

"Let's move. Keep it quie—" the man stepped forward but abruptly lost his footing, crashing loudly to the floor. The impact was awkward enough that his nose smashed against the hard surface.

"Idiot..." someone hissed.

"I don't get it... how did that happen?" The man scrambled to his feet, hurriedly wiping the floor clean. "At least the alarm's off. Let's keep going."

The group spread out. Two focused on the safe, working with deft hands, while the other two investigated the hidden compartments. One was embedded in the floor, requiring careful handling to avoid triggering traps. But just as one of them began to open it...

"Ah, crap!" he cursed, accidentally slicing his finger on an automated mini-saw. "Ahh... cut through nearly half my finger! Bone's nicked..."

"Idiot! How could yo—" Before he could finish berating his companion, the man working on the safe with an electronic device was suddenly struck by a jolt of electricity. Something short-circuited, causing the device to spark violently. A moment later, the man collapsed, smoke rising from his mouth.

"Worthless fools!" the mage snapped.

"This place is cursed! Nothing's going right." The man with the broken nose rushed to help his fallen teammate, only to realize the truth. "He's dead. How is he dead?"

"Well, he's dead, whatever! Let's hurry. We still have to wipe out this fa—" The mage abruptly fell silent and turned around, but it was too late. His head toppled cleanly from his shoulders.

"Shit!"

The remaining intruders drew their blades, panic setting in. But their weapons were utterly useless against the skeletal warrior that now loomed before them.

CHAPTER 6

I WOKE UP IN THE MORNING only to find out that some scumbags trashed my entire study. There was blood everywhere! Xena nearly fainted when she saw it all and knew she'd have to clean everything. Honestly, we'd probably have to replace the floor or repaint it at least. But what about the carpets? What on earth would we do with those?

We handed the bodies over to the ISS. Let them deal with disposal. I had no interest in raising zombies from them. As for their souls — one went straight to Hell on its own, while the rest moved on to the afterlife.

Their gear, though, was interesting and probably expensive. I thought it could be useful, so we kept it. The investigators only got a brief look at it, muttered something like, "Nice stuff," and left looking dejected. Or maybe something else happened? I was half-asleep and barely paying attention.

On top of all that, I learned I had two secret compartments in my study! The first held twenty books of ultra-advanced light magic spells. Mastering those felt about as likely as a vacation on the moon.

The second contained the journal of the previous family patriarch. It was a goldmine, packed with records of family affairs: contracts, debts, orders, dirt on enemies, and more. I'd need to go through it carefully. Debts, huh? If I'm not mistaken, the Scully family often lent out money. Maybe this would also explain how Alexander's older brother managed to owe so much and to whom.

Oh, and I almost forgot — the compartment also contained three small artifacts: a ring, a small cube, and a fountain pen.

Ring of Righteous Fury
Rank: A
Description: *This ring absorbs all the pain you've endured over the past hour and releases it tenfold, amplifying both your physical and magical strength.*

Purification Cube
Rank: A
Description: *A mysterious artifact that, when infused with mana, unleashes holy energy to cleanse the surrounding area of evil forces.*

Additional Effect: *Holy mana significantly enhances the artifact's purifying power.*

Simple Ritual Pen
Rank: A
Description: *Any ritual circles drawn with this pen become more effective and require less mana to activate.*

As I understood it, this was Alexander's working kit, the one he used when fighting curses and dark creatures. And let me tell you, the last two items in there cost as much as the entire mansion! But of course, I wasn't planning to sell them. I'd need them myself.

I got a little sidetracked. After signing a mountain of paperwork and reassuring the women that I'd find extra security and everything would be fine, I headed down to the basement. The fact that my altar was already eight inches but still wasn't covered in runes wasn't right. I just never got around to working on it. Well, no big deal, I'd make sure my eight inches were in top shape now.

Soon enough, I was in the basement, sitting in front of my eight inches. The obelisk stood tall, like an unshakable rock, with four glowing runes at its peak. Now, I was about to add one to the middle. Unfortunately, just one for now. The rest I'd save for later, just in case.

I'd spent a long time deciding which rune to place. That was the main reason for the delay. It wasn't like I had a huge selection anyway — the real perks only started at the altar's third level. But even so, this required some thinking. The answer came to me on its own while I was figuring out how to arm my guards. And in the end, I figured out how to arm my entire army!

A lich, who was also a raven, used magic to craft armor and weapons for his undead minions. I could do the same. Was it expensive? Absolutely. But the "Weapon" rune significantly cut the costs and would give my creations a more refined look.

The rune wasn't just for weapons — it could also create armor, like plate mail and all kinds of gear. The more divine energy I poured into it, the better the equipment would be. As a Curator, I could clad myself in black armor, wielding a sword and shield.

The problem was, doing that in public was, to put it mildly, a surefire way to blow my cover. And then? Paladins, priests, a psychotic, deranged goddess hunting me down. A life on the run with no cake!

The rune took 2,100 units of DE. Costs weren't going to be uniform anymore. Some things would be more expensive, some cheaper.

Anyway, I finished up and, without bothering to test the rune, went upstairs. Why waste resources? I thought I'd test it that night, on the other side of the River. I had a slaughter to attend, after all.

Forty minutes later, I was hauling a fresh batch of zombie warriors to the lumberyard. They'd be guarding the area and training for combat. After all, they needed to get used to their new bodies, and that wasn't a quick process. Just yesterday, they had been warped souls and ghosts. Now, they had bodies and consciousness.

Zhanna, the kikimora, and I arrived at the sawmill, unloaded the horde of zombies, picked up some lumber, and headed back to the city. Then we did another couple of runs. And just to note — this wasn't a rented logging truck anymore. It was a brand-new, beautiful one.

A powerful cab with a sleeper for two behind the driver's seat. Insane off-road capability. Reinforced armor, plus various technomagical devices powered by crystals, including the engine. The black-and-red beauty even had a manipulator arm, perfect for loading timber and logs, or even monster corpses. It could also tow a trailer. I had two of those!

This luxury beast had cost me twenty-five million. Though there was a hundred-million model out there, but that wasn't meant for hauling lumber, that was for driving through wastelands, crushing monsters, and slaying dragons.

Thanks to the trailers, two runs were enough to haul everything from the warehouse, including hides, claws, and other trophies. According to Zhanna's estimates, the monster materials alone were worth around four million. Not a fortune, but still, a steady passive income.

What else would the zombies do there? The lumberjacks chopped down trees, which attracted all sorts of creatures. Their fighters took care of them. Oh, and I brought them new axes, some weapons made from shards, and plenty of clothes. Upgraded them all the way!

After that, I took the most experienced zombies with me. They'd be hunting in the wild lands. I didn't bother leaving the skeleton behind — I had already wiped out all the strong monsters in the area and sealed the gates, so there was no need for him to guard anything.

I was sure my advanced zombie, Herman, would handle things just fine. I gave him a full set of gear, including cockroach armor. I was even considering buying ten more sets. Let the zombies wander the forest, scaring people and monsters alike.

That armor had self-repair properties, which was perfect. And it cost next to nothing. So what if it looked disgusting and smelled awful? Honestly, it was debatable who reeked more — the zombies or the cockroach armor.

"That's a good idea," Zhanna confirmed, tapping a new task into her tablet.

And the truck? It was driving on autopilot! Pretty cool, right? You could sleep or read a book while it steered itself and ran over anything that got in its way. Of course, autopilot was banned in within the city limits.

But I got getting sidetracked again. After unloading everything, we set out on our expedition. To do that, we had to cross the bridge over the River and head southwest. To the east, that wild and dangerously turbulent river marked the boundary between settled lands and the untamed wilderness.

The bridge was unusual — it was a drawbridge, and lowering or raising it required special authorization. Then again, all I had to do was say who I was and where I was going.

"In a logging truck? Are you sure?" The soldiers eyed my monstrous beauty of a vehicle with confusion. Or rather, one particular officer did.

"Why not? It's got a manipulator arm, it's got a cargo bed, meaning plenty of room to store the spoils."

"You're planning to take the spoils, too?" His eyes widened even further as he stared at me. "The request was only for heads as proof."

"And just leave all that loot for the beasts to tear apart? Not a chance." I shook my head.

"But the blood and carcasses will attract predators!"

"Even better. Saves us the trouble of hunting them down." I grinned, while the officer froze, likely debating whether I was insane or just unbelievably stupid. Something told me he went with the first option, especially with the way he looked at my warriors in the truck bed.

Before long, the bridge was lowered, and we sped off into the wild lands — territory that had once belonged to the Ming Empire. No one really knew what had happened to them. First, monsters had pushed them away from the River's banks, and after that... well, who knew? Planes didn't fly over this region — it was too dangerous. There were satellites and high-altitude aircraft, of course, but any intelligence gathered that way wasn't shared with the public. So ordinary people and even aristocrats had no idea what to expect in these lands.

We had a map of the surrounding area — provided at the bridge checkpoint — but its monster-related details were next to useless. Most importantly, not a single cemetery was marked. Then again, the way I saw it, this entire wilderness was one giant graveyard.

Soon, we crossed the River. On the other side stood a small fort, and once we passed through it, we had officially left the empire's borders and entered the lands of monsters. I immediately headed southwest, toward the hills, to avoid attracting human attention. No one needed to witness the army of the god of death and the underworld on the hunt.

We quickly found an old dirt road, a relic from the days when the Chinese had lived here. An hour later, we stumbled upon the ruins of an ancient village.

There was nothing interesting left, just the half-buried remains of stone houses. No souls, no traces of life. If people had died here, their spirits had either moved on or turned into undead and wandered off. I just needed to figure out where they had gone, but that could wait.

After scattering some minor creatures with my aura of death, we continued on our way. The lesser beasts still feared us, but my fighters remained on high alert, as did the kikimora. She was already up on the roof, lounging in a swimsuit. Why a swimsuit? Maybe she was shy about strutting around naked in front of the zombies? Not that I minded the swimsuit.

With the second level of the altar, my aura had grown stronger, allowing us to travel about sixty miles undisturbed. We simply followed the road, letting it take us wherever it led. Eventually, it brought us to another dead city.

This one was far better preserved than the villages we had passed. I decided to use it as a temporary base. There was a lake, reinforced concrete buildings — some still in decent condition — rusted-out vehicles, and, most importantly, gates.

By rough estimates, the city had once housed about a hundred thousand people. There were no undead here, but I did spot malevolent spirits. They were likely the reason weaker creatures avoided the area.

We stopped in a large central square, where a tall stone statue still stood untouched. That's where we set up camp.

I had fifty zombies with me, and they immediately began gathering all the wrecked vehicles in the square, turning them into some sort of barrier. Why? I had no idea. That was Zhanna's decision. Whatever, let her have her fun. I even gave her my skeleton to help. Meanwhile, our dear bird took off on a scouting mission.

I ordered it to locate all nearby monsters and any gates. As for me, I turned my attention to the statue. Why was it still standing, looking so pristine? It depicted a powerful warrior, one arm wrapped protectively around a pregnant woman, the other outstretched, gripping a sword. The craftsmanship was exquisite.

I decided to make it even better by turning it into an altar of the Great Me. Why not? Repurposing existing structures was far more efficient and cost-effective than building one from scratch. Within half an hour, the statue bore two runes. As always, Death, which claimed the city as my domain, and Peace, which immediately began drawing in lost souls. But from where? Were there undead here after all?

"Master!" Zhanna ran up to me, visibly alarmed. Understandable — she couldn't see the countless ghosts. And there were many.

The air filled with howling winds, voices speaking in an unknown tongue, and various anomalies — flashes in the sky, distortions in space. The resonance of souls and the sheer force of death was overwhelming.

I allowed her to see what was happening, and she immediately grabbed my hand tightly. For someone who had lost a loved one not so long ago, this must have been especially painful. And I had a feeling I reminded her of her late husband. At least, when she gave me his shirt, it was only slightly too big. Now, I figured, it would fit just right. No point prying into the soul of my only follower, though.

Countless souls were now flooding into my altar, and it looked like I was going to recoup the thousand DE I had spent here. Most spirits dissipated immediately, finally finding the peace they had long sought. The voices — mostly children's, as they were the most emotional — made my assistant weep.

This city had fallen to a monster attack. All its residents had perished. Many hadn't died quickly, which explained the presence of so many vengeful spirits — too much suffering had taken place here. But now, there was peace, and some souls would be reborn, depending on their deeds and the strength of their essence.

Suddenly, the sky over the city darkened. Lightning flashed, thunder rumbled, but no rain fell. Instead, vengeful spirits poured down, twenty of them. Black, amorphous blotches — powerful ones at that — descended toward the statue. I couldn't just absorb them. I would have to fight.

I pushed Zhanna behind me and was about to strike when the spirits suddenly changed shape. Not into twisted shadows of cursed energy, but into something almost alive. They were only slightly translucent. And they were warriors — men and women clad in ancient armor. They knelt, then bowed in a formal salute.

"You wish to serve me?" I asked, surprised.

In response, I received a flood of mental images. They couldn't speak, their souls were too warped from their time as vengeful spirits. But I understood. Even in death, they had continued to protect the city and the souls that lingered here.

"I see. In return, you want me to grant peace to the rest of your kin." I nodded. "I don't mind, but it won't happen overnight. However, sooner or later, I will regain my full strength, and every soul in this world will find peace."

That answer satisfied them. Instead of merging with the altar, they entered my body directly.

These souls were strong and could easily move on to reincarnation. Yet they chose to stay and fight. Noble of them. Too bad I didn't have proper bodies for them. But I'd figure something out.

"For now, get to work!"

The souls could find peace without my help. Meanwhile, I poured five units of DE into each of my zombies. A dark mist enveloped them, gradually solidifying into black armor. They also gained matching black swords and shields. Did they know how to wield a sword? Hard to say. But at least they knew how to hold one. The rest they'd learn through battle. Hopefully.

Soon, we split up. The kikimora took ten zombies to hunt some strange foxes hiding in an old shopping mall. The skeleton led another ten toward a massive pit where oversized lizards had made their nest. A third group stayed behind to guard the truck. And as for me... Well, there just so happened to be E-rank gates nearby.

Twenty zombies stormed through one of the gates and we saw a jungle on the other side. The same kind I had encountered before. The monkeys were absolutely stunned by our sudden arrival. There were eleven of them. It took us about five minutes to deal with them all. We lopped off their heads, tossed them into a sack, and moved on.

That's how we worked — going from gate to gate. I didn't bother trying to predict which gods were behind them. What I needed was mana. Not just for myself, but for Zhanna as well.

The raven had drawn some kind of sigil on her shoulder. It absorbed and concentrated mana. Theoretically, once enough mana accumulated, the sigil would unleash it all at once, awakening her latent magical abilities.

Next, we reached some D-rank gates, where we were met by swine-crocs. The same ones that loved to charge with their snouts and fire air bullets from their noses. It was like a game of bowling, except my zombies were the pins. But once I reanimated the fallen, we tore through the bastards and kept moving.

With armor and weapons in hand, the zombies became much more efficient. Short-term, magic gear was expensive for them, but for a large-scale purge like this, it was a serious cost-saver. And I kept receiving notifications of DE gained by my other squads.

The city had been teeming with creatures, but they had been hiding, lurking in the shadows. This place was essentially one massive hunting ground, where everyone was both predator and prey. The winner was whoever struck first from ambush.

But none of that mattered now. We had filled the truck bed with bodies in no time and hadn't encountered anything truly strong — only D and

C ranks, at best. We tried to capture those. The rest, we just beheaded.

We'd be back. And yet, I couldn't shake the feeling that I had forgotten something...

CHAPTER 7

THE RADIO WAS PLAYING MILITARY SONGS, and Zhanna, in a good mood, hummed along while I simply sat back and relaxed. It was a job well done and I was quite pleased with myself.

I had gained a massive amount of divine energy, so I didn't hold back and pumped a good dose into ten of my zombies, stuffing them to the brim. Soon, they would evolve into advanced creatures, and I'd assign them to guard the mansion.

As usual, weak monsters didn't bother us, and we didn't encounter any strong ones nearby, so the journey back to the River was uneventful. What surprised me, though, was the traffic jam waiting for us.

Two massive combat groups — around five hundred people each, with plenty of vehicles — were returning to the city after a hunt. They, in turn, were quite surprised to see our logging truck, trailers, and the pile of monster corpses on board. Not to mention the fifty fighters in black outfits, hoods, and axes in hand.

We simply took our place at the back of the line, ignoring the many curious glances. Behind us, in the cabin's living quarters, the kikimora was resting, now fully dressed. I had recalled the skeleton. When he would finally evolve into a knight, as long as he kept his helmet on, no one would be able to tell he was undead. I'd could then bring him everywhere and save on summoning costs.

After a while, the bridge finally lowered, and we crossed. Several dozen more vehicles had lined up behind us. They were small-time groups, it seemed, since none had more than fifty people. Most were traveling in off-road vehicles and pickup trucks.

The latter had their cargo beds packed tight and sealed with tarp, probably filled with monster heads. If they hunted like this every day, there wouldn't be a single creature left around the city. No wonder the Emperor was furious. The aristocrats had all but abandoned their duty to fight monsters and protect the empire.

Now, with the threat of the Wave looming over them, they were scrambling to follow the Emperor's orders. I could already imagine the pomp and self-congratulation that would follow. And yet, all they were really told was: "Do your damn job."

"Uh, so, you brought the bodies and want to put them up for sale?" The soldiers on the city side of the River seemed taken aback. They were in charge of logging our kills and confirming monster heads as proof of the hunt. But no one had expected us to bring the whole corpses. We had heads too, of course, but most belonged to shard-beasts.

Now, we were standing in front of my monstrous truck while the officer in charge of tallying the haul eyed everything with confusion.

"That's right. Is there a problem? The order was to bring proof of the hunt," I said, still smiling as he grimaced. Clearly, this wasn't what he had signed up for.

"No... no problem..."

"Good to hear."

My zombies got to work unloading the monster carcasses. Fortunately, the truck's manipulator arm made the job much faster. Once the bed and both trailers were emptied, we finally headed home. There was still plenty of daylight left — we had finished far too fast.

That meant I had time for something important: inspecting the assets of the man who had lost the duel. I had already forgotten his family name, not that it mattered. The old patriarch had died of overeating. His family was small, and most had scattered, given that their clan was in serious debt.

There were two stores, a modest mansion, and a single, rather pathetic-looking car. No artifacts, no valuables. And, just my luck — because of their debts, half of their assets would go to their creditors.

At least I found out who that was. It was just one creditor, in fact — a George Talster. And he was an enemy of my house.

I had an excess of divine energy. Now I just needed to find him. That wouldn't be easy — I needed direct visual contact. Or maybe there was another way...

* * *

A few hours later
Somewhere in the city
A luxurious, but small office
George Talster

A tall and rather plump man lounged in a massive chair, completely naked. Kneeling before him was a relatively young woman, begging for forgiveness. Had Gauss been there, he would have recognized her as the very same girl who had supposedly been defiled by him.

"You idiots! You absolute idiots! Ughhh..." His grumbling abruptly stopped — the woman was a master of her craft. Even his frustration couldn't compete with the pleasure she provided.

Grabbing a large tablet — one designed specifically for people with fat fingers — he turned his attention to business, enjoying the best of both worlds.

His life had everything he could possibly want — money, influence, and, most importantly, power. That was what he loved most: making people do things they did not want to do.

"Hm, Scully went out into the wild lands?! And why am I — ah, right, the report came in early this morning… I was busy," the fat man muttered to himself. "A shame, really… Missed a perfect chance to have him killed. But isn't that too much loot? I'll have to investigate."

He scrolled down. "And what do we have here? The Ratters are trying to muscle into my restaurant business? Planning to open a luxury spot for aristos? Ha!"

"Caw!"

"Hm?" The man jerked his head around — there, perched on the open window, sat a raven. "Why is the window open? I'm sure I'd closed it."

"There's a bird."

"Don't get distracted." He pressed down on the girl's head. "And you — get lost, you filthy creature."

He pointed a finger at the black bird, and something — an invisible force — knocked it clean out of the air. Instead of crashing lifelessly to the ground, the falling creature suddenly flapped its wings and soared away.

·

THE COMING OF GOD OF DEATH

* * *

The Academy
A few days later
Gauss

"Can I try too?"

"No."

"But why?"

I gave Basel a once-over and grimaced.

"You already attract way too much female attention. Then they end up staring at our group and distracting everyone. Polina already has a hard enough time fending off competitors." I grumbled, continuing with what I was doing.

"Competitors? Polina?" He blinked at me in confusion.

"Forget it. Let Zverinski be the center of attention instead. At least that way, he'll be useful for once."

"Go to hell, Scully!" Zverinski said — he was sitting in front of me.

I was training my magic to raise my state of development faster. The parasite seemed like it was on the verge of keeling over from the strain — silver strands were already appearing in my hair.

"Why him and not one of the girls?" Basel asked, looking around. The girls looked rather upset as they watched us. Anna, meanwhile, sat nearby, smiling sweetly.

Her hair shimmered with vitality, and her skin

9 2

looked so soft and smooth that she was practically glowing. Give it a little more time, and she'd be radiating light like a human lamp from all that holy magic. I needed to find another test subject.

"I don't know. I asked — they all refused." I shrugged.

"Not a single one wants to participate," Anna chimed in, looking quite pleased with herself.

"Well, maybe Polina will agree. Is lunch soon?"

"No, not Polina." Basel winced at the mention of his girlfriend.

"Fine, fine. I'm not forcing anyone. Right, Zverinski?"

"You threatened to beat me up if I refused!" the long-haired blond shot back.

"Did I? Don't remember that. Anyway, your hair isn't absorbing my energy anymore. I'd say about seven more sessions, and you'll be a real beauty."

"No, thanks! I don't want to be a beauty!"

"Oh? Then why are you growing your hair out?" Zverinsky's golden locks reached the middle of his back. He was on the lanky side, though he insisted he was slim, not skinny.

"Because it looks good," he huffed, standing up and pulling out a folding compact mirror. Seriously?

"Well, damn!" He let out a heavy sigh, then flicked his hair dramatically before looking at the girls around.

There were gasps. Someone even let out a quiet "eep."

"How am I supposed to go to beauty salons now, knowing they'll never achieve results this good, no matter how much I pay?" I just shrugged and resumed my search for a new test subject.

And then, one walked right in. Miss Yana Orinofsky — our runic magic instructor. Not the most popular subject among students since runes were both difficult and time-consuming.

"Good afternoon, everyone, please take your... Scully? Do you need something? Maybe you should step out?" She smiled at me.

"A volu — uh, someone for magic practice."

"You were about to say volunteer, weren't you?" She narrowed her eyes, while someone in the class snickered.

"Possibly. I want to combine two healing spells, and unfortunately, Zverinski is all used up." I gestured toward the blond, who promptly tossed his hair again, earning more sighs from the girls.

"What about your classmates?"

"They don't want to participate," Anna answered before I could. The teacher turned to her.

"Winters, maybe you should return to your own lecture hall?"

"I'd rather not, not while Alex is still looking for volunteers." She shook her head and shot a pointed glare at the other girls. And suddenly, like a prisoner who, after four days of incarceration, finally realizes that one of the walls in his cell was missing, I understood why none of the girls had agreed. It was Anna's jealousy!

"Besides, my group has Ritual Magic right now, and I've already passed the exam."

"Then fine." The teacher nodded. "Just don't disrupt the lesson. Today's topic is… What, Scully?"

"Practice." I raised my hands, letting them glow. What, did she think I ate that mana crystal for nothing?

She hesitated, looking at Zverinski, but ultimately couldn't resist. With Anna's approval, of course. I really needed to rein in that jealous streak of hers, it was actively getting in the way of my progress.

So, the teacher took a seat at a table in the corner of the classroom, while I worked on her hair. She always wore her hair tied back, so I had to undo the ponytail first.

I had to admit, she was quite attractive. Well-proportioned, around thirty-five years old, and popular among both teachers and students. She typically dressed in a long black skirt and a crisp white blouse.

At first, she was distracted by my presence. But soon enough, she forgot all about me and even went up to the board. Which meant I had to follow her around the classroom, which was rather exhausting.

Thankfully, she wasn't too tall — just about six inches taller than me, while wearing heels.

The lesson lasted an hour and a half, and for all ninety minutes, I trailed after her, applying Wet Hands and Purification, with just a touch of divine energy. Of course, I used different hands for each spell.

I wanted to test the combined effects and enhanced properties. And it worked! I had finally mastered this magic. It had been an absolute nightmare to get right, but it was worth it. This magic kills viruses and bacteria, removes dirt, and even rejuvenates skin.

It wasn't just skin that could be refreshed, too. This magic allowed for a quick clean-up — removing dirt and blood from clothes in an instant. But most importantly, it made getting rid of the stench of decay effortless!

Yesterday, I went to the cemetery and let my Chinese warriors pick out bodies for themselves. And they were a picky bunch! I took them to the lumberyard, gave them a few of my artifacts, and left them to sustain themselves with divine energy for their evolution.

They had specifically asked for swords, yet they turned their noses up at what I gave them! In the end, they begrudgingly accepted what I offered but claimed they'd find themselves worthy weapons on their own.

BOOK THREE

* * *

Sometime later
Auditorium
Yana Orinofsky — the teacher

"That's all for today. Thank you for being so quiet during the lesson. I wish it were like this more often," Miss Orinofsky said with a dazzling smile before walking out, causing many of the guys to momentarily forget how to breathe. She was going to the teachers' lounge, and then the cafeteria for lunch.

"Why is everyone staring at me?" she muttered to herself, noticing the looks she was getting. "Oh, right, I forgot to tie my hair back. They're just not used to seeing me like this." She continued on her way and soon reached the teachers' lounge.

"Ugh, I'm so exhausted!" she groaned, slipping off her uncomfortable but very stylish heels and changing into slippers. Everyone in the lounge wore slippers — it was more of a break room than a formal workspace.

"Yana?" came a male voice. The woman turned to see another teacher holding a cup of coffee.

"Yes, John?" He was openly staring at her. Usually, he was more reserved.

"I've been meaning to ask for a while but never quite got the nerve… Would you like to have dinner with me?"

"Um… yes?" She liked John, and he liked her,

but neither had ever made the first move. Until now. "I mean, sure!"

"Oh!" A female voice suddenly squeaked. "Ya-Ya-Yana! What happened to your hair? And your face! What happened to you?! Tell me! Where did you go?! What beauty salon is this?!"

A tall, stunning woman — the star among the faculty, adored by both students and teachers alike — rushed toward Yana with trembling hands.

"What are you talking about?" Yana asked. But the other woman grabbed her shoulders and spun her toward the mirror.

"How is this possible?!"

Yana stared at her reflection in disbelief. Her hair was majestic and seemed unreal, and her face... It was hard to believe she wasn't wearing any makeup. Every wrinkle had smoothed out, every skin imperfection had vanished. She looked as if she had been returned to the time when she was eighteen years old.

"Speak!"

"Uh... Scully. He said he needed a volunteer for a new spell or something like that... While I was giving my lecture, he was infusing my hair with magic, but I never thought the effect would be like this!"

The other woman wasn't listening anymore. Nearly tripping over herself, she dashed out in search of Scully.

BOOK THREE

* * *

The Scully mansion
Evening
Gauss

It had been a rough day. The female teachers had all lost their minds! They swarmed me, nearly tearing me apart, all demanding the same treatment Miss Orinofsky had received. I was trying to have my lunch at the time.

But in the end, they managed to bribe me with top grades and preferential treatment during exams. Of course, they couldn't just hand out the grades themselves, since an official commission oversaw the exams. A shame, really...

I worked while Anna fed me. And surprisingly, given my usual appetite, I ate quite modestly. The parasite claimed it was full and couldn't absorb any more energy from food, so I had to limit myself to just four dishes. Not that I had much of an appetite, to be honest. It seemed my ravenous hunger had been caused by the parasite's insatiability all along.

Yet, I still hadn't reached rank seven, despite devouring an absurd number of mana crystals. I guess I'd just have to keep going. Time to find more test subjects.

Luckily, a way to burn through a massive amount of mana presented itself. It was a new job, the one for the Sparrow family. They were ready

9 9

and had invited me to deal with a shard infested with the undead and spirits.

They were very secretive about it, so I went alone — Anna wasn't allowed in for "security reasons." The Sparrows were terrified of revealing the location of their precious shard. Whatever. I didn't care.

Oh, and by the way, the SCU had finished extracting all the gold and valuable materials from that gorilla infested canyon shard. What did I get? Forty million transferred to my account. Not bad!

Now, I was on my way in an armored SUV. The raven flew above, keeping me updated telepathically on our location and scanning for any signs of an ambush. There wasn't one.

A short while later, we arrived at an outpost. It was guarded by six hundred men. Hell of a security force, especially for a shard!

My job was to eliminate all the undead, along with poltergeists, vengeful spirits, and other nasty entities. I needed them all to reinforce my home's defenses. That's why my bag was stuffed with rune stones — handmade, though not without the help of that A-rank pen.

"Are you sure there aren't any people inside?" I asked, standing before a small C-rank gate.

"No, as you requested," the family patriarch said.

"Got it. So, if I do find people inside, that means they aren't yours, and I can kill them." I shrugged and stepped through the gate, which immediately sealed behind me. I wouldn't be able to leave for four hours.

Destroying the core had been forbidden, since that would cause the shard to collapse. As long as it remained intact, the Sparrows could continue harvesting resources. Supposedly, shards gradually regenerated. Not that anyone was entirely sure. If they called me back for another undead purge, that would mean the shards did regenerate. Not that it mattered right now.

I stepped through the gate and found myself standing atop a cliff. Below lay an abandoned mining village. Undead roamed the streets. They were strong, too, which was not surprising for a C-rank gate.

I had my sword, my mantle, and the Purification Cube, which I still hadn't had a chance to use.

"Hm, I can feel a strong will here," I noted as I made my way down the mountain path.

It was short but well-maintained, so I reached the bottom quickly and approached the village, surrounded by jagged cliffs. It was no small settlement, and there were plenty of enemies inside. So, I summoned the skeleton.

I could already tell that controlling the undead here wouldn't be an option. But as soon as we stepped forward, they appeared — skeletal archers perched on the rooftops of the one-story houses. A volley of arrows rained down.

"Ambush!" my skeleton's voice echoed in my mind as he stepped in front of me, raising his shield.

Arrows clattered against his armor, some

piercing through and lodging in his bones, but most struck the shield.

Meanwhile, I conjured a Firefly, infusing it with both mana and divine power. Once it was ready, I hurled it past the skeleton. A moment later, it erupted in a brilliant flash of light laced with black streaks.

Two dozen archers on the rooftops collapsed into heaps of bones. We surged forward, but skeletal warriors poured out of the houses. Side by side with my guardian, I braced for the fight, holding the line against the oncoming wave.

"Rest in peace!" I commanded, exhaling a black mist. As soon as it touched the skeletons, they crumbled into piles of bones. The smarter ones, however, backed away at the sight of the mist, only to charge again once it had dispersed.

"Your master must be strong if you can resist me," I mused. "This should be interesting."

With these words, I deflected a strike from a rusted sword, kicked the skeleton back, and drove my blade into its chest, piercing the corroded armor. It immediately collapsed into a pile of bones, and I rushed at another one.

And then, something I hadn't expected appeared — animated armor warriors! These were towering, headless figures, standing over six and a half feet tall. Their bodies were made of assembled metal plates, resembling suits of armor. They wielded massive swords, and black mist seeped from the gaps in their plating.

"Interesting!" My eyes gleamed with excitement as I exhaled black smoke to drive back the lesser undead, then reached into my bag and pulled out a custom-made piece of metal.

It weighed about four pounds and had a honeycomb-like structure — steel on the outside, copper on the inside. I hurled it at one of the animated armors. A loud "Boom" echoed through the air, and the entire cloud of black mist was sucked into the object! Perfect. The spirit trap worked flawlessly, which meant I could keep going.

We threw ourselves at the armored warriors, and as we fought, I prepared a Flash Burst. We were pushed back toward a house, and the number of our enemies had grown to around forty.

That was when I unleashed the spell. The skeletons were swept away as if by a wave. They were flung back, and by the time they hit the ground, they were nothing but scattered bones. Right after that, more enemies appeared. It was as if they were attacking in small groups on purpose, trying to wear me down.

Unfortunately, there were no zombies or any other creatures with flesh, which meant I had nothing to raise as a puppet. Using skeletons would just be wrong.

We kept fighting, but the enemies only got stronger! Flash Burst was our saving grace, and I was beyond grateful that I had stocked up on mana crystals. Still, I could hold out for a long time.

Every undead I destroyed was absorbed into my underworld, where most of them found peace.

DE trickled in slowly, but my overall expenditure was still higher.

It made me wonder — where were all these undead and wandering souls coming from? I found it hard to believe this was just a fragment of a divine plane. Or had one of the gods created a whole world here and populated it with the dead? That seemed entirely possible.

"So, you're the strong ones, huh?" I muttered, watching as four knights survived my Flash Burst. The regular skeleton warriors had all been reduced to bones. The whole village was already littered with them! "How many more are there?"

The fully armored knights didn't respond and, raising their massive swords, charged at us. My guardian met them head-on, knocking three to the ground, while I went for the last one.

I dodged as its huge blade came crashing down, then slashed at its leg. But the armor was so thick that I had to strike again. This time, I infused the blow with four DE. However, before I could land it, the knight nearly kicked me, then followed up with another sword strike, this time at an angle. I barely managed to duck in time.

Now it was my turn. My first attack was deflected, the second nailed the skeleton in the chest, the third was blocked by its left arm, but the fourth finally pierced through its armor, sinking deep into its core.

A moment later, its bones and armor collapsed to the ground, and I immediately rushed to help my guardian. The battle was brutal, but with my aid, the remaining three knights finally fell. It seemed that was the last of them. I channeled energy into my guardian to help him recover from his injuries, retrieved my spirit trap, and we headed toward the cave.

As soon as we stepped inside, two more animated armors appeared, but they immediately collapsed, falling into heaps of scrap metal. We continued onward without resistance.

Inside the cave, torches flickered along the walls, the wind howled through the tunnels, and then...

You've absorbed an evil spirit and get 30 units of divine energy.

There were many vengeful spirits and ghosts here, but how was I supposed to hit them with a chunk of metal? The bastards kept dodging! I hadn't considered that when designing the traps. So, I had no choice but to absorb them instead.

And so, we continued forward, wiping out the undead until we reached a massive cave, which was the boss's lair.

"Well, hello there, my friend. And why the hell are you so huge?"

CHAPTER 8

A MASSIVE, NEARLY TEN-FOOT-TALL zombie with arms as thick as tree trunks stared down at me. And I stared back. In my hand, radiating darkness, lay my sword. Beside me stood my skeletal guardian — slightly battered but ready to fight. The enemy was undoubtedly strong, but slow and clumsy, which I planned to exploit.

"Mas... ter..." he suddenly dropped to his knees.

Guerilla zombie, the keeper of the shard, wants to become your guardian.
Accept?
Guardian maintenance will cost you 6 units of DE daily.

"You are smart and strong, and your am-

bushes were effective. I won't refuse such a guardian, so be it!"

The kneeling zombie was swallowed by a black
blotch that appeared behind him. And with that
the shard was cleansed, and the barrier surrounding the pedestal with the core collapsed.

Except, without destroying the core, I still had
a few hours left to sit here and wait. Bored, I decided to explore the cave and came across a vein
of strange bluish ore. It had a faint glow and felt
warm to the touch. Whatever, it wasn't my con-
cern. My job was done, and the rest didn't matter.

Returning to the village, I found a half-decent
house with a bed and collapsed onto it. It was hor-
ribly uncomfortable, but I fell asleep surprisingly
fast.

* * *

At the same time
Talster mansion
George Talster

Throwing on a robe, George Talster stepped out of
the bathroom, where two beauties had just
washed every piece of his fat body and given him
the proper treatment. He was in a fantastic mood,
and even past failures couldn't get him down. After
all, a new day meant new opportunities!

He went into his study and headed for his desk
as usual, but suddenly, he accidentally stepped on
the belt of his robe! He never tied it, because it felt
uncomfortable around his belly.

"Ah, shit!" George lurched sideways, tripped over the edge of the desk, and, toppling over it, crashed face-first onto an unfortunately placed metal briefcase.

A loud "clang" echoed through the room, followed by a string of curses. Moments later, two naked women burst out of the bathroom, still dripping wet. They rushed to their master's side and helped him up. One of them immediately ran off to fetch the mansion's resident physician, who was kept nearby exclusively for the patriarch.

"Looks like I got up on the wrong foot," George grumbled, rubbing his bruised nose and forehead. The petite girl, barely a fifth of his weight, tried to lead him to the couch. But the floor was slippery from the water that dripped off the girls when they ran in to help.

She managed to walk just fine, but the man shifted his full mass onto one leg, only for it to slip. With a thunderous crash, the fat man hit the floor, shaking the entire building, and at that very moment, a massive, elegant chandelier came crashing down on top of him! A split second before impact, he shoved the maid aside to keep her from getting crushed.

"Ah, shit!" he cursed again. "Looks like even the goddess herself is telling me I should take it easy today."

For a mage of his caliber, a mere chandelier wasn't much of a threat. With a grunt, he lifted it off himself and sat up.

"What a mess..."

BOOK THREE

*   *   *

Somewhere
Sometime
Me

"Master Scully! Wake up! Master Scully!" A voice buzzed in my ear, relentless and persistent. I had no choice but to open my eyes, only to find the face of the Sparrow patriarch staring down at me.

"Hmm? Has the gate opened?" I asked, yawning loudly. Just when I had finally gotten comfortable...

"It's been open for an hour! We were worried since you didn't come out and decided to check."

"I see... The shard is cleared," I said as I got up and stepped outside. There were quite a few people around, tidying up the area and gathering bones — probably to prevent them from rising again. I could also hear the noise coming from the mine. They were quick, I had to give them that.

Some time later, we made our way back to the gate. It was being forcefully held open; otherwise, it would have locked itself for several more hours. I stepped through without issue and immediately asked to be taken home. It was already late, and I wanted to get this over with quickly so I could get back to sleep.

I had three traps, each containing vengeful spirits. They were strong enough to interact with physical objects. Now I just needed to motivate them properly. That didn't take much effort, thanks to well-crafted seals. However, maintaining them required two DE per day, and I needed at least ten of them to fully secure the mansion. Oh well, I'd just have to capture more spirits and set up additional altars.

I used the amulet-traps to protect the sisters' and Tatiana's rooms. Any intruder attempting to enter either their rooms or their assigned section of the mansion would be met with an aggressive poltergeist attack. That wouldn't stop a powerful mage, but would buy time.

And let's not forget the Fortress rune. It had worked wonders on those would-be thieves and burglars last time. But that could wait. Right now, I needed sleep. And so, that's exactly what I did.

The next day, I practiced magic, consumed mana crystals, and, of course, napped during lectures. Before I knew it, it was Friday, meaning time for another field exercise. Just like last time, we were given a D-rank shard.

The advisor looked on edge when we arrived, probably worried there'd be another incident. But we surprised him and cleared the shard without a hitch. Basel and I made a good team, and Polina did well. Whenever necessary, she summoned her mist to shield us from enemies with ranged attacks, specifically, the spitting spiders. Despite her fear of arachnids, she held her ground. And Anna? She was her usual self, looking like spiders, or rather cutting off their legs, were what she did best in life.

We successfully cleared the shard, earned a D-rank magic staff as our reward, and returned to the Academy, where, for some reason, I was summoned to the head's of school office.

"Oh, Scully? That was fast! You wrapped up the shard already?" Surprisingly, the head of school was in the middle of a yoga exercise, rather flexible for his size. "The reason I called you is because Chita's governor reached out to me. He wants to reward you."

"Hm? A reward? For killing the Wave's main beast?"

"Yes. You basically saved the whole city back then. The SCU confirmed the monster's death — just before scavenger swarms completely devoured it," the director said, stretching toward his feet — first one, then the other.

"I like rewards, but I'm planning to head into the wild lands for a hunt this weekend."

"Understood. Then let's schedule it for Monday after class," the head of school suggested. I nodded in agreement.

Soon after, I was free to go and get back to my own business — specifically, a trip to the factory. Zhanna was already waiting for me in the parking lot.

"Caw! Caw!" My raven circled above, looking way too excited.

"Good evening, Master," Zhanna greeted me with a smile. The kikimora was sitting in the car, giving me a brief nod.

"Evening." I climbed into the car, and Zhanna

briefed me on recent matters, including the Sparrows payment: fifteen million. Not bad, considering that was just for a small shard. How great it would be to find more just like it.

"As you ordered, I purchased ten full sets of cockroach armor. Additionally, all the trophy armor has undergone a full cycle of repairs and maintenance."

She was referring to the armor taken from the people who had attacked us on our way to the lumberyard — forty-seven sets of old armor, along with an equal number of basic technomagical rifles.

"Excellent," I nodded, satisfied. Now I could further reinforce the mansion's security.

When we arrived at the factory, we were immediately greeted by two zombies standing guard, clad in that same armor and bearing my family's emblem. They had rifles, though I wasn't sure how useful those would actually be.

Dressed in a sharp black suit, the kikimora stayed by the car while Zhanna and I headed inside, nearly colliding with a blonde zombie in the process.

"Oh! Sorry! I almost ran into you..." Before us stood a young woman in a black security uniform. On her hands, she wore D-rank gauntlet-knuckles — the same ones I had acquired. What stood out even more were her striking light-colored hair and the rather prominent breasts at my eye level. If I recalled correctly, she was one of the developed ones — the same one that old pervert had his eye on because of her "outstanding" features.

"It's fine. No problem." I let her pass, and she quickly hurried outside. She spoke surprisingly well — not something you'd expect from a zombie.

"Master! Zhanna!" Maxim's voice rang out, his gaze lingering on the blonde as she left. "I've prepared everything."

We stepped inside. As usual, the factory was alive with activity. The zombies worked tirelessly, the furniture production ran without pause, and the lumber supplies were depleting rapidly. We'd need bring more lumber tomorrow.

A while later, we arrived on the third floor, only to find utter chaos. Papers were scattered everywhere, and the air reeked of unwashed socks. There was dirty underwear under the table.

"Maybe you should get yourself an assistant," I suggested, barely avoiding stepping on a receipt for a batch of furniture.

"But what about our secrecy? The zombies and all that..."

"Hm... You're right. And zombies wouldn't be suitable for this kind of work." I noted. This required high cognitive ability, something even developed zombies lacked. "Although, I do have a candidate in mind..."

I suddenly remembered the waitress who had become a mage and wanted to serve under me. I wondered if she had enrolled in the school for commoner mages. I'd have Zhanna look into it later.

"I'd really appreciate that!" the old man said, visibly relieved. I couldn't blame him — there was a ton of work, and he was handling it all alone.

We then discussed the order from... what was his name again? The guy I saved from the accident. He had placed a massive furniture order worth 150 million!

According to Maxim, we'd complete it in two months, which was fantastic news. Even better news was that our factory had almost no operating costs. The materials were free, the zombies needed no salaries, and we saved on food and countless other expenses. Plus, the factory ran 24/7.

After discussing business and arranging the shipment, I stepped outside, where a dozen zombie warriors were already waiting for me. They were all clad in battle armor, painted white. Their weapons? Rifles and mercenary blades.

And so, we hauled this brave little squad to the mansion. Ivan was a bit surprised to see these fighters appear out of nowhere, and even more surprised that they didn't need to be registered, paid a salary, or anything of the sort.

But in the end, I was the patriarch, and my word was final. The people at the mansion had gotten a bit too comfortable, so the sight of armed fighters was a wake-up call.

As for those slackers who were supposed to be guarding us before, we suited them up in armor too. They were thrilled, especially about the technomagic rifles. Despite being old, the armor was still pretty solid. Plus, it couldn't be hacked, since it had almost no electronics. Which was good, considering I'd just been informed that some hackers had managed to disable our security system.

We were still trying to figure out how that was done, and on top of that, I'd been reading the diary of the previous patriarch. It was so boring that I could barely manage half an hour at a time. The man had a thing for brevity. His entries were something like: "Visited Jones. Evil spirit. Category 4. Purification cube ineffective. Used rituals. Trapped and dispelled. Success."

He had no shortage of exorcism work, which, in theory, should have meant he had plenty of friends. And yet, not a single one of them stood up for him when the clan wars began. That's why it's always better to take money now rather than promises of friendship and good relations, only to be betrayed later.

That was Friday. On Saturday, we set off for the Wildlands.

First stop, of course, was the lumber mill to check on my Chinese zombies. Those turned out to be defective. When I brought them to the mill, they were all sturdy and powerful. But now? I came back to find twenty short, round-faced, narrow-eyed men and women.

Just like my soul, after landing in Alexander's body, was trying to reshape it to match my true form, the same thing was happening with my servants. If these were ordinary zombies, they would've stayed the way they were. But they were my divine servants, their power granted by a god — namely, me. It was the same way Reyna's paladins and priests functioned.

So, calling them traditional undead was a bit

of a stretch. Their little beards were hilarious, and looking at their height, I started to wonder if Alexander was Chinese too.

"Great One!" The moment I stepped out of the lumber truck, the warriors surrounded me and knelt. There was just one problem — I didn't understand a word of Chinese!

"Forgive... should have guessed... that Great One... not know our language," a woman said so I understood.

It seemed like she was struggling to remember the words. Honestly, it was impressive that she could speak a foreign language at all. She was, after all, an evil spirit, a corrupted ancient soul. Most of her memories should have been lost by now. And usually, the first ones to go are the insignificant ones.

Like trigonometry. Whoever actually needed trigonometry in real life? Certainly not Alexander. But what about his father's drunken ramblings about how they'd rebuild the family by making it numerous?

According to the former patriarch's plan, Lena and Katie would've been pumping out kids like a factory. And ancestral magic could've made that possible. Then again, Alexander already had a ridiculous number of siblings — both of the patriarch's wives had done their part. But I digress.

I looked at the twenty zombies and noticed one was holding a brand-new two-handed axe, another had a horned helmet. Wait, were they actually sealing gates? I figured I would ask. "Can you seal?"

"Yes, Great One," the woman answered immediately. She was quite pretty, I might add.

"Ugh, so much mana wasted on nothing. But whatever. You're doing great. Now, we're going to free your homeland from monsters." The Chinese zombies perked up.

I'd completely forgotten we had to deliver the lumber first. We made two trips and also brought replacement parts to repair the conveyor equipment. That was a request from Joe, the zombie foreman — the one who had managed to get the machinery up and running.

I also brought various materials so the zombies could patch up the holes in the walls surrounding the mill. They assured me they'd handle it, and I'd figured I'd let them.

Then we were back in the Wildlands. Heavy machine tracks were everywhere, and near the bridge there was a mangled APC that looked like it'd been torn apart by claws. Someone had obviously towed it there. Judging by the bloodstains, some of the people inside hadn't survived when that tin can got peeled open.

"Gra-a-a-a-ar!" Suddenly, a massive beast tumbled onto the road between two hills. About ten feet tall and sixteen feet long. Two wolf-like heads, a massive bear-like body, and beautiful silvery fur.

My Chinese warriors immediately leaped out of the lumber truck, like grasshoppers. The other zombies clambered out after them, though far less gracefully.

"Kill the monster!"

"In the name of the Great One!"

The Chinese warriors shouted something in their language and charged the creature. Divine energy instantly poured out of me, flowing into their weapons, filling them with power. And just in time — the beast had a barrier.

"Gra-a-ar!" the creature roared, snapping its jaws and swinging its massive paws. But it didn't even manage to hit anyone. Well, at least not until the other zombies got closer.

I quickly called them back, wanting to give the Chinese warriors a chance to prove themselves. It seemed I hadn't been wrong to take them in and grant them power. The twenty of them moved as a single unit. The beast was constantly surrounded, and the moment it tried to attack, it was struck from all sides.

They didn't leave themselves open, didn't take reckless risks, didn't act foolishly. And also they jumped like fourteen feet in the air! My warriors soared onto the monster's back, slashing at it, wearing down its barrier.

The creature finally lost its patience, both heads glowing as it prepared to unleash magic — one head gathered icy breath, while the other burned with fire. But then, two glowing orbs shot toward its faces. The beast blinked at them in confusion just before they exploded in a blinding flash of light.

The now-blinded creature let out a furious

roar, spewing its gathered mana uselessly into the sky. My warriors seized the opportunity, their weapons smoking with darkness as they struck. And just like that...

Your servant had killed a monster and absorbed its power.
You get: +83 divine energy.

Wait... what rank was that thing? A? That seemed weak for an A-rank, but oh well.

Soon, the corpse was loaded onto one of the trailers, and we continued toward the town where my altar stood. That's where we'd resume our productive and fruitful hunt. I figured, while we were at it, I'd take Zhanna through the shards — maybe she'd finally awaken as a mage.

CHAPTER 9

Fortress by the River
Loot collection point

"YOU'RE BACK QUICKLY TODAY. Any trouble? If so, I'd appreciate any intel on the whereabouts of strong monsters," asked the SCU officer — the same one who had inspected our haul last time.

"Yeah, we had a problem — not enough space in the trucks," I sighed. We had to bury so many carcasses. I wanted to burn them, but then everyone would've seen the smoke column. And if we left them lying around, they'd attract scavenger beasts.

"Not enough?" The man walked past me toward the trailers, then froze in shock. "H-how?!"

His words immediately drew several other fighters over, and they all gawked, jaws hanging open. My lumber truck had two trailers hitched to it, both nearly overflowing with severed heads. We had to decapitate most of the corpses and take only the most valuable parts — eleven B-rank and four A-rank. But these creatures were so massive that they took up almost half the available space!

Honestly, I was upset about the lost profits. We left behind millions in monster carcasses, and it was only three in the afternoon. We hadn't even sealed many gates, Zhanna's magic hadn't broken through, and now... what the hell was I supposed to do for the rest of the day?

"You'll let us handle the sale, right?" the officer asked. Funny, he hadn't wanted to deal with this last time.

Selling them myself would've been a nightmare — I didn't have the market connections or staff like the big families did. So, of course, I let the SCU handle the transaction. Naturally, they'd take a cut, but at least I wouldn't get scammed.

Before long, the unloading was complete, and Zhanna drove the truck to the factory. Maxim was already waiting for us, and he looked upset.

"What happened?" I asked, walking up to him.

"This!" He handed me a document. In short, we were facing some legal consequences for illegal logging.

Technically, we could cut down the trees, but only under specific conditions for forestry workers, like setting up a special insurance fund and more bureaucracy. Apparently, logging was considered a deadly job. And I could see why — there were plenty of lumberjacks buried in cemeteries.

But as long as the pay was good, there would always be people willing to do it. Though, honestly, I doubted the Krasnovs had these so-called insurance funds. They were far too greedy for that.

"Well then, why don't we go have a little chat?" I grinned predatorily, having found a way to fill the rest of my day.

Leaving the zombies and the lumber truck behind, Zhanna and I headed to the city administration building. If they'd delivered a letter today, that meant they were working.

I left my Chinese warriors in the Wildlands. I couldn't be bothered to haul them back to the sawmill, and this way, they could keep hunting and purging their "Chinese" lands of the "Chinese" monsters.

The city administration greeted us with confusion. "But it's Saturday. We're closed."

I shoved the letter with today's date into the receptionist's face, which quickly changed her attitude. She had no choice but to call the genius who signed it. And wouldn't you know it, the guy was at work, though he wasn't supposed to be. From the faint voice coming from the phone, I could tell he was surprised to hear he had visitors. But then his tone shifted to excitement, and he ordered the receptionist to send us in.

She personally escorted us to his office, but the man wasn't in any rush to open the door. Trying to rattle me, maybe? Hoping I'd lose my temper and start throwing insults? Foolish mortals.

"Dear Margo," I read her name from her badge,

"am I correct in assuming that the not-so-honorable Athanasius is making us wait on purpose?"

"W-what? No, I'm sure there's a reason." The girl looked uneasy. I could see on her face that she understood everything but couldn't do anything about it.

"I certainly hope so. Because open disrespect toward the high aristocracy could be grounds for a duel, or a lawsuit." I said the last bit loud enough, and, what a miracle, the door swung open. But we didn't hurry inside. Because suddenly, I had an urgent need to call Anna.

"Alex?" Her voice sounded surprised. "I thought you were still in the Wildlands."

"Already back, and with a good haul. Is your father still there?"

"Yeah, he's scheduled to return in an hour. Why?" Her voice tensed. Did I spook her?

"Well, if he happens to find some undead but doesn't feel like dealing with them, I'd be happy to take that burden off his hands."

"Oh! That's what you meant! Got it, I'll let him know. And Alex, your sisters and I are out shopping, it's kinda hard to talk and try on this really beautiful purple lace bra at the same time."

"Got it. Sorry, I won't distract you."

Ending the call, I calmly stepped into a rather small office and narrowed my eyes — the darkness of this man's soul practically burned to look at. He had taken so many lives...

But that was a thought for later. Suppressing my ability to perceive soul corruption, I took a quick look around. The office was extravagant, everything screamed wealth. This man reveled in luxury and in flaunting his importance, as evidenced by the photographs where he shook hands with various city patriarchs.

One of the walls featured a massive map of the city's surrounding areas, with about a dozen marked spots near the forests. Likely sawmills. Behind a large desk sat a man in his forties, of average height and sturdy build, with an unnaturally thick head of hair. He looked irritated.

In front of his desk stood a wooden stool. Was that meant for me? Bold move. Or was he just foolishly fearless? Fortunately for him, there was an armchair in the corner, and that's where I sat. It was far from the official, but my eyesight was sharp. Though now Zhanna had to stand. I invited her to sit on my lap, but then her back completely blocked my view...

"Why don't *you* sit on *my* lap?" she suggested. I nodded, and... wow, what soft, comfortable legs she had. Not to mention the two large, plush cushions pressing right against the back of my head. So cozy, I almost didn't feel like arguing anymore.

"Are you done?" the official grumbled.

"Hm? Done with what?" I looked at him in surprise. "You only have one chair, but there are two of us. You could've at least provided a couch. And why place the chair so far? It's inconvenient to talk."

"Well then, you could have moved closer!"

"Oh? If you're implying that this stool was

meant for the patriarch of a high-aristocracy family, I'll execute you in a duel right here and now." I gestured toward the cheap plastic thing — it wasn't real wood after all. Zhanna immediately snapped a photo. Smart girl.

The official turned crimson, clearly wanting to fire back but stopping himself each time. Cunning bastard...

"Oh! Where did that come from?!" he suddenly said. "I specifically asked my staff to bring two fine chairs, befitting your status! I apologize for this misunderstanding."

"Let's not waste time on empty talk and get to the point. What's with these ridiculous and unfounded accusations against my factory?"

"Ridiculous and unfounded?!" His face contorted into "sincere" indignation and righteous anger. "According to the Imperial Decree 'insert bureaucratic jargon, dates, and numbers', the harvesting of magical timber in red zones is strictly regulated! You are required to have 'more terrifying bureaucratic nonsense'. Otherwise, you are endangering the lives of Imperial citizens for your own greed!"

"That's all well and good, but I don't have a single human lumberjack," I said, throwing him off completely.

"What? Then where is all that timber you bring in every weekend coming from?!" He looked at me, while I sat back, comfortable as ever. It could be more perfect only if I had a cup of tea and a slice of cake. I think my relaxation was irritating him.

"From deep in the forest. We just go and pick it up."

"And it just lies there untouched? No one needs it?"

"Oh, someone needs it — monsters. I come back with a pile of trophies every time."

"Stop trying to feed me nonsense!" he snapped. "Where exactly do you get your timber?!"

"Lower your voice when speaking to me, bureaucrat," I said in a cold, serious tone, fixing my gaze on him. "As you might have noticed, I don't bring in raw wood, I bring in lumber. Where I get it is none of your business. Consider it found."

"F-found? You just find it?" He was beginning to fume.

"Anything taken from monsters rightfully belongs to Master Scully," Zhanna interjected. The official was about to say something offensive but barely held himself back. A shame.

"Any other questions?"

"Where is this storage site?! It requires an inspection!"

"Oh, so I tell you where it is, and then next time I arrive, it's mysteriously empty, huh?" I laughed.

"Master Scully is under no obligation to disclose or register his trophies. That is a matter of his family," Zhanna chimed in again, making his eyebrow twitch.

"Any other questions?" I asked, smirking.

"No. No questions. For now," he growled.

"Good. But be warned — if any of my words

here are twisted or misrepresented, I will take this to court immediately. And besides that... you might want to say your goodbyes to your family," I added, shaking my head.

"Is that a threat?!"

"We light mages have certain abilities. And you, in particular... the number of lives you've taken puts even the worst serial killers to shame. The souls of those whose deaths you caused..." I stared intently behind him. The official turned around — but saw nothing.

"Well, it doesn't matter anymore. I won't interfere with the vengeful spirits' justice. Good luck," I said with a grin. He had no idea who I was wishing luck to.

You've spent 5 units of divine energy and changed a man's destiny.

We stepped out of the office, accompanied by the receptionist who had been waiting for us. Judging by her pale face, she had likely heard the entire conversation. Without a word, we made our way down to the exit.

The city administration building was massive, housing all the ministries and bureaucratic offices. And according to the evacuation plan posted inside, there was an entire underground bunker beneath it — a hidden little city where officials could ride out a monster invasion. Just as I settled into the car...

"Hello?" I answered the call.

"Alex, we've got a problem. Can you help?" I heard Lena's voice.

I was in just the right mood for some trouble. "On my way!" I said and hung up the phone.

* * *

Sometime ago
The Beaver mall
Anna and the sisters

The Beaver was the best shopping center in the city. Located right in the heart of downtown, it had fourteen floors, making it the second-tallest building in town. It was named after the family that owned it — the Beavers. Naturally, beaver imagery was everywhere, from real-life depictions of the animal to costumed mascots entertaining guests.

Inside one of the fitting rooms, decorated with a beaver poster and a list of changing room rules, Anna stood before the mirror wearing nothing but jeans and a slightly see-through purple lace bra.

"...it's kinda hard to talk and try on this really beautiful purple lace bra at the same time."

"Got it. Sorry, I won't distract you," Gauss ended the call, leaving the girl perplexed.

"So he's completely uninterested, huh..." she muttered.

Just then, Lena peeked into the booth. "Whoa! Now that's gorgeous. And he's just a heartless rock."

"I'd never let him see me like this, but still, that

kinda hurts," Anna bit her lip in frustration as some rather inappropriate thoughts flashed through her mind. But she quickly shoved that wicked part of herself aside.

"What about your wedding night?" Lena giggled.

"No," Anna shook her head. "For that, I'll need something even sexier."

"Hm... then let's pick something out!" Lena's eyes sparkled like two flashlights.

"What's the point? He made it clear — no weddings until after we've graduated. By then, I'll have grown up a bit more." She cupped her rather ample breasts, noting that they were still growing.

"What do you mean, 'what's the point'? So you'll know what you like when the time comes! Trying things on is totally allowed!" Lena grinned, and Anna had no choice but to agree.

"Girls," came Katie's voice from the neighboring fitting room. "I'm not sure about this. Can you take a look?"

Anna quickly threw on her sweater, and she and Lena rushed into Katie's booth. Before them stood a girl in bright red lingerie, some parts sheer, others with intricate patterns.

"Perfect for a brothel," Lena giggled. Katie pouted.

"And why do *you* need something this fancy?" Anna squinted. "You're not trying to seduce my Alex, are you? We agreed he's mine."

"Oh, please, as if I want him! And I'd never show up in lingerie in front of him! Especially this kind! What do you take me for? I'm a respectable girl!"

"That would sound a lot more convincing if you weren't blushing like a tomato," Anna squinted, eyeing the tall, long-legged beauty with a bombshell figure.

"It's hot in here! You guys are breathing too much! Now get out," Katie shooed them away.

Left alone, she stared at her reflection in the mirror and muttered, "Not like I care about him... Can't I just own some nice, sexy lingerie?"

"We can still hear you!" Lena cackled.

"When we get home, I'm going to kill you," Katie hissed.

Just then, a noise caught her attention. Peeking out from behind the curtain, she saw three guys and a girl coming into the store. The store administrator immediately rushed to them, trying to kick them out — men were strictly forbidden from entering. After all, this was an exclusive lingerie boutique for aristocratic women.

"But how else can we pick something for our dear sister? She can't do it alone," one of the guys said. He looked to be around twenty, same as his two companions. The girl, a blonde with an undeniably bitchy face — at least in Katie's opinion — seemed about eighteen.

"You're not allowed in here! I'll call security!"

"Go ahead," the guy shrugged, looking back at a group of bodyguards in sharp black suits.

"You've been asked to leave. Now get lost," Anna said, approaching the group.

In her rush, she'd only thrown on a sweater over her bare chest. It wasn't see-through, but certain parts still stood out. The three guys immediately fixated on her.

"So hot! Want to come hang out with us? We're from the Smirnoff family. You'll have fun, we promise," the one in the center said, flashing a sleazy grin, his eyes burning with lust.

"God forbid I get involved with trash like you," Anna sneered.

The guys' smiles instantly twisted into anger. "You've got a sharp tongue for such a—"

"Short-legged brat!" the girl they were with finished, her voice dripping with contempt.

A second later, Anna's fist buried itself in the blonde's stomach. The girl crumpled, gasping as she collapsed onto the floor.

"Care to repeat that?" Anna crouched beside her. In return, the girl spat out a string of expletives so foul they almost made Anna's ears shrivel.

"Sis!" The brothers rushed to the blonde, one scooping her up while the other two shielded her from Anna. At the same time, security in black suits stormed into the boutique.

"You'll pay for this, you little brat!" the guys seethed, ready to pounce on Anna.

"Think you're strong enough?" Lena dashed up, activating Reinforcement, her body shimmering as her strength surged.

"You'll be begging for forgiveness on your knees after this!" snarled the one on the left — a tall, broad-shouldered guy with an unpleasant face. Then again, all three of them looked like scum.

The brothers lunged, but, to their surprise, were instantly met with resistance. Lena's leg slammed into the leftmost one's side with a sickening crack! His body flew back a few feet before crumpling to the ground.

Anna's fist, fueled by full force, drove into the second guy's stomach, immediately followed by a knockout blow to his head.

"S-security!" the blonde wailed from her brother's arms. But no one came to their rescue.

Turning around, the brothers saw four armored fighters in white standing behind them, rifles aimed at their personal guards.

"W-who the hell are you?!"

"That's our security," Katie said. She was standing their, phone in her hand, having just called their personal guards. By Alexander's orders, the girls were allowed to roam the city only in the company of these four fighters. "Sorry, girls, I took too long changing."

Katie wore a revealing dress, which made the brother still holding the blonde pause his gaze on her, unable to look away.

BOOK THREE

*   *   *

The same shopping mall
Ten minutes later
Gauss

So, I arrive at the lingerie store, and it's a full-blown circus. Mall security, eight bodyguards belonging to who-knows-whom, my four zombie guards, paramedics, and, of course, my trio of troublemakers.

"I'm the patriarch of the Scully family. What happened here?" I stormed in, so to speak, and positioned myself between the girls and what looked like a mall security officer.

The man tensed up after hearing who I was. "These young women are accused of assault. There are three injured," he replied immediately.

"They attacked someone? Is this a joke? Or are you trying to claim this wasn't self-defense? That the attack wasn't provoked? Where's the surveillance footage?" I bombarded him with questions. "Actually, hold on... What were men doing in a women's lingerie store?"

"I... can't say."

"Then I'll find out myself." I turned to the only uninjured guy from their group.

I really ought to praise the girls, they did a great job. Two of the guys were lying on the floor groaning while a medic tended to them.

"Talk," I ordered the uninjured one. "What

were you doing in the store?"

"We were accompanying our sister!" he snapped, baring his teeth in anger.

"Oh, so the sign that says 'No Men Allowed' meant nothing to you?" I asked.

"We were accompanying our sister!" he repeated.

"Ah, I see. So you're not men. Not even boys. Just women in disguise? You should've said so from the start, then there'd be no problem." I smirked as his face turned crimson.

"Y-you—" he hissed.

"Master. You're not even close to being on my level to be addressing me as 'you', lady."

"I'll kill you!" Guess my last comment pushed him over the edge. He exploded in rage, lunging at me with his fist.

I caught his arm, twisted him around, and 'crack' came the unmistakable sound of breaking bones. Seriously? That weak? A fifth-rank trainee? Or even lower? Pathetic.

"Well, you all saw that. An attack on a patriarch of a high-aristocracy family. Please record everything and file the report. And where's that surveillance footage?!"

Whether fortunately or unfortunately, this was just the beginning. A crocodile is a proud bird, it won't fly until you kick it. And right now, this proud bird was gathering all his strength to come storming in. At least, that's what Anna's brother had told me over the phone. He was also getting together some of his fighters — the ones who hadn't gone into the Wildlands — and heading straight to the mall.

But did I really need backup? We'd find out soon enough.

CHAPTER 10

STANDING ACROSS FROM ME was a human triangle. Short legs, absurdly broad shoulders, and arms thicker than his legs. As for his neck — there wasn't one. The man clearly had no idea such a thing even existed — someone should have told him it's actually useful. Without it, turning your head isn't exactly an option. So instead, this massive slab of muscle had to rotate his entire body a full ninety degrees just to look sideways. And so, we engaged in an intense staring contest — or at least, that's how it looked.

Beside me stood the human mountain — Edward Winters. Just behind us were my troublemakers, and my four zombie guards, rifles in hand. Zhanna was there too, along with the kikimora and twenty Winters' soldiers.

The triangle man had several relatives by his

side, plus about sixty fighters. They wore regular clothes, though many had bulletproof vests underneath. What did they expect? Military gear in public areas was a privilege — not something just any family could flaunt. Even the Winters group was unarmed.

"I made it!" A cheerful voice rang out, and a short man in a white down jacket strode toward us, looking rather displeased as he approached. Without hesitation, he positioned himself between me and the triangle.

"Smirnoff, right? Now listen to me, you fuckhead," he said.

The triangle instantly started heating up, like a tank revving up for a charge. But before he could do anything, the man in the white jacket flicked his hand, and down went the giant. First onto his knees. Then face-first into the floor. His forehead and nose smashed against the ground with a sickening crunch. Gravity magic? That's rare. Even rarer at that level.

"You've completely lost your damn mind, you dumbass!" the down-jacketed man snarled, crouching in front of Smirnoff. "You decided to start shit in *my* mall? You thought you could spit in *my* face, disrespect *my* family? You're lucky your degenerate brats are already crippled, or I'd be tearing their heads off myself!"

"S-shame... they're... not guilty..." the triangle wheezed out, only enraging Beaver further. Yes, the down-jacket man was the owner of the shopping mall himself.

"Are you a complete idiot? Or did you not bother checking the security footage?" Beaver snapped. "Your moron sons walked into a lingerie store to spy on the ladies! That's lower than low!" Beaver spun around to look at his security team. "You showed them the footage, right?"

"Yes, Patriarch! But they refused to watch. They said they believed the 'victims' and that video footage can be faked."

"For fuck's sake!" Beaver groaned, then turned back to the Smirnoffs. "So, what should I do with you? Should we start a war? I could just wipe out your entire family and be done with it. Or we can act like civilized people, and you compensate me for this mess."

"C-com... pensate..." the triangle wheezed.

"Good. You idiots scared off a ton of my customers with this stunt, so you'll pay for every single penny of lost revenue!" Beaver flicked his hand again, releasing Smirnoff from his magic, then turned to us.

"And as for you, since you were the victims here, anything you want in the store is covered by Smirnoff today. Isn't that right?"

"We'll pay," Smirnoff grumbled, still sitting on his ass, trying to recover.

"Perfect. Now get out of my mall, and don't ever show your faces here again." He waved a dismissive hand, sending the muscle-brained fools on their way. Not that they seemed eager to stick around.

Beaver then walked up to me and shook my

hand. "Thanks for not turning this into an all-out brawl."

"Fighting in a public space? My family's reputation is still important to me," I shrugged.

"Glad to see there are still reasonable people in this city," he said and shifted his gaze from me to Edward. "Since you're here, I take it your father is still in the Wildlands, carrying out the Emperor's decree?"

"Yes. Otherwise, we'd already be storming the Smirnoff estate," Edward said.

"I'll have a word with your father. And I'll remind the Smirnoffs what happens to those who sabotage an imperial order." A sinister smile spread across Beaver's face.

Before long, he left, and Edward had to go as well — some urgent family matters required his attention. I was about to leave too, but...

"Alex! You barely have any clothes. We need to get you some new outfits!" Lena's eyes were practically burning.

"Great idea." Anna nodded vigorously, a wicked smile spreading across her face. "I also need a guy's opinion."

"This won't take long, right?" I asked.

They responded almost in unison, "Of course not!" And I believed them. I had never gone shopping before. How naïve I was.

They dragged me into a men's clothing store. At first, I thought all this shopping nonsense was a piece of cake. You just sit on a couch while the women run around the store, looking at what's good, and laughing amongst themselves. Surprisingly, Zhanna also ran around with them, and seemed to enjoy herself.

Beside me on the couch sat the raven, engrossed in something on a tablet. I glanced over and nearly passed out from sheer boredom. It was some gigantic, dreadfully dull treatise on magic. The font was tiny, the text was one endless wall, and the bird just kept flipping through page after page with its claw.

Everything seemed fine. I was relaxing, and I might have even managed to catch a quick nap. But that's when the trap snapped shut.

The women returned with a mountain of clothes. A real, actual pile! Which is when I learned the horrifying truth: you actually have to try on clothes in a store. Tailor-made outfits were one thing — those were crafted specifically for me. But at a store? They had to check the fit, the cut, the size — it was complicated!

To try things on, I had to go into a special fitting booth. A tiny and uncomfortable one, I might add. Inside was a soft chair, some hangers, and a large mirror. And the moment I stripped down to my underwear, a hand suddenly appeared from behind the curtain serving as a door. Zhanna's hand — holding three hangers. A shirt on one, pants on the second, and a jacket on the third. I had no choice but to put them on.

Once I got dressed, I had to step out and let the experts evaluate.

"Yeah, Zhanna's right. The shoulders don't

look good, and Alex isn't tall enough for that suit," Lena declared. The girls all nodded in agreement. "Next one."

"I have to change again?" I gave them a look of pure annoyance.

"Well, how else are we supposed to pick something worthy of a high-aristocracy patriarch?" Anna said. "Your clothes wear out quickly. And most of them don't even match your status."

No arguing with that. I had to give in. Besides, Alexander's old clothes barely fit me anymore. I'd gained a lot of muscle and filled out significantly.

And so, I tried on outfit after outfit after outfit. It was just changing clothes, so why did it feel like it was draining the very life out of me? Finally, after stepping out in yet another bizarre suit...

"Nah, looks terrible. Next one," Lena said instantly.

"That's it. I'm done," I protested.

"He lasted longer than I expected," Zhanna remarked. "My late husband gave up by the sixth change. But don't worry, I have a solution."

And honestly, her "solution" worked for me. I just shut down, surrendered my body to their hands, and even managed to doze off. They dressed me, undressed me, and giggled the entire time. I only occasionally tensed my muscles to keep from falling over whenever they propped me up.

At some point, they moved me to a large couch. The store staff was kind enough to set up some portable dividers, giving us privacy from the rest of the shoppers. And in the end, I actually fell asleep.

* * *

Same place
The troublemakers and Zhanna

"How did he go from a scrawny twig to THIS so fast?" Katie grumbled, eyeing the well-built guy lounging on the couch in nothing but his underwear. Her gaze mostly lingered on his torso and strong arms.

"He used to be all skin and bones. But after recovering, he just started bulking up," Lena added.

"I remember being afraid I'd crush him if I so much as touched him," Zhanna confirmed, and immediately, three pairs of angry eyes turned to her. She didn't fail to notice. "Oh, don't be jealous. I'm not after his heart."

"We're not jealous," Katie muttered.

"Well, I am," Anna said. "He's mine."

"Yeah, yeah, yours, all yours. Here, take him." Katie waved her hand toward the guy.

"But how did it happen?" Lena suddenly asked, turning to Zhanna.

"Mmm... I was taking some 'me time' in the park. I was in a crappy mood and figured I'd distract myself by reading outside. And then, out of nowhere, a monster attacked me. A massive, terrifying snake! It coiled around me, lifted me up, ready to swallow me whole. Its jaws were already open. But then Alexander showed up and saved me. And after that, he closed the gate."

"I remember. He went for a walk over a month ago. Right around the time he started acting weird," Lena noted.

"Yeah, that's right." The older sister nodded.

"Well, after that, he kept grumbling about how he never got to eat, so I figured I'd feed him. And since he helped the limping me get home, I offered to wash his clothes since they were filthy. And, well... one thing led to another... I won't go into details."

"Not even a little?" Lena grinned.

"I do not need details about how my future husband is sleeping with other women," Anna said, eyeing the redhead suspiciously. "What's *really* suspicious is how interested *you* are in this."

"How could I not be? You should've seen him back then — just skin and bones! And Zhanna is so tall and, well... juicy. I honestly don't get how it even worked between them..."

"I was on top. And that's the end of that conversation." Zhanna shot the girls a stern look, and they all nodded.

"Still, he's changed so much. Those abs, those muscles... Damn, he looks good. Even his face seems more handsome. And is it just me, or did the shape of his eyes change a bit?" Lena stepped closer to the guy on the couch, studying his face.

"They look the same to me. Not like I've spent much time staring at him," Katie scoffed. But Zhanna and Anna exchanged glances.

"No, you're imagining things," Anna said, her voice slightly nervous.

"They're the same as always," Zhanna added. She tensed up too, afraid the girls might uncover Gauss's secret. But the moment passed.

"You think so? Well... maybe..." Lena stepped back, but her eyes were still fixed on the guy's body.

"Keep looking at him like that, and you'll swallow him whole with your eyes!" Anna huffed. "Can we please finish the fitting already?"

"And start picking out stuff for ourselves!" Lena beamed, as did the other girls.

* * *

The store
A long time later

"Alex, wake up! Come on, wake up, we need your expert male opinion," a voice called out as someone started shaking me. And I was sleeping so soundly...

When I opened my eyes, I found myself in another store. In front of me stood four girls in stunning dresses. Each outfit highlighted their figures and unique features, making them look even more beautiful. Not bad.

"Well? How do we look?" Lena said.

"Magnificent," I answered, and the four of them instantly beamed with satisfaction. Then I drifted off again, but my peace didn't last long. By the third time someone shook me, I finally realized — they weren't going to let me sleep.

The only thing that kept me sane was that I just had to sit on the couch while the women came to me. And that went on for an entire hour! Thankfully, they eventually got tired and hungry. So, after handing over their purchases for delivery, we headed to a restaurant.

The girls were wearing the dresses they had just bought — the best ones from everything they had picked out, all paid for by the Smirnoffs. They were very pleased by the envious stares of other women.

I, on the other hand, was wary of potential problems. Too many people, seeing how short I was, assume they're better than me. Which meant they thought stealing my women was as easy as pie. Like, all they had to do was humiliate me in front of them, and suddenly, the girls would realize how worthless I was and fall for the "heroes" who opened their eyes. At least, that's how I imagine idiots like that think.

Even though it was late, the restaurant — with its view of the night city — was packed. Soft music played, creating a relaxed atmosphere, and a friendly hostess led us to a great spot right by the window.

We all settled in comfortably, but my appetite was pretty much nonexistent. The parasite kept saying that without intense physical exertion, it couldn't enhance my body any further. It was already stuffed to the brim with energy. I hadn't been using it much lately.

So, to the girls' surprise, I only ordered two dishes. Otherwise, I just wouldn't be able to eat it all, even with magic. Or worse, I'd start getting fat and turn into a ball. I needed a good fight, then I could eat as much as I wanted again.

"Then let's order a bunch of different dishes and share," Anna suggested, and everyone eagerly agreed.

Before long, our table was overflowing with all sorts of delicacies, many of which I'd never seen before, along with light drinks and juices.

"To an amazing shopping spree! We really went all out today," Lena toasted, and everyone except me joined in. In my opinion, shopping was just another form of torture.

The food turned out to be great, but we got distracted when a performance started. It was Gloria who came out on stage to sing.

"If she's here, does that mean Basel and Polina are too?" Anna wondered. And sure enough, after scanning the crowd, I spotted a very familiar head. But no, the big guy was here alone, watching the elf singer with reverence. I decided not to disturb him.

"She sings beautifully," Katie murmured, completely captivated. Lena was just as impressed, while Zhanna and Anna — who preferred a different kind of music — quietly chatted among themselves. I wasn't sure about what, though. I was listening to Gloria.

And just when I thought the night might actually go peacefully, a loud crash echoed through the restaurant. Then came shouting. The music instantly cut off, and the elf on stage fell silent.

"Say that again, you bastard?!" Basel practically growled as he punched someone in the face, or at least tried to. His opponent, along with two of his friends, turned out to be tough.

"I said that picking up a no-name, second-rate singer like her is easy as hell," a tall blond in a stylish outfit laughed. Clearly, the guy kept up with his workouts. His two buddies looked just as strong. And, most importantly, they were all Adepts [10-19]. Possibly even close to advancing to Junior Mages [20-29].

"I'll kill you, you piece of shit!" Basel snapped. Oh, Basel, Basel — losing your self-control like that? His barrier was barely holding because of his raging emotions. And those three? They just kept laughing.

"Haha, not strong enough, huh?" The blond smirked, shattering Basel's barrier with a single punch and slamming a fist into his face.

Basel staggered back, and the two guys rushed in, landing blows on his ribs. Basel crashed onto his own table, breaking it under his weight and landing on the floor. The assholes kept laughing.

Meanwhile, the other guests were thoroughly enjoying this unexpected and, without a doubt, far more entertaining show. Even the mall security had arrived to "protect" the guests.

"Three upperclassmen against someone way younger than them? Wow, real heroes. Let me guess, you only go on F-rank shard expeditions?" a voice rang out behind the trio. Naturally, it was me. No way I was going to abandon a friend. Sure, he was only human, but he was my human.

"And what's this little thing?" The blond sneered, pointing a finger at me. "Did you escape from kindergarten, kid?" His two goons burst into laughter.

"No, but you sure came looking for one. Guess you can't handle people your own age, so you try to make yourself feel better by bullying those younger and weaker than you. My condolences. Life must be tough when you're a coward *and* a loser."

Laughter rippled through the crowd. The blond knew how to keep his emotions in check and held his composure. But his lackeys? Not so much.

"You talk too much for a damn runt!" the dark-haired one snarled and lunged at me, trying to grab my shoulder.

"Parasite, crank it up. I want to feast tonight!"

"Oh great... More work... Why me?" the creature inside me groaned, acting like it was some tragic victim.

And then, in an instant, a surge of raw power flooded through me. The energy was so intense that my already snug white shirt burst apart at the seams!

Shreds of fabric flew more than three feet in every direction as my muscles swelled to a size that was honestly a little terrifying. It looked like that bastard overdid it.

"I did exactly what you asked! You're gonna feast tonight!" the parasite shot back.

Gasps of admiration rippled through the crowd, while the dark-haired guy stumbled back, taking a series of blows to the chest. His barrier held, but it couldn't fully absorb the impact.

"Basel, do you really think so little of Gloria that you let these nobodies' words get to you?" I called out, dodging a punch from the third guy. "They're baiting you on purpose, and you, like an idiot, fell for it."

The guy attacking me was a short redhead, and he was very fast. He kept pressing in, striking at an insane speed. But he got tired of that real quick and switched to magic, wrapping his hands in gloves of wind. It was becoming dangerous.

His next strike barely missed me, but two deep cuts appeared across my chest. The wind sliced like knives!

"You're right. Sorry, I was being an idiot. Shouldn't have had that drink," Basel's voice rang out, and suddenly, all eyes were on him. He looked like a living statue now — his massive fists transformed into stone hammers, blazing with fire.

"A dual-element user," the blond cursed under his breath. At that exact moment, the redhead flew back six feet before crashing onto the floor.

The restaurant staff had already cleared away the furniture, so there was nothing left for him to break, except for the shattered remains of Basel's table still littering the floor.

The redhead groaned in pain, clutching his stomach. I might have gone a little overboard. My glowing fist, infused with divine energy, had slammed into his barrier. I didn't break through it, but the sheer force of the hit was too much for it to absorb.

"How?" the dark-haired guy muttered in disbelief.

"Quit gawking and finish him off already!" the blond barked, then lunged at Basel himself.

His hands ignited, but before he even got three feet from Basel, he fired a concentrated blast of flames, like a human flamethrower. Too bad for him. A massive fist burst through the fire, slamming straight into the blond's smug face and sending him flying. His barrier held, but Basel was just too big, and the blond wasn't strong enough to break the laws of physics with sheer willpower. He scrambled back to his feet and launched several fireballs, but Basel raised a wall of fire, completely nullifying the attack.

Meanwhile, I had both the dark-haired guy and the redhead on me. And let me tell you — it was tough. So many eyes were watching that pulling off any tricks was out of the question. But what I did have was raw, explosive physical power. And wounds that healed before their eyes.

I poured just a little divine energy into each of my hits, making their barriers drop faster. But I was taking damage too — these two were experienced and strong. At their level, they were nearly four times stronger than a regular human.

"Damn it!" the dark-haired guy cursed as I landed a solid hit on his jaw. He stumbled back, and the redhead immediately stepped in, blasting me away with a gust of wind.

Blinding them was out of the question, there were too many spectators. So I shifted back. The dark-haired guy immediately fired a jet of water at me, like a damn pressure hose. The magical barrier around us meant he wasn't worried about hitting bystanders. But I was still getting drenched. And the redhead kept striking from the side whenever he got the chance.

"Let's see how long you can keep this up." I reinforced my body as much as I could, then powered through the water and landed a devastating uppercut, launching the dark-haired guy into the air.

At that exact moment, the redhead landed a vicious blow to my ribs. I gritted my teeth, tanked it, then blasted the airborne guy with a punch, grabbed his leg and swung him like a club straight into the redhead, who froze on shock. I kept going.

I swung the guy like a damn sledgehammer. He was cursing, trying to fight back, but he was in constant motion, slamming into things again and again.

"Quack!" the redhead yelped when I finally smashed him with his own partner. Their barriers shattered, as did a few bones.

Just as I turned to help Basel, the blond — his face completely wrecked — crashed to the floor beside me. And damn, there was a lot of blood.

"Nice work," I said, looking at Basel's satisfied face. He was banged up too, but he looked thrilled.

"You didn't do so bad yourself. That was honestly terrifying to watch," he laughed, then suddenly froze.

"Thank you for defending my honor," Gloria said as she approached, flashing a warm smile. She kissed Basel on the cheek, then kissed me too.

Yeah, that was a mistake. The big guy turned to stone, not literally, of course — he probably didn't have enough mana left for that. Oh well. I was starving. And I was about to devour everything in the restaurant.

CHAPTER 11

Townhall
Sometime ago

ATHANASIUS WATCHED SCULLY and his assistant leave, his eyes burning with rage.

Athanasius saw Alexander Scully and his associate off, feeling enraged. "That little mutt dared to threaten me?" he growled, pulling a sheet of paper toward him and grabbing a pen. He immediately started writing up a report that such-and-such aristocrat threatened him with death and all sorts of punishments simply because he was honestly and dutifully doing his jo...

Suddenly, the pen started leaking, drowning the entire page in ink.

"Oh, for the love of — !" He flung the pen aside and reached for another one, his thick mane of hair practically bristling with frustration. But as he bent down, he lost his balance and, to his own shock, tumbled straight to the floor.

In an attempt to catch himself, he threw out his hand, only for it to land right on the discarded pen. It rolled beneath his palm, sending him skidding even harder, making his fall twice as painful.

"Arghhhh!" he let out a guttural snarl, groaning in pain. His shoulder twisted unnaturally — it was dislocated.

There was no one around to hear his cries, but at least he wasn't dying. Once the initial pain subsided, Athanasius struggled to his feet, his fury now fully directed at the treacherous pen. So he kicked it with all the strength he could muster. That was a bad idea!

The pen ricocheted off the wall and shot straight back at him, plunging directly into his neck, as if it was made of steel. With a strangled gasp, he yanked it out and tossed it aside, clutching at his throat.

Thankfully, the pen hadn't gone in too deep. But with only one functional arm, stopping the bleeding was a struggle. Biting into a pencil to keep from screaming, he managed to dial emergency services from the desk phone. Miraculously, he got through.

"Send help..." he rasped. Speaking was excruciating. "Throat... wounded... dying..." He wasn't actually dying, the wound wasn't fatal. But Scully's threats, combined with all the rumors, sent his fear spiraling into full-blown panic.

The ambulance was dispatched and would arrive within minutes. But Athanasius wasn't just going to sit there. He managed to find the first aid kit in his office, pried it open with his toes, and clumsily retrieved a bandage and some painkillers.

It took effort, but he managed to patch himself up. All that was left was to wash the pill down with water from the cooler nearby. He hobbled toward it, which is when the door suddenly slammed open.

Startled, he flinched, and his foot landed right on the same cursed pen. He practically launched into the air. Right in front of the medics rushing in, he crashed through the window, shattering the glass, before plummeting from the fourth floor and landing on the roof of the ambulance.

Meanwhile, the very same pen, ricocheted off the wall again, flew out the window, and landed right into Athanasius's open mouth.

"Holy shit!" one of the medics blurted out. Without hesitation, he jumped out of the window, covering himself in a water barrier before landing beside the wrecked official moments later. "He's alive..." the medic exhaled in relief, then immediately got to work. Saving the life of a VIP client was priority number one.

THE COMING OF GOD OF DEATH

*   *   *

Ancient city ruins
Sunday
Gauss and Zhanna

The sleeping area in the logging truck's cabin was cramped, uncomfortable, and stuffy... It was like a sauna in there! Although, to be honest, I was perfectly comfortable at the moment.

I hate to admit it, but I did it again... Turns out, the massive surge of energy the parasite gave me back at the restaurant had a lot more side effects than I expected.

That morning, I was genuinely shocked when I woke up to find a full beard on my face and my hair grown out past the middle of my back. I would've shaved it all off, but, well the four-inch nails made that a little difficult. You should've seen Xena's face when she walked in on me...

I blamed it all on magic. She seemed to buy it, though she did pointedly mention that her hair was still short, and so were her nails.

Oh, and all my teeth had fallen out! New ones grew in, perfectly straight and even. And let's not even talk about the layer of dead skin that peeled off me overnight.

Long story short, all the bedding had to be thrown in the wash, and I spent two hours getting cleaned up, delaying our expedition into the wildlands.

156

BOOK THREE

There we were, in the ruins, where I had decided to give Zhanna a gift. After all, I had finally gone through all the loot from... what, forty? No, maybe even fifty gates.

Most of it went to my zombies. Something went to the sisters, a few items were set aside for sale, and a special something was reserved just for Zhanna.

Gogo's favorite wife's corset
Rank: *B*

Description: Gogo deeply loved his wife. He crafted this corset to protect her from enemies while also enhancing her beauty. Not only does it generate a protective barrier whenever the wearer in danger, but it also preserves her beauty, health, and vitality.

Zhanna tried on her gift right in front of me. That's when my body suddenly remembered yet another side effect of using the parasite, and my magic completely shut off. I couldn't even summon the simplest Light spell.

Luckily, my assistant was understanding. But she had no idea just how bad things really were. So while everyone else was out hunting and fighting, we... well... spent the next two hours like wild animals, driven by nothing but instinct and sheer lust. I thought I was going to die.

"Parasite, next time, only release that much energy if things are really bad. Actually, better yet, ask me how much to use first."

"You did get to eat almost everything in the restaurant afterward. Just like you wanted."

"Huh. Sounds like I'm not giving you enough work," I snickered mentally.

"I'll definitely ask from now on! Every. Single. Time."

"See? That wasn't so hard."

Once I made sure my magic was back to normal, I climbed off the bed and pulled a blanket over the exhausted woman. I was a mage, she was just a regular human. It had been way harder on her. But when those primal instincts take over, you stop thinking entirely.

No wonder elves see themselves as superior to humans. They don't suffer from this kind of thing and have no animalistic urges. Or, maybe they just hide them really well.

Fully dressed, I stepped out of the truck cabin. The air was cold — October was already halfway through. Winter would come soon, and most monsters would go into hibernation, which meant there'd be no more Waves. We just had to hold out until then.

But according to the military guys I'd talked to before heading out to the Wildlands, the chances of a Wave were only increasing. Too many signs pointed to it happening soon.

As usual, my camp was set up in the city center, right by the statue. It was busy, in its own weird way — zombies were everywhere, hauling in loot. Some loaded carcasses onto trailers, others carried them by hand. I also noticed the kikimora sitting off to the side. In a swimsuit.

She looked deep in thought, absentmindedly playing with some kind of construction set, except instead of building blocks, she was assembling zombies from a pile of dismembered bodies.

"Who did this to them?" I asked as I walked up.

"A monster. Rank A with wind magic. We barely managed to take it down," the monster-woman muttered, looking both battered and exhausted.

Since I had nothing better to do, I decided to help her out putting the zombies together, which turned out to be a lot harder than I expected. The zombies we were working with were low-tier, meaning they weren't smart enough to say things like "Hey, this isn't my arm, it's a woman's hand!" So we winged it with a lot of parts.

As I was dealing with this fascinating task, Zhanna finally woke up and climbed out of the truck, bringing me hot tea and sandwiches. We ate, rested a bit, then set off to close the last gate in these ruins. There were barely any monsters left there.

After this, we'd move to a different location, and my "Chinese group" would find a suitable spot. At least, that was the plan right up until a massive explosion went off nearby. Two tall buildings started collapsing, throwing up clouds of dust.

"Caw! Danger! Caw! A monster! A huge monster is coming!" The raven circled above, screeching its warning. I only needed a brief look through its eyes to understand the situation.

"Load up and move out!" I ordered immediately, sending out a mental command to all my zombies.

The Chinese were the only ones who refused to retreat. They held their ground, doing their best to slow the creature down. But did they really stand a chance? Not likely. It was a giant crab, as tall as a four-story building.

Its entire shell was covered in strange spines that shot out different kinds of magic. Mostly fire. Could I kill it? If I had thousands of B-rank monster bodies under my control, maybe. But with just zombies? Not a chance.

I hated feeling weak, but there was no winning this fight. Unless, I burned every last drop of my divine energy. And then some asshole in the city would take the opportunity to stab me in the back. Instead, I poured extra power into my Chinese guys and told them to try to survive. Their bodies were expensive, after all...

Soon, my skeleton unit returned with the fighters. We didn't even bother loading the corpses, just bolted straight for the city.

"Hello?! It's Scully! Pick up the damn phone!" I cursed, dialing. What was the point of emergency satellite phones if no one ever answered them?!

"Scully, what's the issue? This better be important."

"Oh, I don't know, maybe the fact that there's a four-story-tall crab attacking and firing off every type of elemental magic?"

"Haha, very funny. What's the real problem?"

"The real problem is exactly what I just said. And your problem might be losing your damn job if you don't take this seriously." I heard nothing but silence in return.

Then, a nervous stammer: "Y-you're not joking? That thing must be at least an A+ rank!"

"Yeah? Then start writing down these coordinates."

The satellite phone had a handy function — it could display my exact location. However, right now, I was already five minutes out from the city. Luckily, Zhanna had saved the city's coordinates of the monster on her tablet.

"Get out of there immediately. They'll probably carpet bomb the place."

"I've been calling you for five minutes. I'm already long gone."

"U-understood..."

What exactly was an A+ rank? It was when no one could decide whether a monster was an A or an S. Though, technically, you could say the same for B+, D+, or any other "in-between" ranks. Lower-ranked creatures were easier to classify. They almost always dropped fixed magic crystals — ones, twos, and so on. But the higher the rank, the less predictable things got.

Less than a minute later, I got another call. This time, the voice on the other end was deep and commanding. They wanted details. And, apparently, they liked what I told them. Maybe — just maybe — killing this beast would prevent the Wave from happening? I seriously doubted that. If the crab was leading the Wave, where was its horde? Still, taking it down would definitely weaken the Wave if it came. With an army backing it up, that walking magic tank would be an absolute nightmare.

I hadn't gone too far and stopped on a large hill overlooking the city. My zombies were still holding out, and explosions continued to rock the ruins. And then, the bombers arrived. Three massive aircraft, flying high, escorted by a dozen fighter jets. But even they weren't safe.

A flock of something monstrous appeared in the air. The battle was brutal. The fighter jets — clearly piloted by mages — pulled off impossible maneuvers, attacking with both traditional weapons and magic. Their opponents were something like a mix between pigeons and peacocks, but each one was the size of a fighter jet. They had strong barriers and outnumbered our forces.

That said, the planes had barriers too. It was a tough fight, but the air force managed to keep the creatures away from the slow-moving bombers. Not that the bombers were helpless — far from it. They were flying fortresses, each armed with over a dozen turrets spewing fire and hundreds of pounds of lead every second.

Finally, they reached the city. The crab was clearly visible, making it easy for the pilots to aim their payloads. A storm of massive bombs rained down. Immediately, some of the birds lunged at

them, and the crab fired back with its magic —
lightning, wind blasts, even fireballs. But the
bombs were protected by barriers. Some didn't
hold under the heavy fire and exploded prema-
turely, but luckily, not at full force, so the surrounding bombs weren't affected.

Not that it mattered anymore — several bombs
still made it to the ground, and the resulting explosions were so powerful that even from my van-
tage point, far outside the city, I was hit by a wave
of scorching air. Though, what city? There was no
city anymore. But it seemed like my altar was still
standing. People were going to be very surprised
when they found an untouched statue in the middle of all that ruin.

The monster was dead, as were my zombies,
though their souls were already returning to the
altar. Great. More bodies to find. More money to
spend.

The city was burning. There was no point in
sticking around, so I decided to continue hunting,
this time in the forests. But then, one of the planes
got shot down. The aircraft lost a wing, trailing
smoke as it spiraled toward the trees. The pilots
couldn't eject because there were three of those
flying freaks after the plane. I could see a black
mist rising, meaning the pilots were still alive. Did
I need to save them? Not really. But my family's
reputation could use the boost.

I glanced at my zombies. All clad in black armor. The skeleton still looked like a skeleton. The
kikimora? Adorable as ever in her swimsuit. She'd

even managed to wash off all the monster blood. Though I'd seen how she did it — like a cat, with her long tongue. The real problem would be if she ever decided to clean me that way.

I roughly estimated the crash site and set off. The road soon ended, so I left Zhanna, the skeleton, and part of my zombies behind. The raven went ahead for reconnaissance — through its eyes, I'd see everything.

Pouring out waves of death aura, I pushed through the forest. The weaker monsters had fled, frightened by the city's explosions. The predators, though, were pissed. Turns out, my aura wasn't quite as effective against them right now.

"Raaaar!" Three wolves snarled. Each the size of a bear. No barriers, but electricity crackled along their fur.

"Attack!" I commanded. My black-armored zombies formed a shield wall and advanced, with the kikimora and me behind them.

"Awooo...?" one of the wolves howled, then suddenly whimpered.

I had to burn a little divine energy, but my new diarrhea ring worked like a charm. I had bought a set of five at an auction. I mean, they were very useful and could be even lethal with enough divine energy poured into them.

As one wolf struggled to empty its insides, the other two lunged, scattering my zombies like bowling pins. The undead slashed back with their black swords, but every time they landed a hit, they got electrocuted. Hard. Their eyeballs literally burst. Not that it mattered. I'd grow them back later. I had zero interest in my own eyeballs bursting, though, so I attacked from a distance.

Meanwhile, the kikimora had climbed a tree. She waited for the perfect moment, then pounced onto a wolf's back. I quickly funneled a burst of divine energy into her, shrouding her in a dark mist. Just in time — a massive electric shockwave blasted out and she barely escaped it, her claws tearing into the wolf's side.

At the same time, my black crescent attack shot straight into its open mouth. Then the zombies swarmed in and finished the job. That was rough.

While we were fighting, the plane had crashed. I needed to hurry, if I wanted to save those pilots. But there was a problem with that — most of my zombies were still missing their eyes. My power was already working to regenerate them, but it would take time. For now, I took only the kikimora and five fighters with me.

Luckily, there were no more monsters along the way. Unfortunately, there were plenty at the crash site. Well. It hadn't exactly been a clearing before. The plane had simply plowed through the trees like they were nothing.

The pilots were another story. One lay slumped against the wreck, completely still. The other was fighting for his life — sword in one hand, submachine gun in the other, he desperately held off seven clawed monkeys.

They had barriers — weak ones, but barriers

nonetheless. Two of them were already dead, but I seriously doubted the pilot could take down the rest. He didn't look like he believed it either. And then...

Two mana crystals dropped into my mouth. The five rings on my fingers flashed. The monkeys froze, their faces twisting in terror. The pilot's hands trembled. When your enemies suddenly stop and look terrified, it usually means something even worse just arrived, you just can't see it yet.

Lucky for him, this time, it was me — the ally. Leading my undead squad, I charged onto the battlefield.

With two swift swings, I decapitated the shitting monkeys. Their barriers had collapsed thanks to the diarrhea ring and they became easy prey. The fight was over in seconds, but the stench was absolutely vile.

"You are the reinforcements?" The pilot sounded stunned. His helmet hid his face.

"Yeah." I nodded, sheathing my sword.

You've changed the destiny of two men and saved them from death.

You get: +121 divine energy.

"We need to get out of here. It's too dangerous."

"Just a minute! I need to activate the emergency beacon so they can recover the aircraft later," the pilot said, quickly scrambling into the cockpit. The plane was in rough shape, but the main structure had held together.

"Sorry, do you have any crystals?" he turned to me, and I generously handed some over, earning a grateful nod in return. Now the plane would be protected from monsters for a while.

After that, he hoisted his injured comrade onto his back, and we rushed toward my truck. The zombies followed behind, dragging the wolves' corpses. Thankfully, their vision was almost fully restored by now.

The logging truck was still undisturbed. Using my raven, I sent a message to Zhanna that we were on our way, so by the time we arrived, everything was ready to go. We piled into the cabin, and the truck roared to life, heading toward the city. Just in time, because the forest's wildlife had gone berserk.

CHAPTER 12

"THEY'RE COMING!" voices shouted. And *they* really were. But that wasn't my problem. I was a pancake, my job was to just lie there. A very, very sad pancake. My beautiful, glorious logging truck was badly damaged, and those bastard monsters were swarming from all sides. Now I'd have to send it in for repairs. No idea how long that would take. Not that it really mattered, since heading into the Wildlands anytime soon wasn't a great idea.

We were stationed in front of a bridge on the River. It had been raised specifically to keep us and the other aristocrats from abandoning this side and retreating. We were expected to defend the bridge and the forward post. And now, groups of monsters were closing in from the south and west. It wasn't enough to warrant artillery support, but more than enough to make things difficult for the aristocrats holding the line.

In front of the bridge, two rows of armored vehicles formed a defensive semi-circle. Between and around them stood infantry and mages. What was I supposed to do there? Oh, and the pilots? I had already handed them over to the military. So honestly, I wasn't all that interested in the situation.

The important thing was that no one needed rescuing anymore, no one was trapped, no one needed help breaking through monster hordes. Because on the way here I had to save two separate groups. Which was why I was now exhausted and pissed off.

My evolved zombies were all gone! Every artifact they had recovered was gone. My truck was damaged. Our haul? Pathetic. And now, I was wasting time here.

Then, something exploded nearby. I didn't care, it was probably nothing. Then, there was another explosion. This one was closer. And a third — this time so close that I nearly rolled right off the bed! Bastards!

I dragged myself to the front seats, then stepped out of the truck. Zhanna was already outside, standing next to the kikimora in her suit. My armored zombies were positioned alongside the soldiers, swords and shields at the ready. Ready to welcome anything that broke through the line. The soldiers, however, were looking at us like we were lunatics. Heading into battle without firearms?

"What's with all the explosions?"

"Suicidal monsters. The troops are holding for

now..." Zhanna didn't look convinced they'd hold for long.

Fine. I threw on my cloak, grabbed my sword, checked my rings, and sprinted toward the nearest APC. The ground around it was littered with spent shell casings, and the soldiers were firing non-stop. Someone was shouting something. I ran up to one guy, who was standing in front of the vehicle, firing a machine gun. I tapped him on the shoulder.

"Not now! We're about to get overrun!" he barked, not even looking at me before going back to firing.

Alright, fine. I grabbed him by the shoulders, climbed up over him, and jumped onto the top of the APC.

"Whoa!" I let out a breath. The battlefield was insane. There were corpses everywhere! But there were still plenty of enemies left. Small birds swarmed from above, while all sorts of beasts charged from the front. Bullets and magic poured down on them relentlessly, keeping them from getting too close.

I was on the western front, and things were rough, but not as bad as on the eastern front. There had already been several breaches there — nothing catastrophic, but still. Helicopters kept flying in to provide fire support, though they were terrified of the smaller birds.

"Well then, let's begin," I muttered, cracking my fingers. My rings shimmered as I raised my hands. The targets? Bloated, screaming pigs the size of small elephants. Their skin was an eerie shade of green, and their tails burned like fuses. They were walking bombs.

Most of the firepower was concentrated on them, but their hides were so tough that even technomagical weapons struggled to pierce through. At least, not right away. But the pigs had no barriers.

"Oink?" Five of the monsters suddenly let out confused grunts, then sped up. Panic erupted among the soldiers. But before the pigs could reach them, they started deflating like balloons and collapsed about a hundred yards short of the line, leaving behind a trail of blue sludge.

And then, some bright spark of a mage decided to toss a fireball at it. The entire battlefield erupted in explosions. I popped a large chocolate sphere into my mouth, savoring the mana crystal hidden inside. Zhanna had come up with the idea and even made them herself. My genius girl!

My rings flared again, and I targeted another group of pigs further away. And yeah, I had to burn divine energy for this — without it, my puny F-rank rings wouldn't have been able to handle C- or even B-rank monsters. It was such a waste... I'd have to treat myself to some cake when I got home.

"You shouldn't be treating yourself to cake! You should be exercising so I can keep strengthening your body!" the parasite grumbled.

Hey, nothing was stopping me from doing both: eating cake and training.

The battle continued, but nothing major happened after that. The army held strong, no more breaches occurred, and the tougher monsters had already been dealt with. So I went off to get some rest.

On the way, I overheard soldiers talking about my rings. Looked like their price was about to sky-rocket. Too bad for them. Without divine energy, they'd never achieve the same effect I did. Although, certain shamans, necromancers, and dark mages might be able to get close. Their magic worked exceptionally well with curses. Or at least, that's what the books said.

"I'm so tired and hungry!" I whined like a little kid, flopping onto my bed.

"I'm sorry. I thought I'd cook something fresh once we got back," Zhanna said, climbing into the cabin with a guilty look. "Would you like a massage instead?"

"I would. Thank you." Soon, I was lying on my stomach, groaning in satisfaction. The battle was still going on outside, but it was obvious that it was almost over.

I was right — twenty minutes later, the bridge was lowered, and we were among the first to cross into the city. Everyone else still had to divide up the loot. My fighters hadn't participated in the battle, so I wasn't getting any of the spoils anyway.

After unloading, I once again surprised the SCU troops with my trophies — specifically, the electric wolves. Apparently, they were insanely dangerous, and insanely valuable. Their hides provided excellent insulation against electricity and lightning. This material wasn't just used in combat gear but also in various technological devices.

That lifted my mood. And later that evening, it got even better. According to reconnaissance, we had pushed the monsters back significantly, and the Wave wouldn't come until at least spring.

To celebrate, the governor hosted another banquet. Of course, I went. Pretty much every aristocrat in the city was invited. The sisters and Tatiana came too. After all, they had just gotten a ton of new dresses the day before. They'd been complaining for ages about having "nothing to wear." Which was weird, because I distinctly remembered them having mountains of clothes.

How did I know that? No idea. Maybe I had seen it somewhere. Maybe I had peeked. Who knew? My memory had nothing to say on the matter. Lena and Katie were still young and growing — maybe they had just outgrown their old outfits. I, on the other hand? I had grown in a different way.

And so, we arrived at the banquet, along with the vast majority of the city's aristocracy. The sisters attracted a lot of attention in their new dresses, and somehow, I ended up surprisingly popular too. But then...

"I heard he's a master of curses — especially the diarrhea curse. His enemies die horrible deaths," a dark-haired girl whispered nearby, thinking I couldn't hear her. Her friends seemed to think the same.

"That's horrifying," added a long-legged

blonde. "But isn't he a light mage? How does he have such a talent for curses?"

"Who knows? That Scully guy is such a mystery..."

"Oh, but I heard..." the third girl — a slightly chubby one, shorter than the others — leaned in conspiratorially. "The four men accused of trying to kidnap the pocket patriarch's sisters? They nearly died so many times... and then suddenly wrote full confessions, admitting they were hired for it!"

"No way, that's nonsense," the blonde scoffed, shaking her head. And then... There was a loud rip and her delicate pink panties fell to the floor, slipping out from under her very short skirt. The same thing happened to her friends.

"Alex!" Anna's voice rang out just as she approached, looking very pleased with herself. Her brother was with her, staring in shock at the trio of girls clutching their ruined underwear.

They instantly crouched down, snatched up the torn fabric, and bolted. The blonde was sobbing in humiliation.

"Weirdos," Edward muttered, shaking his head. He walked up to me, shook my hand, then burst into laughter. "You're famous now!"

"Yeah, I heard... and the nicknames they've come up with," I sighed. The nicest one was Diarrhea King.

"It's just fear. Trust me, you'll have way fewer enemies now!" Edward roared with laughter.

"Alright, go already," his tiny sister grumbled,

trying to shove him away.

"But I wanna hang out and talk!" he protested.

"You can talk over the phone!"

Edward just laughed and finally left me alone with Anna. Fortunately, she wasn't acting up and behaved herself.

Some time later, the governor made his entrance — massive, broad-shouldered, and imposing. He launched into a long, boring speech, which I, of course, didn't listen to. That is, until my name came up.

"Only thanks to the Scully family did we learn about the crab lurking some ninety miles from the city. It's terrifying to think what could have happened if that creature had reached the River."

Huh. I hadn't thought about that. If the monster had gotten into the River, killing it would have been nearly impossible. It could have easily surfaced to attack with magic, then vanished beneath the water. Or worse — crawled onto shore and turned the city into a living hell.

"Alexander, please come up to the stage."

Sighing, I put down my half-eaten slice of unusual cake and made my way forward. And there I stood, next to this giant, while he grinned at me. Suddenly, he extended a massive hand. I shook it. Guys like him should be shaking hands with bears, not regular people.

"The pilots reported that your warriors bravely held the monster back, preventing it from escaping into the nearby lake. They gave their lives for that. As I understand, your unit lost twenty men."

I didn't respond, just grimaced at the sheer loss, not just in numbers but in divine energy and artifacts. But the crowd saw it differently...

"I can see this weighs heavily on you, but know that their sacrifice was not in vain. Through their heroism, they saved countless lives. Let us honor their memory with a moment of silence."

The hall fell silent. People stared at me. Then they brought up my rescue of the two pilots and their aircraft. To my surprise, they decided to reward me.

"Considering your role in saving a large SCU unit near Chita and your recent contributions, the government has decided to grant you a diamond account on the SCU site! With it, you will have free access to any information. I repeat, any — even S-rank. However, you are strictly prohibited from sharing it."

The hall erupted in murmurs. My eyes widened. The cost of A-rank information alone was astronomical. And S-rank... Oh boy!

"Additionally, you will receive priority when reserving shards, and the auction house will take a significantly smaller cut from you. And most importantly, all taxes on your trophies are now waived, and the commission on extracted resources from shards is halved!"

"Thank you. That's... quite generous," I said, still processing.

I wasn't the only one shocked — the entire room was buzzing. The SCU was notoriously greedy. And yet, here they were, throwing this much at me!

"This isn't just my decision — it's also thanks to the governor of Chita. He wanted, and still wants, to personally thank you for your help. If you hadn't taken out the Wave leader, the city would have suffered greatly. Some say it might have fallen, though reinforcements were already close. The Empire will never allow its cities to be destroyed by monsters!" The governor cast a stern look over the crowd.

"Glory to the Empire!" someone shouted. The crowd immediately picked up the chant.

Soon after, I returned to the hall, only to find myself swarmed by people! "What do you want from me?! Why the congratulations?! Who are you people?! I don't even know you!" I thought to myself.

"Alexander! I'm Georgy, I used to work with your father," came yet another new voice.

The moment I shook off the crowd, this guy appeared. He was older, standing next to a petite, sweet-looking girl who kept sneaking shy glances at me.

"Hello, Georgy. Unfortunately, I don't remember you. What exactly did you do with my father?"

"Hah! I caught bullets, and he pulled them out of me!" the man chuckled.

I immediately understood. The previous patriarch had served in the army and built quite a career for himself.

"Hedgehog?" I asked.

"Yes, yes! That's exactly what he called me. Too

many bullets in me," he grinned. "I just wanted to congratulate you. It's good to see that despite the heavy losses your family suffered, you're doing well. And that his son has grown into a fine man."

"Thank you." I nodded.

"Now, the reason I came over... I'm sure you're sick of all these congratulations, but my granddaughter here hasn't been able to sit still — she says you've stolen her heart!"

"Grandpa!" the girl protested, hammering her tiny fists against him while he laughed heartily.

"May I ask you to give one dance to Daria?" Hedgehog requested. The girl looked at me with hopeful eyes.

"Sorry, but I have to decline. After the Wildlands, I'd rather not exert myself physically," I shook my head.

Sure, I could have danced with her, but why would I? There was no point in dealing with the family's former partners. They had already proven themselves useless as allies.

"I understand, I didn't consider that," the man nodded, while the girl's face fell. "Well then, we'll look forward to the next banquet."

Hedgehog and his granddaughter left, but my mood had soured. I wouldn't be able to keep rejecting people without hurting the family's reputation forever. Why did humans have to make things so complicated?

"Left you alone for one minute, and already these harlots are throwing themselves at you," came Anna's grumbling voice. She had been standing off to the side, not interfering, and only approached once I was alone. "And judging by the looks in this room, there will be plenty more."

She scanned the hall, noticing just how many girls were eyeing us. Had the Scully family really become that interesting to everyone? Unfortunately, yes. People were doing everything they could to separate Anna from me. Mostly using her father for that.

The patriarchs and noblewomen kept piling on me, swarming me non-stop. Half an hour passed, and my slice of cake hadn't gotten any smaller. That was the last straw. I left for home. Tatiana could look after her daughters herself. Not like anyone was going to bother them now.

I had built up a nice stockpile of divine energy. It was time to create a new rune. I had decided a long time ago which one I needed. It would be the Body rune this time. It would help me fight against humans more effectively. The battle at the restaurant proved that point well.

If I was ever caught without my magic and artifacts, facing Adepts or anyone stronger would be brutal. But with this rune, I'd be tougher, stronger. And since Body-2 aligned perfectly beneath Body, their synergy would boost each other significantly.

By the moment I finished carving the rune, my entire body ached. Like my bones were being twisted apart. It wasn't pleasant at all. Eventually, it passed, and I exhaled in relief. If the parasite hadn't been asleep, he could have helped, but the bastard was actually snoring!

Meanwhile, I was stuffing myself with mana stones, finally pushing through to the seventh rank. Just a little more, and I'd become an Adept. Then, I'd have my own barrier, and life would get so much easier.

But that was for later. Right now, I needed to soak in a hot bath, stretch out, and fully enjoy the warm water. And then, cake and sleep. Sure, I had promised the parasite I'd start training, but that could wait. Tonight, I had definitely earned my cake and rest.

* * *

City hospital
Special room
Athanasius and company

The door to the hospital room opened, and a nurse entered, followed by two priests of Reyna's church. They looked around in surprise at the soft walls and floor. There was no furniture, so the patient lay on the ground, covered with a blanket.

The man woke up immediately and, upon seeing the priests, nearly screamed: "You're here! Save me! Please, save me!"

"Quiet," one of the priests ordered. He was already aware of the situation.

In just two days, the man had been impaled by a metal rod, electrocuted, choked nearly to death, had his life-support machines explode, and had almost been poisoned by carbon monoxide. And that wasn't even counting the smaller incidents, like the pen lodged in his throat, a cut from a piece of bread crust, and many other misfortunes.

"I've been cursed! Scully cursed me! Save me! I beg you! I'll pay! I'll pay a lot!"

The priests exchanged glances. "What do you think?" asked the one on the left. Their robes and hoods concealed their faces.

"I sense no curses," the one on the right replied. "But I can see his sinful soul. It's so black that even a weak priest like me can see it. Disgusting."

"He's in the logging industry," the priest to the right added. "Forestry, lumber work... I don't even want to imagine how many lives he's ruined to stain his soul this deeply."

"What are you talking about?! Save me! I've never killed anyone!"

"We refuse. Our church aids only the needy and the suffering. And you, it seems, have earned your punishment." The priests turned toward the exit, leaving Athanasius in shock.

"Wait! What?! You can't! Don't leave me! I'll pay! I'll pay a fortune!"

"Wipe your ass with your blood money," the priest scoffed, shaking his head before slamming the door shut, leaving Athanasius alone with his millions and his despair.

Suddenly, a team of doctors rushed past the priests and stormed into the room. The patient had suffered a heart attack. But of course, he was a VIP client. The best doctors were always at his disposal, and that kind of care wasn't cheap. Considering how often they had to drag him back from the brink of death, Athanasius's millions would soon be flowing straight into the hospital's accounts.

CHAPTER 13

THE BOARDING SCHOOL for commoner mages was a rather disgusting place, if you ask me. It looked more like a prison than an educational institution. High walls with watchtowers, a barbed-wire fence around the perimeter. And notably, the fence wasn't outside the walls, but inside the so-called "protected" territory.

It was obvious that they were training cannon fodder here. Proper aristocrats trained their own mages. And as I had learned, this place also allowed hiring commoners for shard-clearing missions. But that only interested weaklings — after all, commoners rarely amounted to anything special. In the end, it was cheaper and more efficient to train and equip a squad of guards instead.

For the army, though — where most commoner mages ended up — it was a decent support system. Those who managed to prove themselves had a shot at becoming aristocrats. And why not? I'd read that occasionally, true talents emerged among commoners.

I went there for that waitress... what was her name again? Lily, I think. Initially, I had planned to fly to Chita, but the governor was dealing with urgent issues. The monster uprisings had reached them too.

Something was happening in the Wildlands. A territorial shift among the monsters, maybe. Or some especially nasty creatures had broken through, driving the others north. And here we hu

— Well, look at that! I was already starting to think of myself as human. What a joke.

"Master Alexander? Master Alexander!" A woman's voice pulled me from my thoughts.

"Yes, sorry, I was just thinking," I nodded to the woman in front of me. I was in the office of the school's headmistress. We were negotiating the "purchase" of a student.

Buying out a mage wasn't cheap. Which was exactly why she was being so polite. The army would lose a recruit, but the school would make a hefty profit. And who cares about the army, right? At least until the next Wave came, and there weren't enough defenders to hold it back. Then, suddenly, all the blame would fall on the military.

As one god supposedly said, "Cats are better." And so, he created the beast-folk. But they turned out half-wild. All they did was sleep, eat whatever they could find, and cause havoc in the middle of the night. They loved settling among other races, but for some reason, those races weren't particularly fond of them.

"Master Alexander?"

"Apologies, got lost in thought again. Yes, I'm sure. As you probably know, my family is rapidly regaining its power after the last noble war. I'm in desperate need of capable people."

I looked at the woman — she was around forty, stately in presence, but exhausted. Wrinkles lined her face, her skin was dry, and her hair was splitting. A workaholic, without a doubt.

"I understand. But will you be able to give her the proper education? She's only a branded one, but she already shows strong talent in wind magic. If you're willing to pay extra, we can provide you with training materials up to the Adept level."

Her eyes gleamed. There it was — she was trying to squeeze more money out of me.

"Why not," I shrugged. I was certain it wasn't classified information. Otherwise, she wouldn't be selling it. And my bird might find it interesting and perhaps even learn something from it.

"Wonderful! Our best teachers crafted an individual training plan for Lily. We had great hopes for her," she went on, inflating the price as we waited for them to bring the girl.

The door opened, and an unpleasant-looking woman in her fifties stepped in, her face bulldog-like, her elaborate hairstyle resembling the Leaning Tower of Pisa.

"Come in," she ordered as she walked into the

office, and a slightly nervous girl followed behind her.

"G-good afternoon, Headmistress. Good afternoon, Noble Sir," she said, bowing. Her words sounded rehearsed, as if she had practiced them over and over.

"Hey, Lily." I nodded at her, and a brilliant, joyful smile bloomed on her face.

"Lord Scully! You came to take me with you?!"

"Lily! What kind of behavior is this?!" the bulldog-woman barked, making the girl flinch and shrink back in fear.

"Yes, I came for you. I need more helping hands."

"Then perhaps—"

"Lily!" the woman snapped again.

"Please do not interrupt or interfere in our conversation." I shot the bulldog-woman a sharp look, and she immediately shut her mouth. "Go on, Lily, what did you want to ask?"

"There are two girls who also want to work for you. They say you saved them," she said hesitantly, still looking a bit nervous, but as she realized no one would scold her for speaking, she grew a little bolder.

"The goblin dungeon... yeah, I remember. Their team abandoned them to die."

"They did abandon them! Oh, sorry..." Lily quickly covered her mouth with her hands when she saw the bulldog's furious glare.

"If they want to join me, I don't mind. As I said, I need all the help I can get." I glanced at the headmistress, who looked rather pensive.

"They're graduates. They already have contracts to serve in the army. The penalty for breaking those will be significant. Are you sure?"

"I'm sure."

"Sir, one of them also has a brother studying here. He's a graduate too and a talented mage..." As soon as Lily said that, the headmistress's faces twisted in displeasure.

"He's not that talented. And he's very problematic," she said, but I raised my hand, cutting off her lies.

"I'm taking him as well. I don't want to separate families."

"O-okay." She sighed heavily, as if tearing out a piece of her soul, and picked up the phone. "But first, I need to call someone in the army. They might refuse to terminate the contract, and they'd be within their rights. I need to check first..."

I had no objections, so she made the call. The people on the other end were clearly unhappy — after all, the Wave was nearly upon us, and now they were losing their mage recruits. And not just any mages — Adepts [10-19].

"Who's buying them out? Alexander Scully... What? Hang on? Alright..." The woman looked surprised, and for nearly two minutes, we waited for them to make a decision. And then... "What? What do you mean he doesn't have to pay the penalty? What? Saved the pilots and helped prevent the Wave?! I see..."

She looked at me as if I had suddenly turned

into a pacifist red dragon. She couldn't believe that the small guy in front of her had done so much. "Yes, yes, I am that amazing. And I deserve some cake," I thought to myself.

"So, the army is willing to terminate their contracts, and you don't need to pay any penalties. Just compensation to the school and, if you'd like, the training program up to Junior Mage [20-29]."

"It's a pleasure doing business with you, and I'd appreciate it if you informed me of any young talents in the future. But for now, allow me to thank you as only a light mage can," I smiled as my hands began to glow.

"Ms. Semyon, leave us and prepare the documents!"

"Yes, Headmistress," the bulldog said, pushing Lily out into the hallway. I got to work. I really wanted to try out this new idea...

Soon, we were both seated, and I began. It didn't take long, since I was using divine energy, but just a tiny bit.

"Oh..."

"I can stop if this makes you uncomfortable."

"N-no, please continue..." she murmured in a sultry voice as I ran my hands along her back, then over her stomach. After that, I asked her to stand so I could work on her legs.

"And... my butt?"

"If that doesn't bother you," I shrugged and focused on the requested area, then went over her entire body just to finish the process. When I was done, I stepped back, nodded in satisfaction, and turned her toward the mirror.

"Huh?" She rubbed her eyes with her fists and stepped closer to the mirror, unable to believe what she was seeing. Her hair now shone like polished gold, the wrinkles on her face had vanished, and it looked like she had just shed ten years. Heh-heh-heh... I had a feeling that this magic could conquer the entire world!

You've changed the destiny of a woman, making her life much better.
You get: +9 divine energy.

"Perfect! It works!" I thought. "If I crunch the numbers: out of fifteen people, three had already given divine energy. One in five, huh? Not bad. If I open a clinic, just how much energy could I be collecting per day?!"

"I'll wait outside," I said out loud, but she didn't hear me. The headmistress was furiously stripping off her clothes, and that was not something I wanted to see. Slamming the door shut, I walked out into the hallway.

From inside came delighted laughter, cries, shouts, and all sorts of other noises. Now I just needed to figure out how much to charge for this procedure. A million? A million of millions? "Heh-heh... I really should just open a clinic..."

"Wait! What if the sisters get married and leave? I had to eliminate that possibility. Their husbands had to be local, then the girls would work at my clinic. I could set up contracts or something along those li—"

I didn't get to finish that thought, because the door burst open, and the headmistress lunged at me with a hug. Fortunately, she was dressed again.

"This is incredible! Absolutely magical!"

"I've saturated your body with life. If you don't want the effect to fade quickly, make sure you get plenty of rest, eat well, and stay physically active."

"I will! I promise!" She beamed.

We returned to the office, and barely a minute later, the bulldog-woman entered. Her jaw dropped. She just stood there, mouth agape, staring at the headmistress.

"Madame, you look positively stunning today. As if the Goddess herself had descended from the heavens before me." Came her syrupy voice.

I turned to see a blond pretty-boy, and behind him, a familiar tall blonde and a slender dark-haired girl.

"Allow me to introduce our guest: this is Sir Alexander Scully. He is buying out your contracts. As of today, you are servants of House Scully," the headmistress announced with satisfaction.

"Master! Thank you for saving us!" The tall blonde stepped forward. She had a generous chest, a shapely backside, and a narrow waist — her figure was practically an hourglass.

Beside her stood a thin, delicate, dark-haired girl, reserved and quiet, like a young birch tree.

"And I want to thank you for saving my sister and Xenia." The young man also bowed.

BOOK THREE

"We light mages don't abandon people in distress," I said and gestured for them to straighten up. "As my servants, you will receive good salaries, full medical coverage through my house, and support for your families. I won't be using you as cannon fodder or sending you into shard-clearing missions. We'll discuss your responsibilities later. First, I need to know what you can actually do. Any questions?"

"If not for shards or battle, what do you need us for?" the young man asked, suspicion in his eyes.

"My guardians handle combat. As for shards, I can clear them just fine on my own — anyone else would just get in my way. I need you because I desperately lack trustworthy people. Mostly for leadership roles, business management, and administrative work."

"I'm good with accounting, got only straight A's in it," he said, and the headmistress nodded in confirmation.

"That's true, Stephan is a highly talented accountant and clerk. Irina, well..." The headmistress turned to the tall blonde, then grimaced. "She's... beautiful and... resilient. And Xenia is a good lawyer. Though she could use a bit more confidence."

"Yeah, I can see that. But we'll fix it." I took a good look at the group.

Stephan immediately impressed me. I saw a determined man, someone willing to sacrifice for his loved ones. Strong-willed, he'd go far.

We wrapped up the paperwork and headed for the exit, but there was a problem. I had come in an SUV, and everyone couldn't get into it. So I called Ivan.

"You guys packed so little?" I looked at my new group. Only Lily had a suitcase, the rest carried small backpacks.

"The school provides everything, and all of it belongs to them," Stephan said.

"Got it. Tomorrow, my assistant will take you shopping. Buy whatever you need. Don't worry about the cost."

"You're not going to deduct it from our salaries later, are you?" Stephan eyed me warily. It was too good a deal — he probably thought there had to be a catch.

"Stephan, you saw what I did to the headmistress. Tell me, how far would women go to get my service?" I looked at him carefully.

"Anything. Probably kill for it!" He laughed dryly. And I laughed with him. Because it was true. The Academy's teachers had been ready to blackmail me with failing grades just to get me to make them beautiful. That madness in their eyes... Women would go to great lengths for youth and beauty.

I had been human, and an aristocrat, for nearly two months now. And in that time, I had learned one thing: many problems existed because of women. Though, to be fair, they were usually not the ones at fault.

One man desperately wanted a woman and

ended up causing trouble for everyone around him. Another simply desired wealth and a harem of stunning women to serve him day and night. And then there were those who would do anything for their wives, daughters, or sisters. Those were the ones I would target.

Once women learned about my magic, they would demand my services, pressuring their men to secure them a rare appointment. Was this not a brilliant plan? They used to call me the Evil God. Might as well be one for a bit! "Bwahaha!"

"Then you understand our potential," I said to Stephan.

"Wealth, fame, and reputation." He nodded.

"But first, we need to handle immediate problems. My family suffered a brutal war and lost. Now, I'm rebuilding our house from the ground up. I hope you'll help with that." I looked at the four of them. Stephan suddenly knelt. A moment later, the others followed suit.

"We wish to serve you for the rest of our lives, Master. We will do everything in our power to aid you, I swear it by my magic," Stephan said.

"I swear by my magic!" the girls echoed.

Interesting oath. I'd never heard it before. Though my memories told me it was a standard mage vow. Rarely spoken, because breaking it could actually strip a person of their magic.

"I accept your vow. Welcome to the family," I grinned. And right on cue, Ivan pulled up.

We all piled into the cars and headed home. My new employees would be living in the mansion

— after all, they had nowhere else to stay. If they wanted, I would buy them an apartment closer to Zhanna. I told them that right away.

When we arrived at the mansion, it looked far more intimidating than it used to. Twelve armored fighters, weapons at the ready, and within city limits — it looked very impressive. Later, I would get something even stronger and expand the guard, but that could wait.

For now, I remotely connected to the Fortress rune and added the newcomers to the "partially trusted" group. They were free to move around the mansion but couldn't access critical areas.

Xena and Valeria were waiting for us at the entrance, along with the ever-curious sisters. "Valeria, take in the newcomers."

"My God, I've never seen such enchanting creatures. You're mesmerizing," Stephan said, turning on the charm with the sisters, but they were immune to such flattery. At the last reception with the governor, they had already heard every compliment imaginable. Still, the girls smiled.

I introduced my new crew, then introduced the sisters, after which Valeria whisked the four of them away. She had already been informed that there would be three more servants and had ordered their rooms to be prepared.

The mansion was huge, full of unused rooms, and keeping them all tidy while maintaining order was no easy task. How did Xena and Valeria manage it alone? Must be magic...

Then came the long-awaited dinner, though

unfortunately, I couldn't eat much. As the parasite had already mentioned, my body had reached its limit, and converting energy from food into muscle wouldn't work anymore. That explained my loss of appetite.

"Alex, are you feeling sick? You're eating so little," Tatiana said. For the record, I had already finished three plates and was planning to tackle the fourth. Meanwhile, the sisters ate calmly, quietly discussing the newcomers.

"On the contrary," I said. "I'm perfectly healthy now, so there's no need to keep consuming food in industrial quantities."

"Should I cook less?" Valeria asked, standing near the table beside Xena. They had even dressed Lily in a maid outfit, which suited her.

"Yes, sorry for not mentioning it earlier." I glanced over the table, packed with delicious dishes, and sighed regretfully.

"Don't worry, you have four new servants with ravenous appetites. The food won't go to waste," she chuckled. She had a point — no need to throw away perfectly good food, plenty of dishes hadn't even been touched yet.

"Alex!" Tatiana pounced on me like a bear and once again smothered me with her large breasts. "I'm so happy you're finally completely healthy!" Alright, I could endure the smothering for a bit.

I didn't train after dinner, but rested. It had been a long, exhausting day. After my rest, I gathered all the newcomers and the sisters in the training hall. The sisters had been restless for a while, begging to start training again.

Stephan, Xenia, and Irina were still wearing the same clothes they had on when they left their school, since they had nothing else. Lily was in a sports top and shorts. I had to admit, the former waitress was quite attractive. The sisters and I were in our usual training outfits. Nearby, the training equipment was neatly arranged along the wall.

"Now, we're going to have a little sparring session. I want to see what your school has taught you. But first, state your age, rank, and element. Let's start with you, Irina." I pointed at the blonde, and she immediately stepped forward.

"Irina Elissis, twenty-four years old, third-state Adept, fire magic." She raised a fist, and her brand flared to life with fire on the back of her hand. A bright pattern of twelve small dots spiraled across it. It was a strange choice, putting a mark in such a visible spot. An enemy could easily see it and gauge her strength.

"Alex Scully, twenty years old, seventh-state Apprentice. Pick a weapon and fight at full strength."

The girl didn't move, too stunned to react. The others seemed just as bewildered, probably wondering how I had single-handedly cleared out that goblin shard.

"Don't mind my rank. I'm stronger than everyone in this room combined. And just so you know, Katie and Lena are fifteenth rank. Now grab a weapon and attack," I gestured to the weapons by the wall. The blonde nodded silently and picked up a large wooden club.

The fight began, and let me tell you, there was a lot of work to be done. Irina coated her weapon in flames and swung at me like I was an annoying mosquito. She was as strong as an ogre but clumsy. Her generous proportions made her sluggish in battle, but if she were suited up in heavy armor, she would make an excellent "crusher." In the end, she never landed a single hit, and I easily shattered her barrier.

Stephan stepped forward after Irina. "Stephan Elissis, twenty-four years old, fourth-state Adept. Like my sister, I wield fire magic."

He grabbed two swords and lunged at me. He had decent combat instincts and moved well, but his magic was absolute trash. His control and power were both terrible, same as his sister's. He lasted only slightly longer than Irina.

"Xenia Knight!" the dark-haired girl nearly shouted. "Twenty-four years old! Third-state Adept! Fire magic!"

"Caw!" came the furious screech of a bird. "Fire?! Who the hell trained you?! Who in their right mind would waste such a beauty on fire magic?!" The raven swooped around the training hall, cursing up a storm, leaving everyone gaping. Even the sisters were surprised.

"Meet your magic instructor. Call this bird whatever you want. If it gets too annoying, feel free to smack it like a mosquito or roast it. It's tough, but its personality is unbearable. And you," I said, turning to the bird, "I've never heard you call any-one 'beautiful' before."

"Caw! Of course, she's a beauty! Slim, cute lit-tle face, barely any chest, long legs, and short stat-ure! A loli! A perfect loli!" the raven squawked, still circling overhead.

Xenia instantly covered her chest with her hands and puffed out her cheeks in indignation, which only seemed to excite the bird more.

"Caw! Adorable! Loli! Caw!!! Oof!"

I hurled a shield at it, knocking it out of the air, then walked over and grabbed it by the neck. "Focus. What's wrong with fire magic?"

"What do you mean, 'what's wrong'?! She has the element of darkness! Those idiots slap a fire brand on everyone! Even that cow over there — they turned her into a fire mage, those morons! She's an attribute of life! Even a fool should under — krk!" I had to squeeze a little harder to make it shut up before it insulted anyone else.

"Now, calmly explain everything to us," I or-dered, pulling its soul slightly toward the Under-world.

"Yes! Of course! Mercy, Master!!"

And so, the stunned audience sat down across from us, and the long, rambling lecture began.

CHAPTER 14

SIX ARMORED, WELL-ARMED SUVs sped down a long-abandoned road. Each was painted white with lavish gold detailing, making them instantly recognizable as a church cleansing squad.

Before long, a village appeared on their path. It had already been cleared out, and quite some time ago.

"Stop the vehicles!" ordered the bishop from the passenger seat of the lead car.

The SUVs came to a halt in the center of the village, and from them poured warriors clad in golden armor. Their reinforced technomagical plates gleamed in the light, each carried a sheathed two-handed sword, and a powerful shotgun strapped to their back. For now, none of them reached for their weapons.

"Bishop, is there an enemy here?" one of the warriors asked. They all looked nearly identical in their armor.

"There's nothing here," the bishop replied firmly.

"So, we leave?"

"No. You don't understand. There is *nothing* here!" The man, who appeared to be around forty, removed his helmet, revealing a face that had grown noticeably younger. Of course, everyone was already aware of this, but his words... It took them a moment to grasp what he was saying.

"How is that possible? No souls?!"

"None!" The bishop closed his eyes and focused. A golden wave of mana radiated outward from him in all directions. It was warm and soothing to everyone it touched. "No one at all... I was here after the dead of this town rose from their graves. We put them to rest, but their souls were too filled with rage to disperse peacefully."

"I read about that incident," another paladin spoke up. "Monster attack. The village leader fled, leaving the people in terror and despair."

"That's exactly what happened. I could feel their pain. But now, there's nothing but peace and purity here. I don't understand how that's possible," the bishop muttered, then abruptly opened his eyes. "Search the village!"

"Yes, sir!"

The warriors scattered, but it didn't take long

for them to find something unusual — an obelisk standing in the center of the village fountain.

"What is this?" the bishop murmured in confusion, running his hand over the stone structure. He channeled mana into it but felt nothing. "Drawings..."

He noticed that the obelisk was covered in carvings depicting heavenly light and joyous souls ascending toward it. "Who could have created this? Incredible... It's so peaceful near it... Could this have helped the souls find rest?"

"Bishop, look at this." One of the paladins handed over a phone displaying several photographs. "An identical obelisk was discovered at the city's first cemetery."

"Then it's no coincidence! We need to visit that cemetery. If my senses are correct, no undead will ever rise from that cemetery again, and no filth will ever take root there!"

The paladins erupted into cheers. "This is a blessing from the great goddess!"

"Glory to Reyna!"

A few of the more zealous warriors fell to their knees, their armor clanking, and began to pray.

"Are we returning to the city?"

"No," the bishop said, replacing his helmet and gazing into the distance. "We continue onward. We must see what's happening in the cursed lands. They're like a festering wound on the goddess's body, and we must find a way to heal them."

The squad pushed northward, though the journey was anything but easy. The region teemed with monsters. But these were no ordinary warriors, they were warrior-priests and part of a cleansing squad. They were more commonly known as paladins.

Several hours later, six slightly battered vehicles reached the cursed lands, and the priests froze in shock. Where once there had been blackened earth and nature twisted by unholy power, now there was life. Rotten trees had sprouted new shoots, and young saplings were already growing in their place. Some trees had even managed to restore themselves, their branches budding with fresh leaves. Though, not everything had recovered.

"The cursed lands have shrunk by half," the bishop murmured, staring at the blackened soil beneath his feet and the ruins of a bone fortress. "And it looks like they're still receding. But who could possibly be powerful enough to destroy a lich? No one else could have built that fortress of bone. And I shudder to think what would have happened if that creature had waged war against humanity."

"Bishop! We found something! We found it!" a voice crackled through the armor's built-in speakers. The bishop replaced his helmet, where an internal screen displayed a blinking marker on a small map. His paladins hurried to the location, only to be met with —

"Another obelisk! This one is enormous!" one of the warriors exclaimed in astonishment. The rest of the squad was equally stunned. The obelisk towered over them like a colossal tree.

"Yes! This is it! I can feel it!" The bishop rushed to the obelisk. "This is why the cursed energy has left these lands. And life! I can feel life radiating from it… Could it be? It transforms curses into life itself! A miracle! Truly! Who is this great paladin who has graced our land?!"

"Should I send a request to the High Church?" one of the paladins asked.

"Yes, please do. I wish to kneel before this holy person and kiss their hand. This is a deed of the highest order!"

"Shall we collect photos and video evidence for the High Church?"

"Yes," the bishop nodded. "If the great paladin shares their secrets with us, we can save the world!"

* * *

Scully Mansion
Training hall
Great paladin for some, Alexander for others
And company

We sat on the rubberized floor, listening to the black bird in the center. And oh, how I wanted to swat it with a slipper — too much pointless chatter.

"So, our low compatibility with fire is due to the fact that we actually have a talent for other elements?" Stephan summarized.

"Bravo, you finally got it!" the bird said. "But

let me point out — it's not a talent, caw, but a natural, caw, inclination. It's like if this short—" The bird pointed a wing at me, but before it could finish, Lily smacked it with her sneaker.

"Don't insult the master, you nasty bird!" she huffed.

"He just wants to spend the evening in my company," I grinned wickedly, and the bird flinched.

"F-f-forgive this fool, caw!" The raven hopped onto its feet and bowed, spreading its wings.

"Continue."

"Y-yes! Caw! What I meant was that if, caw, the Master tried to wield any other element — any at all — it wouldn't matter. He'd turn out to be a useless, caw, hack, not a mage. His natural affinity for white, caw, magic is too strong."

"I see... But how did you figure out that my element is 'nature'?" Stephan asked. The others also looked at the bird.

"Oh, come on, caw..." The raven froze when it saw my expression and seemed to swallow hard. "It's obvious to the naked eye. Look at Irina," it gestured with its wing toward the blonde. "Women with, caw, generous proportions tend to have a strong 'life' attribute. And sweet little Xenia — she's definitely darkness. Just look at her black eyes. The darker they are, the stronger the affinity."

"And me? Why 'nature'?"

"Because you're a pretty, caw, boy that everyone finds annoying!" the bird cawed bitterly.

"Those with an affinity for 'nature' always have perfect looks. But in your case, it's all about 'fire.' Caw! It's like you're burning on the inside, which makes you weak."

"Got it. Yeah, I do feel something like that." The blonde nodded uncertainly. "So, what do you suggest?"

"Destroy the, caw, brand and make a new one, what else?" The raven looked at Stephan like he was an idiot.

"So we have to start over? From rank zero?" Xenia looked about ready to collapse.

"Would you rather stay, caw, weaklings? Have you even seen your magic? Your barriers are brittle, your attacks are pathetic, even your physical enhancements are useless! Caw! Such talent, wasted! Your teachers were morons! Idiots! Caw! Degenerates!"

"What about me? I was assigned 'wind'." Lily waved a hand.

"Then they actually, caw, tested you properly. But even without a test, it's obvious you're, caw, wind. As flighty as the bre — quack!"

"You're so annoying," Lilia hissed, raising her sneaker again.

"I agree to change my brand," Stephan said firmly, his gaze resolute.

"Master should take you through the, caw, shards. You'll regain your strength quickly. The body remembers everything and will absorb mana like a sponge."

"I agree too," Irina declared.

"Me too," Xenia said quietly.

"Good. Then by Master's will, I'll prepare custom brands for each of you. I need time to get ready — two days."

"What about the stages? How far will we be able to develop?" Stephan and the others were clearly concerned about this. It was understandable — brands varied in quality. The foundation of the brand determined the limit of one's rank and stage.

A weak foundation meant the brand wouldn't be able to handle much, limiting a mage to a Junior Mage level [20-29]. If someone needed to mass-produce mages quickly, they could use an even weaker foundation, boosting ranks fast but capping out at peak Adept [19].

In short, it was complicated. The foundation — the original brand of my bloodline — allowed all its members to reach the pinnacle of magic. That was the case for most powerful families. As for the imperial family, rumor had it that their brand was so mighty it not only made rank advancement easy but also granted terrifying magical strength.

"What kind of stupid, caw, question is that? I'll make a brand so strong that nothing will limit it! Caw!" The raven flapped its wings. "You've built up a massive amount of, caw, mana. When I break your current brand, I'll channel all that energy into the new one. It'll settle in perfectly despite its complexity. I am a, caw, genius! And you better not underestimate me!"

"What about me? I'm still rank zero," Lily said.

"I'll figure something out for the chicken... quack!" The bird got smacked again. And it deserved it. Life never taught it a thing.

We talked a little more and then continued training. Now the sisters had sparring partners, and they were very pleased about it.

The next day was quiet, peaceful, and uneventful. I spent my time at the Academy handling various matters and thinking about potential purchases. But then, during lunch, Anton Vecher found me.

He looked much better than the last time we met. The dark circles under his eyes were gone, he had gained a bit of weight, and overall, he seemed like a completely different person.

"Alex," Anton said, sitting down at our table. "We've been thinking for a long time about how to repay you for saving us. Your assistant suggested magical devices."

He handed me his phone, displaying a picture of an unusual contraption. It looked like a tripod with something resembling a drum in the center, covered in golden engravings and magical inscriptions.

"A diffuser?" Basel asked.

"Yes, an artifact from a shard. Rank A."

Basel's eyebrow shot up, Polina's mouth fell slightly open, and Anna... Well, today she had apparently decided I didn't need my left arm, so she was clinging to it with a death grip. In short, she was just as surprised.

"This is a family heirloom, and we want to offer

it as payment for your work."

"Don't you need it yourselves? Isn't this an incredibly useful thing?" I asked in surprise.

"Incredibly useful, but..." Anton made a guilty grimace. "It devours mana crystals like crazy. Technomagical diffusers are much more efficient, though they can't generate mana concentrations as high as this one."

"Now I see. Alright, I accept it as payment." I nodded and shook his hand. The guy looked genuinely happy.

"That's an expensive trade," Basel mused, while I, on the other hand, was pleased.

Crystals weren't a problem for me, and considering the parasite's ability to absorb mana from the surroundings, this might actually be more effective than giving myself heartburn by consuming crystals.

"Well, I collect a lot of crystals, so I can afford it."

"Then I should come visit sometime!" the big guy laughed.

"No, definitely do not come visit. That would be a headache," I thought to myself. Aristocratic etiquette and all that nonsense — hosting guests, giving them attention, wasting time and energy, and worst of all, sharing food. I'd rather spend my time productively — or better yet, sleep.

"Why is everyone so worked up?" I asked, glancing at the commotion in the cafeteria.

"Oh, right! You slept through the announcement," Basel burst into laughter again. He was really getting on my nerves — I was going to go deaf at this rate. "Long story short, since the monsters have gone berserk, the practical training on sealing gates has been temporarily canceled. Instead, we're getting field practice!"

"I don't want to go anywhere," I grumbled. That's a massive waste of time! And I already had plenty of things to do.

"Like sleeping?" the parasite joked in my head.

"Haha, you're comedian of the year."

"Teleportation," Basel grinned widely.

"Well, in that case..." I nodded. "What exactly are we supposed to do?"

"Hunting monsters outside the gates, scouting, learning to drive military vehicles, shooting machine guns, and training in combat tactics."

"Sounds like a pain in the ass."

"Oh, come on! There'll be gates, tents, field kitchens, forests, adventures, youth!" If we were sitting closer, he would've clapped me on the back. Good thing we weren't!

"Tents..." Anna's eyes sparkled. So did Polina's.

Yeah, Basel was definitely getting assaulted on this trip. Though I wasn't worried about Anna — she was clingy, but smart and reasonable. "No funny business before marriage." But still, that look of hers... She had the expression of an Amazon who had just caught a warrior-man. Hopefully, I was imagining things.

The rest of the day passed as usual — lessons, then my personal errands. Specifically, a trip to the cemetery. At night, of course. I revived my Chinese zombies but didn't evolve them because it was too costly. I figured I'd let them hunt monsters and grow stronger on their own.

After that, I headed to the lumberyard with Zhanna, unloading twenty freshly raised, foul-smelling zombies, along with construction materials. I also reinforced the security a bit and let the skeleton out to roam. No point in him just lazing around in the afterlife, right?

Meanwhile, I collected hides, claws, and other trophies from the monsters my zombie guards had taken down. Plus, I loaded up a full truck and both trailers with lumber.

I was leaving for field practice soon, so I had to stock up in advance. The next day, right after classes, I made two more trips for materials and also quickly cleared a couple of fresh shards.

Well, "cleared" might be an overstatement. I just told the zombies and skeleton, "Sic 'em," and they wiped everything out. Just two D-rank shards. I only took the crystals — they were meant for helping my incompetent mages become real mages.

And so, a day later, on Thursday, we gathered in the training room. The raven used its beak and blood to carve a magic circle into the floor, while the diffuser hummed beside it. Crystals were placed on top of the device, while a blue mist drifted out from below. The sisters, Anna, and I sat off to the side, watching, careful to keep our distance so we wouldn't accidentally absorb the mana. It wasn't meant for us.

Stephan was the first to sit in the circle — it had been drawn using his own blood. And then...

"Alex, how can I not laugh?! I can't! I'm gonna die!" Lena was pounding the floor with her fist, howling with laughter. The others weren't far behind. Even I couldn't help but smirk.

The raven was dancing as it cast its spell. The whole thing looked so absurd that even Stephan was barely holding back his laughter. And then, it began.

The blue mana mist surged toward the circle, and the mana crystals at its edges began to sizzle. Then came Stephan's agonized scream. His sister immediately made a pained expression and tried to see through the mist, but all she could glimpse were the raven's black wings occasionally flapping. The screaming only grew louder...

A minute passed. Then another. Five... Ten... And then — silence. Irina's face turned pale with fear, as did her friend's.

"He did it," I stated confidently. And I was right. The blue mist was blown away by the raven's wings, revealing Stephan — red-faced, drenched in sweat, and grinning. He stretched out a hand and released pure mana that glowed green.

"It... really worked. This is my element..." His voice was filled with awe. "And I'm a fourth-rank Apprentice, but I feel way stronger than before. This is amazing!"

"Of course, caw! Now your, caw, mana is in harmony! And your magical, caw, channels have been cleansed and restored! Whoever branded you before was a clumsy, caw, ass! They should be turned into a zombie!"

Soon, the raven began drawing a new circle, this time using Irina's blood. The process went much faster — life magic was gentle and forgiving, so she barely felt any pain. In the end, her rank dropped from twelfth all the way to third. It was different for Xenia.

"My dear, my beautiful lady. Everything will be just fine. Caw! You won't feel a thing, caw. My poor heart couldn't handle your, caw, cries and tears," the raven cooed while inscribing the circle. This time, the design was twice as large and far more intricate.

The process took half an hour, but not once did Xenia scream. Her rank fell to fourth. Oh, how I wanted to smack that damn bird.

"What? Caw! It doesn't affect the final, caw, rank! Just the process speed and its, caw, pain level. Xenia is not only, caw, beautiful but also tal—" The raven suddenly froze, and a second later, its legs buckled as it collapsed. It was staring at Xena, who had just walked in carrying tea and snacks.

"Goddess... Goddess of all lollies! I love you! Marry me! Caw!" The bird darted toward Xena as she set the drinks on the table, only to be met with a tray to the beak.

"M-Master! What is that strange bird? It talks?" Xena clutched the tray to her chest and hid behind me.

"Yes. It's a very strange and very perverted bird. If it bothers you, just hit it. You can stab it with a knife or scald it with boiling water."

"U-understood..." Xena left, and the raven remained sprawled on the floor, slowly coming back to its senses.

"Happiness... It was so, caw, close..." it moaned before passing out completely. Damn, Xena really got him.

We cleaned up, and I sent everyone off to rest. Lily had already gone through the branding process, she was first, in fact. But since she was rank zero, it had been quick and painless.

The next day, I took Irina, Xenia, and Stephan to the factory, which would be their office. Lily, meanwhile, would serve as a maid at the mansion, helping Xena and Valeria with their duties.

"This place has a weird vibe," Stephan noted.

"A little, yeah," I shrugged. We were inspecting the factory with Maxim, his smile so wide, it was about to split his face in two. He clearly liked the sight of the curvy blonde, though he tried not to stare too obviously. Xenia, on the other hand, seemed completely invisible to him.

"They look and move like robots," Irina muttered.

"And now you're about to learn a little secret," I grinned. The others stopped smiling. "No one can know about this. It's a trump card for light mages."

"Undead?" Xenia suddenly blurted out, stunning everyone.

"You think they're zombies? That's impossible!

How can zombies work? And how come they don't stink?" Stephan asked in disbelief.

"Because they're not ordinary zombies. They weren't created by cursed magic, but by my magic," I explained, shocking them even further. "I can not only banish the undead and cleanse filth but also control them. And since I have issues hiring living workers, because everyone is too scared, I decided to use the dead."

"That's hard to believe," Stephan examined the workers closely. I called one over, and he stripped down.

Underwear wasn't part of the uniform, but that didn't seem to bother the girls in the slightest.

"He really is dead," Irina placed her hand on the man's cold, pale chest. "His heart isn't beating."

"They don't need rest, sleep, wages, and, most importantly, they won't betray me," Stephan mumbled to himself before suddenly looking at me with admiration. "This... This is genius! These are perfect workers! This factory will make a fortune!"

"Exactly!" I grinned. I liked this guy, he was quick-witted and business-minded. Maybe I'd set up another enterprise in the future and make him the CEO.

After finishing the tour, we got down to business. Stephan immediately teamed up with the old factory manager to go over documents, while Xenia handled the legal matters, though she had to check the internet constantly for reference.

As for Irina, she started cleaning. Yeah, the

place was a mess. No one had mopped the floors, taken out the trash, or maintained basic cleanliness. It was disgusting, in fact.

The trio was officially hired, with a salary five times the city's average — 100,000. The human workers nearly fainted when they heard that. Before long, I left them to their work. I had my own preparations to make.

Tomorrow morning, we were teleporting to the training grounds, located on the other side of the country. There was even a chance we'd be allowed to visit the imperial capital, which was nearby.

We were advised to bring our own supplies — personal gear, tents, and so on — since military-issued ones might not be to the taste of "pampered aristocrats." And honestly? I had grown very fond of comfort.

I went shopping with Zhanna, who was good at this stuff. I also asked Valeria to prepare a travel cake for me, one that would stay fresh for several days in a special container.

"So, a week-long trip," Zhanna mused as she browsed the options. "It'll be cold, so you'll need a warm tent. Two-person or solo?"

"You think Anna will try to sneak into my tent?"

"I wouldn't rule it out. At the very least, she'll sit with you for a while before heading back to her own."

"Two-person, then." I sighed, and Zhanna smirked.

There were so many things to buy! A gas stove,

boots, camouflage clothing, gas canisters, and a ton of other stuff. It was an absolute nightmare! By the end of the day, my head was pounding from information overload.

Then Zhanna helped me pack everything up. We worked late into the night, and she ended up staying over. Not that it mattered — she'd be driving me to the Academy in the morning anyway.

* * *

Scully mansion
Late dinner at the dining hall
Zhanna and the rest

"How are you settling in? Everything alright?" Zhanna asked my four new employees.

"Everything's amazing! This place is so cool!" Lily beamed, while the others simply nodded.

"After the boarding school, it feels like we've stepped into another world," Stephan added.

"Zhanna, is it true that aristocrats... you know... do things with their servants?" Lily hesitated, clearly embarrassed, while the others perked up — especially Stephan, who shot his sister a sharp glare.

"It's true, but don't worry. Master isn't the type to sleep around. Only when his hormones get completely out of control. Then he comes to me," Zhanna said with a smile. "And how did you all handle stress and hormones back at the boarding school?"

"Meditation," Irina raised a hand.

"Same," Xenia nodded.

"I'd rather not say," Stephan said.

"He slept with every adult woman in the school," Irina outed him without hesitation.

"Sister! It's not like I had a choice! I had to endure it, force myself, suffer through humiliation — just to protect you!"

"From whom? The teachers?" Zhanna looked horrified.

"No," Stephan shook his head. "There was no coercion. That would land someone in prison, or worse. After all, we're mages, and they weren't. But sending someone on a mission they won't come back from? That was easy."

"I see."

The mood plummeted instantly. The rest of dinner passed in silence.

* * *

Morning
The Academy
Gauss and company

The crowd was buzzing with excitement, and a lot of people had gathered. Both the second and third years were heading out for field practice at the same time. The fourth years would leave tomorrow, but to a completely different training base, somewhere in Siberia.

Everyone had brought a ton of stuff, all labeled, numbered, and tossed into a pile. We were waiting in a massive training hall, having already been checked for artifacts and other restricted items.

This time, we weren't allowed to bring anything, except socks. My socks were approved. Also, minor things like communication artifacts and cosmetic items.

"I'm so nervous!" Polina clung to Basel's arm, grinning, while he looked miserable. Poor guy was going to miss Gloria's concert... I almost felt bad for him.

"Tell me about it," Lena sighed. "The forest... tents... It's a nightmare."

"We're aristocrats! Why do we even need this?" Katie grumbled.

"Oh, come on, it's an adventure!" Polina purred, her eyes practically glued to Basel.

"Attention, students! Step forward to the teleportation point! No more than ten people at a time!" the headmaster's voice rang out. He was personally overseeing the process to make sure everything went smoothly. Our belongings had already been teleported. Now it was our turn.

Group by group, students disappeared, transported away. Finally, it was our turn. We stepped onto the portal. Anna let go of my hand. Polina released Basel's arm. The sisters unlatched from each other. A flash of light, and then — I was falling.

"What the hell?!" I barely had time to curse before I crashed into the deep blue sea.

CHAPTER 15

The Academy
Training hall, where teleportation takes place
Headmaster

A SLIGHTLY CHUBBY MAN in a strict suit, his gaze as sharp as a hawk's, closely observed the teleportation of the trainees. Any Academy staff member who made a mistake — or, as people liked to say these days, screwed up — would get personally reprimanded by the director. But so far, everything seemed to be going smoothly.

And yet, unease gnawed at him. He was anxious, but he couldn't figure out why. He kept scanning his staff for potential errors when, suddenly, his phone rang.

"I'm listening."

"What's the holdup? When are you going to resume?" A mildly irritated voice came through the speaker. At that moment, the headmaster nearly lost his balance.

"Stop teleportation!" he bellowed so loudly that the windows rattled.

"Shit. Are we in it?"

"Completely! I've already sent off several hundred people…"

"We've only got seventy…"

Meanwhile, Academy instructors and staff were rushing toward the headmaster, eager to find out what had happened. Judging by his expression, they weren't going to like the answer.

* * *

Somewhere
Deep blue sea, no sharks around
Gauss and company

I smacked onto the sea surface with a loud "splat", full body impact.

"I can't swim! Or can I?" Before I could even finish that thought, something heavy crashed down on top of me. Then another something. And another. Then, an actual bomb hit the water right next to me! The impact propelled me into the air, giving me just enough time to look around. And yeah, this was bad.

We were in the middle of the ocean, surrounded by a ton of people. Everyone was screaming, panicking, some were drowning. And I was one of them. Just like that, the legendary tale of the reincarnated god of death and the ruler of the underworld was coming to an end.

I hoped Zhanna would start a cult in my name and initiate new followers. I really didn't want to reincarnate into her — I didn't want to destruct her soul and body.

The water was warm, and I could see pretty and colorful fish. Suddenly, someone grabbed me by the shoulders and pulled me upward. A moment later, I broke the surface, coughing and gasping for air.

"Alex!" a familiar voice cried. It sounded like Katie. And then I felt like I was being murdered.

I don't know what kind of training Tatiana put her daughters through, but she definitely taught them the boob-stranglehold. And it was deadly. I was about to suffocate!

With great difficulty, I tore myself free, gasping for breath, and immediately started sinking into the water again. But something wrapped around my waist from behind, pressing soft and familiar against my back.

That was Anna. She had latched onto me so many times from behind that I could recognize those two soft curves anywhere.

"Don't panic!" I yelled, wiping salt water from my eyes and scanning my surroundings.

The sisters were in front of me, Anna behind. About five yards away, Basel surfaced, dragging Polina with him. Looked like she couldn't swim either, but at least she was alive, coughing up water but breathing. Wait...

Why the hell was everyone naked?! I felt my socks were still on, but other than that, none of us had any clothes on. Though, I did see someone's scarf floating by.

I told myself to focus, but it was difficult, considering I was being tortured by a bunch of naked women.

"Alex! Where are we?! What's happening?! Are we all going to die?!" Katie was panicking hard.

"I don't wanna die!" Lena was sobbing, absolutely terrified.

"Shut up for a second," I snapped, scanning the water. I saw two dark shapes — someone was drowning!

"Anna! Girls! We're heading over there. Someone's about to go under!"

I pointed in the direction, and the girls immediately swam toward it. Seemed like giving them a clear objective snapped them out of their panic. Anna swam smoothly while pulling me along, while I... flailed around like a maniac, trying to paddle. I couldn't tell if it was helping her. But I did have an excellent view of the sisters in front of me. If we weren't in a life-or-death situation, this could've been very dangerous. I reminded myself to focus.

We reached the first drowning victim — a girl thrashing weakly in the water. Katie and Lena got to her just in time. Meanwhile, Anna and I swam toward a very tall, very skinny guy. He was barely conscious, struggling to stay afloat, choking on seawater, unable to even scream anymore. I grabbed his shoulder, lifting his head above the water while activating Warm Hands with a boost from DE.

"Th-th-thank you…" he choked out, eyes full of gratitude. Then he passed out.

You've changed a man's destiny by saving him from death.

You get: +1 believer, +35 divine energy.

"Anyone else need help?" Anna was still behind me, holding onto both me and the half-drowned guy.

"I don't see anyone in critical danger, so they'll have to manage on their own. But there're a lot of people here." I scanned the area as best as I could, but being neck-deep in water made it difficult.

"And everyone's panicking so much that they can't even use magic," Anna added.

"By the way, can you make an ice raft?"

"Hm… My magic control isn't great yet, but I'll try."

"Then tell your little ghost to help."

"Giving it access to my mana…" she grumbled, then sighed. "Fine. Just for a little while."

One of Anna's hands let go of me and stretched out, and soon, ice began forming on the water's surface. Having so much water available meant she didn't need a lot of mana, it was more about manipulating matter rather than creating it.

And thanks to that method, the ice wouldn't just dissolve, because it wasn't purely magical but solid, real ice — I got this from the books I'd read.

Also, the raven had drilled this stuff into my brain. That damn bird was a magic-obsessed maniac.

The ice quickly expanded, growing to about ten by twenty feet. Anna couldn't make it any larger, her mana had run out.

We hoisted the unconscious guy onto the raft and swam toward the sisters. The poltergeist was the one pushing the ice raft.

You've changed a man's destiny by saving him from death.
You get: +27 divine energy.

I saw that the girls had also managed to save someone — they were tending to a very skinny girl. Frail people had the hardest time staying afloat.

"She's stable now, get her onto the ice." We swam over to them, and the sisters immediately dunked themselves deeper into the water, leaving only their heads visible.

Now they decided to be shy about being naked. They had great bodies, but that was obvious — they were light mages, after all. They used Warm Hands and Wet Hands on themselves every day. Once they got stronger, the effect would be like mine when infused with divine energy.

I sighed heavily, looking at the sisters, then — with Anna's help — reached the barely conscious girl. And one question came to mind. Why the hell was her chest so big? Double D at least! Way too big for someone who was all skin and bones.

Actually, no, she wasn't just skinny, more like

delicate and fragile. I thought she should have been floating better, having built-in buoys like that, though.

With some effort, I pulled her onto the ice and rolled her onto her stomach, so the water in her lungs could drain naturally. We wouldn't want her choking to death. This way no one would be staring at her chest, too. Though, honestly, I doubted modern girls cared much about that. Considering their obsession with "satisfying basic instincts."

Standing on the ice, I immediately noticed how warm the weather was. Straight-up tropical heat, sun blazing down. This ice wouldn't last long. But that was a problem for later.

First, I scanned my surroundings and saw what looked like an island. I cleared my throat and prepared to shout. Needed to be louder than the panicked mob.

"Shut up, all of you! There's an island ahead! We're going to be fine! A big island! Everyone, swim toward me! The ice will be your landmark!"

I was loud, but not everyone heard me. So, I repeated myself. The people who did hear passed it on. Like fish in a pond when you toss in a piece of bread, people started swimming from every direction!

The good thing was, they were helping each other. Well, most of them. Some groups had been scattered, but those who landed near each other had quickly organized.

I didn't see the rest of the sisters' team. I remembered they had been with us — a ranger and a mage. But when we got teleported, there was only the six of us.

"Scully! Are you sure there's an island?!" A familiar voice rang out. It was Ivanov Ivan, in the flesh. The same guy whose little gang had tried to kill me with an artifact.

Ivan hadn't changed since our last encounter. Still a tall, well-built blonde, still the ladies' favorite. Though right now, he looked a bit rough around the edges.

"Well, then swim over here and see for yourself! And while you're at it, all ice mages — get to work! Make this raft bigger! I want a goddamn iceberg! We've got a ton of people who can't swim or got injured during the teleportation!" Judging by the murmurs of agreement, my idea was well received.

"How the hell did you make this ice?! We're all so stressed right now we can't even activate barriers!" Ivanov shouted.

"Because you shouldn't be an idiot. Why is everyone panicking? We're alive. We're mages. We'll figure it out," I answered loudly.

"So... we're going to survive?" A woman's voice, filled with hope, called out.

"My special ability as a light mage lets me sense when someone is approaching death. Everyone who was about to drown, because they couldn't swim, we already saved. There's no one here who will die in the next few hours!" I declared.

Of course, it would have been smarter not to reveal that, even if it wasn't too big of a secret. But

I had no idea what was waiting for us on that island. The more of us who made it there, the better our chances of survival and of getting rescued.

You've changed the destiny of 47 people, saving them from future mistakes, which would have caused their death.
You get: +219 divine energy.

I tried not to smile. I didn't know it was possible, but it seemed like people were actually listening to me. And then the ice mages started to perk up. At first, it was difficult for them, but gradually, people began to calm down and pull themselves together.

Those who couldn't swim — a whole eleven people — were all placed on the ice raft. Another seven had gotten injured when they fell into the water. Probably crashed into someone else, the way someone had crashed into me.

The ice was expanding quickly, but it could never fit everyone. There were just too many people. How many exactly? Two, three, four hundred? I had no idea, but it was a lot.

So, we only put the weakest on the raft. It was about a mile to the island. Polina was among those placed on the ice. And since I couldn't swim, I became the navigator. Or maybe the captain of the iceberg? Yeah, that sounds better.

In the end, seventy people gathered on the ice. The water mages became the driving force, pulling the raft toward the island. I took charge of navigation and kept an eye on the situation, as well as on Anna and the sisters. But they were fine. Basel was helping push the raft — he was raw power incarnate, after all. His legs thrashing in the water sent up waves and foam, like a tsunami.

Suddenly, on the right flank, a plume of black smoke rose!

"Enemy on the right! Ponytail girl, put up a barrier!" I shouted and hurled a Firefly in that direction.

The crowd panicked, while some of the braver guys rushed to save the poor girl. Not that she needed saving. She blasted the water with lightning, and a moment later, a small shark floated belly-up. It looked like I was wrong about there being no sharks. Though, actually —

"Food! Grab that shark! We'll eat it on the shore!" I shouted again, and the crowd loved the idea.

We continued forward at a slightly slower pace — people were being more cautious now. And for good reason! We soon got a few more sharks. Small ones, though, no more than five feet long. Not monsters, just regular sea creatures.

I wondered if shards could appear underwater but hoped not. So I continued monitoring the situation, while also noticing the way some of the girls kept sneaking glances at us. I was at the back of the ice raft with the guys. The girls were at the front, sitting with their backs to us. Given how hot the sun was, being on the ice was absolute bliss. That sun was merciless.

BOOK THREE

The mood of the crowd had improved. Everyone could see the island now — it was just ahead. And it looked big, which meant there was a good chance people lived there. Or monsters... Though, probably not strong ones — otherwise, there wouldn't be much of an island left.

Disrupting an island's ecosystem was ridiculously easy. And once it was thrown out of balance, everything would just die out. Well, maybe not everything, but a lot of species would disappear. If herbivores overpopulated, they'd eat all the vegetation. If only predators remained, their numbers would shrink, because they'd have nothing to hunt and would start eating each other.

It looked like we had a real shot at survival. But there was one huge problem — the island didn't have cake.

I looked at the sisters. They were exhausted, and so was Anna. Then again, everyone was drained. Luckily, we were almost there.

Ahead of us lay a small bay with a beach, surrounded by trees and cliffs. I had chosen this place because it seemed like the safest option. But there were other beaches, one of them stretching for quite a distance.

The moment the ice raft touched the shore, the crowd rushed onto land. Some people collapsed onto the sand. Some fell to their knees, sobbing with relief. Others just stayed in the water, like the sisters and Anna. Actually, about a dozen other girls weren't in a hurry to leave the water either, since, well, they were naked.

But that was a minority. Most of the girls weren't that concerned about modesty. They just wanted solid ground under their feet.

I jumped off the ice, quickly scanned the area, and spotted a plant with huge leaves. I immediately ripped some off and ran toward the shore. The girls were crouching in the water, only their heads peeking out. The water was crystal clear and perfectly transparent.

"Anna, help the girls cover up with your 'secret' spell," I said, handing her a stack of leaves big enough to cover someone's head. Actually, I should make myself a hat. The sun was brutal, and I was starting to burn.

I turned away so I wouldn't embarrass the girls, and in just a few minutes, they stood up, looking a little surprised. The massive leaves covered them well. Still, they were basically naked.

Or were they? I remembered Alexander and his family vacationing by the sea. People at the beach wore swimsuits. And not like the kikimora's swimsuit, which actually covered a lot. The sisters had worn those string bikinis, making Alexander suffer immensely. These leaves covered way more than those swimsuits.

"Thanks!" The girls were embarrassed, but Anna was not. She looked extremely serious, turning her head as she scanned the area.

"Maybe you should cover up too?" Katie suggested. I thought she could just not look at me, and we wouldn't have a problem.

"Not a priority right now. Help the others get

dressed. Come here," I led the girls to a patch of large-leaved plants.

I showed them how to make holes without tearing the leaves, quickly tied them together with thin stems from another plant, and created a necklace with leaves hanging down to cover the chest. The same technique worked for panties. Though, a two-layer leaf skirt would be better.

"How do you know this?" Lena asked, genuinely surprised. The others looked just as baffled.

"I was into survival documentaries about indigenous tribes when I was a kid. They showed stuff like this." And I wasn't lying. Seriously, how else would I have known how to make a leaf chest wrap? Or a skirt?

"Scully!" I turned to see Ivanov approaching with a small group of guys.

"Cover your head. You're an ice mage, you'll get heatstroke," I said, shaking my head before quickly making him a leaf hat. He looked genuinely surprised but took it.

"Thanks…" he muttered, immediately relieved once his head was shaded.

Meanwhile, Anna just had a leaf resting on her head, held in place by the poltergeist. It looked hilarious. The poltergeist looked like a little octopus, stretching out its limbs to hold the girl's makeshift clothes. And yes, it was suffering. Anna, of course, was enjoying its misery.

"Scully, you've always been kind of a nerd. No offense, but it's true. Tell us, what do we do next?" Ivanov asked.

"First, shelter," I said without hesitation. "We have cliffs. Earth mages can dig out caves for us to stay in, but before that, we need simple shelters from branches and palm leaves. Let everyone rest and recover their mana first."

"You're right. We should build palm shelters first, then caves," Ivanov shot an annoyed glance at a guy beside him, who awkwardly smiled. Probably someone who had been stubbornly arguing with him earlier.

"Second, we need to find a fresh water source. That's more important than food. I doubt our mages can conjure enough clean water for everyone. In this heat, dehydration will hit fast," I explained. Then I looked at our melting iceberg. "Though, we could use ice. It's easy to make, and it's fresh water."

"Then earth mages should make containers for storing it," Ivanov noted.

"Better to use clay, if we can find some. Cheaper and easier to carry."

"Smart. What else?"

"The most important thing..." I frowned. "We need to be quieter. There are a lot of us, and everyone's yelling. That could attract monsters. We should start organizing a defense team right away. Most of these second-years can barely handle F-rank beasts without artifacts or weapons."

"Got it. Thanks."

They left, and I turned to the girls. They were looking at me like I was some kind of a legendary dark-skinned high elf, which, by the way, don't exist.

"What?"

"Nothing..." Katie, who had been staring at me, blushed and turned away.

"We're just surprised," Lena shrugged and smiled. "You look really cool and reliable right now. Ow!" She winced and started rubbing her butt, shooting a glare at her sister.

"Alright, go on. I'll try to find us shelter." I waved them off.

The moment they left, it hit me — I needed to hurry. There weren't enough palm trees for everyone. Then I spotted Basel. Finally.

He was carrying Polina in his arms, and she was pressed up against him. And judging by certain indications, carrying a naked girl was very appealing to him.

"Polina, here, cover up. Otherwise, I doubt Basel can cast anything right now," I laughed, pointing at the sisters nearby, who were still making clothes.

"Mm..." came a shy little murmur, and Basel carried his tiny girlfriend over to the sisters.

He set her down on the sand and hurried back, though he threw a few looks at Polina's "rear assets". She turned to look at him, then instantly turned back around.

"You perv. We almost died, and all you can think about is women," I shook my head.

"Can't help it." Basel grimaced, looking embarrassed.

"Help me build shelter first, then I'll help you."

"Alright. What do we need to do?"

We had a ton to do and needed to move fast. First, I demonstrated my kung fu by using a few units of divine energy, and to Basel's shock, as well as pretty much everyone else's, I took down a palm tree with just a couple of strikes. Then another. And another.

After that, we dragged them to the cliffside. Basel carved out two holes in the rock, and we wedged the halved palm trunks inside, supporting them with the second halves. The end result? Two "L" shapes turned ninety degrees. That was just a test fit.

After that, we pulled everything back out and started using old-school wood-working construction techniques — no nails, no ropes. We cut slots into the logs and locked them together tightly. The ground in front of the cliff was rocky, so we dug deep holes to firmly anchor the logs. We added side supports and reinforced the top for a sturdy roof.

I built the shelter to fit eight people. Well, "fit" was a stretch — there was barely enough space for us to lie down, but for now, it would do.

Next, palm branches and leaves became the walls, ceiling, floor, and even the door. We finished everything in about two hours. I don't even want to mention how much divine energy I burned through.

"Holy crap..." was all Katie managed to say. The three of them had helped too. They quickly handled clothes for the most embarrassed ones. And the whole group was bustling around, inspired by our example.

"No kidding," Lena added.

We all squeezed inside, but it was cramped. Basel took up too much space.

"It's so nice and cool in here," Polina groaned with relief.

"It is nice, yeah. But you two need your own den," I smirked, looking at Basel.

Polina instantly turned bright red with embarrassment. I had also made Basel a skirt, because seriously, he needed to stop walking around swinging that thing like a weapon. Someone could get a concussion from a surprise headbutt. The last decent leaves in the area went to him, I didn't even save any for myself.

We kept building, but now everything went way faster. And we needed fewer palm trees this time. Basel's hut built about five yards from ours.

After that, the big guy crafted some clay pots, and we filled them with ice. It was perfect, providing cooling and drinking water all in one.

Then we ran into an unexpected, but serious problem. Aristocrat girls didn't know how to go to the bathroom outdoors. And with so many people around, they were too embarrassed. So much for getting any rest.

With a sigh, I dragged Basel off to find some broadleaf trees. We broke off the straightest branches and started making a latrine. Basel's magic let him shape stone into makeshift nails, so we easily built a wooden box, dug a pit, and covered it with leaves and branches. It was simple but effective!

It had no roof, so things could air out. We dug the pit deep enough so that after doing your business, you could just cover it with dirt. But then it turned out aristocrat girls didn't know how to squat over a hole.

Basel fixed that by sculpting a stone toilet. It wasn't bad, actually. Then we gathered rocks to set up a proper fire pit, tossed down some logs to sit on, and realized we barely had any food. The sharks we caught weren't enough for even a quarter of our group.

"Raa-aa-aar!!!" a roar echoed from outside. It sounded like food had come to us. I just hoped it was tasty.

CHAPTER 16

"FIRE MAGES, DON'T SET EVERYTHING on fire! For the love of — what the hell is this sloppy magic?! Idiots!" Ivanov was shouting furiously. We heard him as soon as we ran out of the shelter, and I couldn't blame him — a group of Adepts was flinging fireballs around like clueless first-year Apprentices. Their aim was off, their attacks were weak, and their technique was just painful to watch.

In front of them stood a team of larger guys, wielding wooden clubs and shielding their bodies with ice, stone, or water. They were holding the line against five predatory zebras.

Alright, they weren't actually zebras, more like hyenas, but bigger, about the size of a horse. Their fur was white with black stripes. Or maybe black with white stripes? Doesn't matter. The creatures had long necks, hooves, and teeth that looked dull but were clearly dangerous.

We were on the eastern side of the beach. This area had far more open space between the sea and the cliffs compared to the western side, where I'd built our shelter. There was also a narrow pass between the cliffs leading deeper into the island. That's where the creatures had come from.

Suddenly, a scream rang out as one of the zebra-hyenas charged a guy in ice armor. The beast slammed into him like a bull, sending the third-year flying. His armor shattered into shards, and his body crashed into two fire mages, knocking them over.

"They're too strong! We can't win! We have to hide in the water!" one moron screamed, spreading panic among the already terrified crowd.

"Stand your ground and fight!" Ivanov roared, launching ice spikes at the zebras.

The fighters were barely holding the creatures back. One of them had already lost his barrier, and his arm bore a nasty bite mark. But despite the injury, he kept fighting, slamming his wooden club into the monster's face while it snapped at him.

"Anna, no! Bad! Stay put!" My shout made a few people turn to see me holding back my blood-thirsty little troublemaker. "Your job is to protect the girls! Don't forget, if you stray too far from them, those leaves will vanish, and they'll be standing there stark naked." I whispered that last part in her ear, and she sighed in frustration but backed down.

Meanwhile, Basel, now covered in stone armor, charged into the fight. His massive fist came crashing down on the nearest zebra-hyena's skull. Its legs buckled, and the monster flopped onto the ground like a stunned starfish. Of course, Basel didn't stop there — he jumped on top of the beast to finish it off.

I had my own problem to deal with. Another creature had broken away from the main battle, circling around to flank Basel from behind. Too bad for it, because I flanked it from behind. Grabbing the monster's tail, I let my right hand glow brightly as I secretly infused it with divine energy. A single strike, and its barrier shattered. My fingers dug into its leg, tearing out a chunk of flesh.

Thanks to the Body rune, I was feeling much stronger. With my divine energy reserve sitting at over three thousand, I probably had the raw power of an Adept right now.

The monster let out a pained howl and tried to kick me, but I took out its second leg in response. Then I toppled it over, climbed onto its back, and severed its spine at the neck.

You've absorbed your opponent's power and get +8 divine energy.

I'd forgotten to turn off automatic absorption. It would have been better to get mana crystals. I figured I'd keep that in mind.

"Damn it! Get off me!" a guy's voice suddenly screamed. One of the zebra-hyenas had tackled him and was mauling his leg.

Basel rushed in at full speed and slammed his massive foot into the zebra's ribs, sending it flying. The moment it started to recover, the big guy pulled off a full wrestling move, leaping into the air and elbow-dropping the monster to finish it off. Even I winced at that one. That thing just lost all its ribs.

"Yeah!!!" three fighters cheered, having just finished stomping the last zebra into submission. In short, we won.

"Healers, take care of the injured! Drag the bodies to the shore! Can anyone get rid of all this blood?" Ivanov barked out orders. He looked like he was about to collapse, but he was still in command and giving damn good orders, too.

I ran over to the guy whose leg had been shredded. He was lying on the ground, gripping his wound. Two more guys were standing by him, looking lost. We had no bandages or medication.

"Get some water and leaves!" I shoved them aside and got to work. Purification, Wet Hands, and a little divine power were my everything.

The guy's whimpering quieted almost instantly, but this was just the start of the healing. Meanwhile, the sisters and some other girl took care of another injured guy. A fourth person, a water mage, worked on the third wounded fighter. He finished quickly and ran over to me. His name was Nikita, and he was a rather weak water healer. Still, our magic combined well. Wet Hands and Healing Water proved to be a solid combo.

Soon, someone brought fresh water. We

pressed a leaf over the wound, and Nikita used Sticky Water to secure it. That would keep out sand, bacteria, and anything else. We couldn't fully heal the injuries, but with natural regeneration and a few more treatments, the guy would be good as new in a day or two.

After that, I checked the other wounded, used Purification to clean out dirt and bacteria, and sealed their wounds with leaves.

The sisters did a great job on their patient, and he was already in a much better shape than the others. Though they did burn through nearly all their mana like a couple of reckless idiots.

"All done here," I straightened up and stretched with satisfaction.

I had received eleven units of divine energy. No wonder I was feeling good — almost every action I took here was changing people's fates. I had a feeling Purification was playing a huge role in that. Seriously, getting sick on this island would be dangerous.

"Scully!" Ivanov's voice rang out again. He looked exhausted and anxious. "Thanks! You and Basel showed up at the perfect time. How the hell did you two not freak out? I was so stressed and scared, I could barely fight!"

"Experience," I shrugged.

"I heard your team only clears D-rank gates," He trailed off, studying me closely. "Either way, you saved our asses. Thanks! We'll give you two of the hides. You'll probably find a use for them."

"Hm, could make a nice floor mat," I nodded.

"I was thinking clothes, actually," he chuckled and glanced over at the sisters.

Ivanov wasn't the only one staring, practically everyone was, which only made the sisters more self-conscious, which was understandable, given how many guys there were on this island.

"Don't be too hard on them," Ivanov said. "They've been through a lot, and looking at beautiful women is the best way to take their minds off the fear and stress. And really, how can anyone not look? Girls like them are a rarity. If you can get them some proper clothes, you'll be doing everyone a favor."

"Easy for you to say. Like I know how to sew," I grumbled.

"You don't?" He looked genuinely surprised. "I figured if you could whip up outfits from leaves so easily, you'd have no problem working with hides."

What did he think I was, some kind of survival expert? To make anything out of hide, you need to treat it, dry it, and go through a bunch of other steps. Alexander had never paid attention to that kind of stuff.

"The leaf thing? Saw it on TV. Hides? No clue," I shrugged.

"I see..." He sighed, then suddenly burst out laughing. "Well, in that case, lucky us! We get to enjoy the view a little longer."

The sisters, of course, had heard everything and wished they could sink into the ground and disappear. So, the moment they finished helping the wounded, they bolted straight to the shelter.

"Sorry. Hope I didn't offend them." Ivanov sighed again. He really liked sighing.

Before long, Basel, myself, and about a dozen other strong guys got to work. Our goal was to block the gorge. We chopped down trees while the earth mages carved grooves into the rock.

The gorge stretched about two hundred yards inland, sloping upward. It was something like six or seven yards wide, though it was hard to tell without a measuring tape.

Either way, we found enough palm trees and other tall trees for the job. We stacked them into the grooves, forming a wall — sturdy, reliable, and full of big cracks.

Small monkeys could squeeze through. Some of the skinnier girls probably could too. Hell, I could fit through these cracks!

We finished before nightfall, and it felt great! With that burning sun gone, the temperature dropped dramatically, and the cool breeze from the sea made everything so much fresher. It was perfect.

Then came the best part — roasted meat. Turns out we weren't the only ones working. While we were gone, some of the others had butchered the zebra-hyenas and started cooking. Someone even found sea salt! They also butchered the hides, which was a pity, but oh well.

Four guys were in charge of grilling and plating the meat on clay dishes. Anyone who wanted some grabbed a plate and found a spot to eat. Most of the girls ate with other girls. I couldn't blame them

— it was hard for guys to focus on eating when naked beauties were sitting right in front of them.

Though quite a few girls had copied the leaf outfits. Some used seashells instead. Others covered themselves in clay. Creativity was thriving. And some just didn't care and enjoyed the attention.

At least everyone was starting to calm down. We'd beaten the monsters, built a wall, and survived. Now all that was left was waiting for rescue.

"If someone comes." Ivanov sighed again, this time full of despair.

We were sitting around the fire on two logs — my team, the sisters, Ivanov, Nikita (the water healer), and a girl named Angelina. Turns out she was 16th rank, the strongest among. A little more, and she'd be an official Junior Mage. And she was only twenty-one.

"No idea how long it'll take them to find us," Nikita muttered, shaking his head. He sounded like he'd already lost hope. "We're definitely somewhere in the south. Probably near the equator. And we were supposed to land near the capital."

"If this island's uninhabited, we should prepare for the worst. We might be stuck here for years," Angelina said, turning to stare at me as she straightened her posture. And in doing so, her ample chest was suddenly aimed right at me.

She was completely naked, except for a single leaf stuck to wet clay over her lower half. A shameless woman, through and through. And yes, she was definitely a fire mage. A powerful one.

The raven had talked about the way elemental affinity influenced people. Like Stephan, for example. His nature affinity was so strong that it completely drowned out his ability to use other elements. Even though his original fire brand had suppressed his nature attribute, it still affected his body.

Elemental attributes mostly affected personality. Wind mages were flighty, free-spirited, live-in-the-moment types. Fire mages were hot-headed, impulsive, lustful, and reckless. Water mages were calm, composed, and often highly intelligent. Lightning mages were decisive and fast-acting. Ice mages? Self-explanatory. And so on.

Of course, that was just a general idea, but even from that, it was obvious — Ivanov was a terrible ice mage. Maybe he had talent, but his elemental affinity was weak. Either he'd made a mistake choosing his element, or his family had pressured him into it. I felt like he had more fire in him than ice.

Angelina, on the other hand? Her fire was burning through her, practically pouring out of every pore. And don't even start with the dirty jokes. I'm not talking about that. Even her hair was fiery red, like shiny copper.

After Angelina's words, Anna latched onto me, shooting a furious glare at her.

"No need." I shook my head. "I already dispatched a message and described where we landed."

"What?" Everyone stared at me like I was some

kind of bearded high elf. And yeah, I'd sent word the moment we landed on the island. I did have a way to communicate with my guardians. I just re-layed a message through the kikimora. Though the distance had made it incredibly costly. So I'd only reach out again if it was really urgent.

"Wait... I hadn't mentioned that?" I gave an awkward smile. "Guess I forgot."

"Alex!" Katie lunged at me, but thankfully, she had the sense not to move too fast and risk losing her outfit. "It's true?! We're not gonna die here?!"

"Why would I lie?" I gave her a serious look. "They're already looking for us. We just have to hold out. I don't think they'll find us fast. So once we're settled, we'll need a signal fire or something."

"Alex," Anna had to make way as both Katie and Lena were now latching onto me, sobbing in relief.

"Scully," Ivanov spoke up, watching me closely. "When we got here, we lost all our arti-facts, and every spell on us — barriers, detection charms — everything was wiped clean. How did you contact your people?"

"Wait, everything?" I stretched out my legs, which still had the wool socks on them. It should have been way too hot for them, but nope! They were truly a divine artifact.

"How?" Ivanov asked the question on every-one's mind. Except Anna's.

"You just noticed?" I raised a brow before spreading my arms. "Well, there you go."

"If you really sent a message, then it changes

everything…" Ivanov mused, then jumped to his feet. "I'll gather everyone right now and tell them exactly what you told us!" Then he ran off with Nikita and Angelina following him.

"Hooray, silence at last!" I cheered and dug into the meat. Unfortunately, it tasted awful. But with some salt, it would do.

"So, you really did contact home?" I guess I jinxed it. Now Basel wouldn't let it go.

"Yeah, but I can do it only rarely. The distance practically rips the spirit from my body."

I kept eating, and with such an appetite that the others followed suit, tearing into the meat. But we didn't get to eat for long. Soon, the whole mob arrived, and damn, there were so many. Yet only ten actually fought off the monsters.

I climbed up onto a tall stump. A lite breeze was pleasantly cooling my… well, everything. Almost everyone here was naked. The girls tried to cover themselves as best they could, while the guys didn't care. Oh, wait, I lied — Zverinski covered both his crotch and his chest. Creepy.

So there I stood, letting everyone stare at my big, beautiful, fluffy… socks. Then, I briefly explained how I had contacted my people using super-secret light magic. In a day or two, I'd reach out again and get instructions on what we were supposed to do next.

You've changed the destiny of 62 people, saving them from future mistakes that would lead to their death. You get: +520 divine energy.

This island was growing on me. Not even a full day had passed, and I'd gained so much energy! Though I did spend nearly an hour being interrogated before I could finally eat my meat.

"Angelina, isn't it time for you to go back?" Anna asked with barely concealed aggression. Even the sisters seemed oddly irritated.

"Go back where?" Angelina replied with a smile. "This is a public beach, and I'm really hoping you'll let me stay. A poor, delicate girl like me… You wouldn't leave me to sleep under the open sky, would you? What if monsters come? And you have such a nice house."

"We would totally let you to that," Anna said with a grin, and the sisters nodded in agreement.

"You're all so mean. Alex, tell them! I'll make it worth your while tonight…" She grabbed her breasts and started squeezing them suggestively, pressing them against herself. But honestly, I was so exhausted that all I wanted was to eat and sleep. This miserable feeling — fatigue — I hated it.

"He's not even looking at me… That's just rude," she pouted, staring at me like she was trying to burn a hole through me. Actually, why "like"? Her fiery mana was practically stabbing into my chest.

"Angelina, if you want to stay with us, find yourself a spot in the corner, just don't disturb my sleep. And don't lie down by the entrance, because when monsters attack us at night, I'll need to react fast." I shot her a serious look, and her smile vanished in an instant.

"You think they'll attack?" She suddenly turned serious and looked like a completely different person.

"The odds are almost one hundred percent. Most small predators hunt at night, and we've made a hell of a lot of noise. Not to mention the smell of meat and smoke has probably traveled for miles. We'll have guests, and possibly a much worse kind than a frontal assault."

"I see… Thanks for the warning." She bit her lower lip, sat there for a while, then got up and left.

"So we're really getting attacked tonight?" Katie asked, a little nervous. Lena and Polina looked worried too.

"Most likely, but Anna will set up an alarm spell on our house," I said. Anna looked a little surprised, then caught on.

"Yes, I'll set one up, but I can only cast a single spell. Still, it'll cover your place too," Anna said and looked at Polina. The girl sighed in relief, and there was even a hint of mischief in her expression.

A little while later, Ivanov returned and said that Angelina had passed on my message of the guaranteed night attack. He wanted advice on what to do.

First off, night predators fear fire. Well, "fear" is a strong word — they avoid it. Ivanov knew that already, but he looked so exhausted that he wasn't thinking straight. Second, we needed a night patrol. Guards to keep watch and protect the ravine until dawn.

"And third, sit down," I said, pointing to a log beside me.

"Why?" He gave me a weird look.

"You're exhausted and barely thinking straight. I'll give you a little boost." I made my hands glow, which convinced him. Then, I used Warm Hands, with two units of DE. A little for the head, a little for the heart, a little for the stomach. "Done. How do you feel?"

"You know... like I just had a full night's sleep..." He stared at me in surprise. "Didn't think light mages could do that, but... Shit! We forgot about the shore! What if something crawls out of the water?! Or sneaks along the coastline or the shallows?!"

He bolted off to deal with it, while I just smiled in satisfaction. Thank the gods this wasn't my problem.

"Can you do me too? I'm on patrol tonight. I won't let the monsters get to my friends," Angelina said, her voice serious and even a little anxious.

"Alright," I sighed, too tired to argue.

She sat across from me, covering her chest so she wouldn't distract me or mess with the spell's effectiveness.

"Better turn around," I said. She nodded and obeyed. Warm Hands again, but this time I poured in three DE — enough to last her till morning — and much more mana. I nearly drained myself.

"I mean, on one hand, I'm glad you didn't lose focus by feeling me up, but on the other, that's kind of insulting!" When I finished, Angelina turned back to check if my "dragon" had woken up and crawled out of its cave. Nope! The dragon was fast asleep, which is all I wanted to do. I wasn't even thinking about cake, just about crashing.

"Face it, girls are at the bottom of Alex's priority list," Anna said, half amused, half disappointed. How did she manage both at once? Women are strange.

"Damn, that sounds like a challenge!" Angelina's hair burst into flames, and she locked eyes with me. Then, out of nowhere, she lunged forward and kissed me. Right as I was yawning!

She caught me completely off guard, her tongue slipping into my mouth like a snake. I tried to push her away, but she twisted and dodged like some kind of wriggling creature. I had to grab her shoulders and pry her off me. Luckily, Katie and Anna jumped in to help.

"Ow!" Angelina was literally thrown a few feet away, landing flat on the ground. "Idiots! That hurt!" She jumped to her feet, but Lena immediately got in front of her, blocking her path.

"You lost your leaf, moron," Lena hissed.

"Huh? You mean... oh... oh no... oh crap..." Angelina quickly dropped to a crouch and covered herself with her hand. Then she looked at me. "Are you kidding me?! Not even that turned you on?! Do you even like girls?! Or are you into guys?! Or are you just impotent?!"

For the record, I hadn't even looked at her. I saw nothing.

"Right now, the only things I like are a bed and sleep," I muttered, shaking my head as I dragged myself toward the house. Inside, the zebra-hyena pelt was already spread out, with little mounds of leaves here and there for pillows.

I could have replenished my energy using the parasite, but I decided to save my reserves for a real fight. Gods, it felt amazing to lie down.

The second my head touched the soft fur, with leaves tucked beneath, I blacked out, slipping straight into the realm of dreams.

*   *   *

"He does like women, but he has two servants for all that," Lena said before heading into the house. Katie shot her an angry glare but followed suit.

"Looks like you're not his type. Or maybe, you're just not pretty enough," Anna added with a smirk.

"Not pretty enough?!" Angelina's hair, and not just on her head, flared up in flames. "I'll show all of you... He's just tired... Yeah, that's it... But whatever. I can hold a grudge, you know."

Angelina left, heading back to her own group. There were seventeen girls in total, all crammed into a makeshift den of dirt and leaves. She ducked inside. Even though it was late, nobody was asleep yet.

"Get some rest, girls. I'm taking beach patrol. Marina, you guard the house," Angelina said, looking at a dark-haired girl sitting by the wall. The girl nodded in response.

Before long, Angelina found Ivanov. They discussed patrol zones, but there was a problem.

"Bastards," Angelina hissed.

"Some aren't physically capable, others are too weak or just plain scared," Ivanov said, clearly frustrated himself. "The main thing is surviving the night. Tomorrow, we'll deal with the fallout and figure out what to do next."

"No work, no food," she growled, snatched up a spear with a stone tip — crafted by the more skilled hands among them — and stormed off.

The night was peaceful, the sky was clear and breathtaking, and the sound of the waves was calming. But not for Angelina. She was too deep in thought, pacing and grumbling nonstop. Time seemed to fly.

"Not pretty enough, huh? Not arousing? He doesn't look at me? No reaction at all? That little—" She suddenly spun around but saw nothing. "I'm imagining things."

"R-a-a-a-a-AR!" A deep growl came from behind her, and a split second later, a piercing scream echoed across the beach.

CHAPTER 17

Academy
Sometime before, the day the students disappeared
Tatiana, the headmaster, and others

AROUND THIRTY PEOPLE had gathered in the conference room — not just Academy staff, but also the governor, a representative from the SCU, and the patriarchs of several families whose children had gone missing.

"So, you're saying the children are alive and well and currently on some tropical island?" the director asked, his voice filled with both relief and anxiety. His hair had gotten a few more grays in the past few hours.

"I can't say for certain that all of them are, but my son hasn't seen anyone die. He also didn't have time to count how many there were. However, they've all lost their belongings and artifacts," Tatiana said, looking as if she might faint at any moment, holding herself together purely through willpower.

"Tracking spells have either dissipated or the distance is simply too great. We can't locate them," one of the patriarchs muttered.

"But how is this possible? Why did some make it to their destination while others didn't? Even people who were traveling together — some arrived at the right spot, while many did not!" another patriarch protested.

"A magical anomaly," the governor spoke slowly and quietly, yet everyone heard him.

"Are you sure?" The headmaster fixed his gaze on the imposing man, who nodded before elaborating.

"Most likely, the rampage of monsters in the wildlands triggered a magical storm, which escalated into an anomaly due to the high mana concentration. This caused disruptions, altering the coordinates of the teleportation. Something similar happened fifty-nine years ago during the evacuation of a large group of people."

"This is just a theory for now, and it needs to be verified first. What if you're just trying to cover for the Academy? I still believe this was sabotage!" one of the patriarchs snapped. He looked awful — nervous, jittery, his whole body trembling.

"It's only a theory for now," the governor nodded. "And it's already being investigated, isn't that right, Alexei?"

"Yes, Your Grace," answered a frail-looking,

average-height man wearing oversized glasses. Adjusting them, he gave a brief report. "Our specialists are already collecting data using the most advanced equipment, while reconnaissance teams are surveying the area for signs of large-scale battles involving high-ranking monsters."

"Any findings?"

"Preliminary data supports your theory. However, we are not ruling out the possibility of an attack. It's entirely possible that someone placed a magical barrier or interference along the teleportation route."

"That would only be possible if someone knew the route in advance," the director sighed.

"The interrogation will reveal if there are any traitors within the Academy," the governor replied. "And everyone will tell the truth. A team of inquisitors has arrived from the capital specifically for this."

"Mind-breakers," the headmaster flinched at the word, the rest of the room sharing his discomfort.

Inquisitors were psi-mages capable of digging into a person's mind. And they did it so thoroughly that the victim would be nauseous and disoriented for a week afterward. More importantly, they could extract any secret, no matter how well hidden. And if someone had a strong enough will to resist, they would be the ones to suffer.

That was why inquisitors had another nickname — Butchers. They would keep torturing their subject until their willpower collapsed, allowing them to pry into the deepest corners of the victim's soul and extract whatever they wanted.

"Tatiana, contact your son, find out how my son is doing — he's my only heir!" one of the patriarchs suddenly demanded.

"I can't. He will contact me himself within a day or two," Tatiana shook her head. "He says the distance drains too much of his strength."

"Well, he is only sixth rank," the headmaster nodded.

"Seventh," Tatiana corrected.

"Already? What kind of monster is he to go from zero to seventh rank in just two months?" the dean blurted out. Like the headmaster, he was also plump but shorter.

"Family secrets," she shook her head, though she was just as baffled herself.

"Alexander regularly clears shards on his own, including C-rank ones," the head of the city's SCU stated calmly, adjusting his glasses.

"What nonsense! How is that even possible?" the dean shouted.

"Are you implying that I'm lying?" The man's intelligent face took on a predatory look behind his glasses, and the dean immediately shrank into his seat.

"No... Forgive me, it's just... that's so unbelievable, it's hard to accept..."

"Enough. We'll discuss this later." The governor raised his hand, silencing everyone. "Tatiana, I want you to relay a series of questions and some instructions to your son. And one more thing: did

THE COMING OF GOD OF DEATH

any of the missing students study astronomy?"

* * *

The Island
Night

I was sleeping soundly when a woman's scream woke me up. It sounded like someone was being eaten alive. I jumped to my feet and burst out of the house, yelling, "Anna, protect the girls! Basel! Get Polina to them, then follow me!"

Basel was already peeking out of the hut, so he reacted instantly. He grabbed Polina, who was still fast asleep, curled up in her outfit made of leaves, and rushed her into our house for safety.

People were waking up fast, voices filling the settlement, but I was already sprinting. Where to? By the shore, there was a pillar of black smoke. The beautiful full moon and clear night sky made it easy to spot.

Pushing through bushes and palm trees, I burst onto the beach and ran straight into a monster. Its spiky side was facing me, which wasn't a big deal for me, since I had my indestructible socks.

I could use four DE for an attack, maybe even five, though there'd be some side effects. Naturally, I went for five, and suddenly I got a good look at the thing. It was a weird, spiky turtle on long legs! It was the size of a lion, with a crocodile-like snout, and a shell that looked like a metal pipe covered in spikes, even on the underside.

"Raaaar!" the creature growled, pressing down on Angelina. I couldn't see her clearly, but the smell of blood was thick in the air.

Good thing I crashed in when I did. My kick shattered its barrier and even broke some spikes, though the shell itself held firm. The monster flipped over, its spiked back sinking into the sand under its own weight. Ha! The way it roared and flailed its legs was almost funny. But there was no time to laugh.

I stepped up to its head and broke its neck with two solid kicks. A moment later, a crystal dropped nearby. I grabbed it and popped it straight into my mouth. Where else was I supposed to keep it?

There was no time to think. Three more of those things crawled out of the sea, and just a couple of feet away, Angelina collapsed, losing consciousness.

I shot over to her and blasted her with magic infused with divine energy. My eyes felt like they were about to burst from the strain, and I was glowing like a giant lightbulb in the middle of the beach.

On one side — three bloodthirsty beasts. On the other — something even stranger peeking out from the bushes, screeching in pain from the brightness. Angelina had been bitten pretty bad in the stomach. How the hell did she even escape that thing's grip? Her wounds were brutal.

Still, with the amount of mana I was pouring

into her, blood loss wouldn't kill her. At least not yet. The main thing was getting her conscious again, which I finally managed to do. Otherwise, I'd be fighting three monsters while defending a wounded person.

"Behind you!" she yelled the second she came to. Stretching out her left arm, she unleashed a blast of fire.

I was on her right, one hand supporting her back, the other pressing against her stomach. There were a ton of wounds on her back too. But damn, that fire! Why couldn't she do this before? The spiked turtles recoiled, and Angelina, now standing firm, ignited completely. Her entire body wreathed in flames.

"I'll kill you!" she screamed and charged at the trio. And she did.

Like a living inferno, she crashed into them, burning them alive despite their barriers. She did it so fast that by the time backup arrived, all they could do was gape in shock.

"Quaaack!" A weird noise made everyone whip around toward the forest. And then Basel stepped out, carrying a massive duck.

The thing was the size of a boar, its beak full of sharp teeth, with two massive fangs sticking out. Guess that was the thing lurking in the bushes.

"Holy hell, the monsters here are insane," someone muttered.

I wasn't listening. Angelina was losing consciousness again, so I sprinted toward her.

BOOK THREE

"Angelina!" Ivanov rushed toward her, but I had already grabbed her and lifted her into my arms. It didn't look very heroic — she was quite a bit taller than me.

"She'll live. Get some fires going along the shore, and don't forget about those ducks." I nodded toward Basel. "If there are any more wounded, bring them here."

I could've given them more smart ideas, but this wasn't the time. Just because Angelina wasn't bleeding on the outside anymore didn't mean she wasn't bleeding inside. How the hell had she even managed to fight?

As I ran, I heard another "Quack" followed by human screams. Looked like we'd be busy all night. Sure enough, shouts started coming from the ravine.

I just hoped no one died. A single casualty would crush morale, and that could seriously hurt our chances of getting rescued. We needed to get off this island as soon as possible.

My factory wouldn't run without materials. And what if someone attacked while I was gone? Or worse, hit the mansion? My altar was there, after all. Worst-case scenario, I'd just raise some puppets, claim I'd tamed a monster, and set sail to find help.

"Holy hell!" The whole gang was waiting for me

by the house. The fire was still burning, keeping everything well-lit.

I set Angelina down on a tree stump, and the three of us immediately started healing her. Before long, a girl with nature magic arrived to help. She was weak, but every bit counted. Even with her limited power, combined with our light magic, Angelina's regeneration kicked into high gear.

Not twenty minutes later, they brought in a guy with a gaping bite wound on his neck. It was a duck bite! Somehow, we saved him. But after an hour of healing, we were completely drained. Thankfully, no one else was seriously injured, and we could just collapse from exhaustion.

Anna volunteered to stand guard and keep the fire going. Well, she had the poltergeist, it would protect her.

The moment I lay down, I was out like a light. And what a dream I had. It was like I was back at the governor's cake duel. The cakes had been brought straight from the capital — so magical, they were beyond imagination.

Just as I was about to taste the food of the gods, something bit me. My eyes snapped open. It was Angelina, biting my neck. Thankfully, not hard. And judging by her closed eyes, she was still asleep. Damn it, why did I let her stay the night?

Wait... was it already morning? Or maybe mid-day? The air outside smelled like roasted meat, and it was pretty noisy. I wanted meat too, but how was I supposed to get up?

To my left, Angelina was latched onto me, her

arms and legs wrapped tightly around mine.

"Mmm..." she moaned sweetly the moment I moved my fingers. So I figured I'd better not move my left hand.

As for my right... I had definitely not expected to find completely naked Katie clinging to me. Her large breasts had trapped my arm, and she was gripping it tightly with both hands. My whole arm was numb, I couldn't feel a thing.

But the biggest surprise was Lena. She was lying a bit farther away, wrapped around Anna like a spider with its prey, her face buried right in Anna's breasts. I couldn't figure out why the hell they were all naked.

"I recommend claiming the females, as your current state is negatively affecting your magical abilities," the parasite's voice suddenly cut into my thoughts.

Before sleeping, I'd ordered it to help me get some proper sleep. That was probably why I felt so well-rested. Aside from my numb arm and the pain in my neck.

He recommends... "It's not that simple with humans. Humans are just... problematic," I grumbled mentally.

"May I remind you that you are human? Which makes you just as problematic. And I must note, out of all the humans you have encountered, you are by far the most problematic of them all."

I ignored it and tried to free my hands. Which immediately earned me two soft moans. And damn, they were sweet... The beast inside me cracked open an eye, teetering on the edge of waking up.

"Growl..."

"Growl?"

"Growl!"

My stomach let out a fierce growl, and Angelina's and Katie's stomachs answered in return. It almost seemed like they were having a conversation, while mine just nodded along. And then, out of nowhere, Anna's stomach roared like thunder. It was so loud that all the girls woke up at once.

"A monster?" Katie mumbled sleepily, forcing her eyes open. A moment later, she froze, and panic started creeping onto her face. She was staring at me, and I was staring at her.

Letting out a startled yelp, she pulled her hand away from mine and tried to scramble to her feet, but she lost her balance and fell straight onto Angelina, who had also just started sitting up.

The two of them smacked their foreheads together and collapsed onto me. Katie's shoulder crashed into my head, while Angelina's skull struck my knee. A second later, her heel slammed into my chin! I barely managed not to bite my tongue off.

Why was this happening to me? I'd done so much good yesterday, yet karma still decided to hit me with bad luck. And on top of everything, I didn't even get a single bite of cake.

"You still alive over there?" Angelina laughed, her voice full of mischief.

I groaned something unintelligible in response, which only made her laugh harder. But Katie wasn't in the mood for jokes. Somehow, her chest had ended up pressed against my face, suffocating me all over again. Letting out another panicked yelp, she tried to crawl away, but her foot got caught on Angelina's leg, and she tumbled down again.

A loud "Ouch!!!" echoed through the room, and my numb arm was flung to the side. Katie's face twisted in panic, and she looked like she was about to burst into tears.

Lena rushed over to help, but her own legs had gone numb from sleeping in such an awkward position. And of course, as soon as she tried to stand, she lost her balance and fell, straight onto Angelina. What did Angelina do in response? She kicked me again and, naturally, started laughing all over again.

"Zhanna, you're so smart. And Xena, you too. Hopefully, Anna won't be the next to fall on me and finish me off," I thought to myself.

Luckily, Anna just looked confused, covering her breasts as her eyes darted around the room, probably searching for some leaves to cover herself with.

"And what do we have here? Heh-heh... oh... n-no!" Angelina's laughter suddenly turned into a panicked squeak.

She'd just realized that her legs were spread wide open in my direction. In other words, I could see everything, absolutely everything. And yeah, the hair there was the same fiery shade as the hair on her head, though well-groomed. After seeing that, how was the dragon supposed to stay in its cave?

Flustered, she scrambled up in a panic and, a second later, was sitting in the corner of the hut on her knees, covering herself with her hands. I couldn't believe she was embarrassed. Showing off her chest was fine, but everything else wasn't? Women are such strange creatures…

"It looks like I'll have to meditate instead of eating. Or should I just say to hell with it all?" I thought. A familiar fire sparked in my eyes as I stared at the girl. I knew a popular method to calm hormones and restore inner peace.

"And what are we going to do about this?" I pointed at my jade staff and looked at Angelina. "I seem to recall someone promising to thank me for letting them stay the night?"

Wow, I'd actually asked for sex myself. What's next? Was I going to start asking for kisses? "Oh, Gauss, how low have you fallen? What is this human body doing to you…"

"I-I was just joking… I'm sorry. I like teasing and messing with guys, but that's all…" She looked serious and a little scared. I couldn't figure out what kind of person she was, it was annoying.

"Then don't bother me for an hour, I'll be meditating." I shook my head, sat down against the stone wall facing her, and focused on clearing my mind. Instantly, a wave of calm washed over me. All the stupid thoughts vanished, and even the women behind me no longer distracted me.

Katie was asking Lena if there was any bleeding "down there." Was she hurt? But judging by the conversation, there was no blood, so she wasn't. Anna was still looking for leaves to cover herself and the others. Angelina, judging by her voice, had completely lost her enthusiasm. And outside... the smell of food... Oh, I was starving...

Thankfully, the hour passed quickly. As soon as I stepped outside, the girls greeted me with guilty looks on their faces. And they'd even made me a skirt out of leaves. Well, thanks for that, at least.

"I'm sorry," Angelina spoke up, walking over to me. Miraculously, she'd actually covered her chest this time. "It was really stupid of me to provoke a healer and mess with his concentration. And just, in general. Please don't think I'm crazy or some kind of pervert. It's just that my power burns away my clothes, so nudity is normal for me. Though, my underwear usually survives."

"We got you some food," Anna cut in and pointed at a large palm leaf piled with meat: duck, turtle, and some zebra-hyena. I really wanted to see how those tasted.

"Thanks," I nodded at everyone with a satisfied smile and dug in. The duck was really good! The turtle was okay, but definitely better than the hyena.

The girls had already eaten, so while I devoured my meal, they told me about what had happened at the camp. Everyone had made it through the night safely, but there was going to be a debriefing soon, and they wanted me there.

So, after finishing my meal, stuffing my belly until it bulged slightly, I headed over to Ivanov. He was still asleep since he'd been up all night. Then again, a lot of people had been.

Eventually, they woke him up, and ten of us gathered to talk. After a short discussion, he called everyone together and started giving them hell.

"We didn't have enough lookouts last night to spot the monsters in time! As a result, two people almost died — one of them being one of our strongest fighters. She just didn't have time to react. And all because of the cowards who refused to go on patrol!" Ivanov sat on a boulder about six feet high, surrounded by the surviving students. "So here's the new rule: if you don't work, you don't eat. Do whatever you want, but we're only sharing food and water with those who contribute."

"Who gave you the right to decide that?! Are you just going to let people starve?!" a tall, slightly hunched guy with short black hair protested.

"I didn't decide anything, we all did." Ivanov gestured toward the group of fighters and patrol members. "We gathered the food. We fought. We got hurt. Give me one good reason why we should share with you."

"Because we'll starve!"

"And?" Ivanov looked at him like he was trash. "Go get your own food. What's stopping you?"

"I could die!" The guy still wouldn't back down.

"Oh, and we're immortal, are we?" I finally lost it and laughed.

I hadn't thought about it before, but after hearing Ivanov say it out loud, it stung. You risk your life, fight, and then some random nobody acts like it's just the way things should be, and even dares to complain about it.

"Stay out of this, shorty," the guy snapped at me.

"This 'shorty' you're talking about," Ivanov scowled, "killed a bunch of monsters on his own and healed dozens of people who got mauled by them. And what did you do? Besides tucking your balls between your legs and ceasing to be a man?"

Oh, the guy was fuming now. I didn't even feel like cursing him anymore.

"I'll say it again: if you don't work, you don't eat, and you won't be protected either. We're not dying for pathetic nobodies like this one." Ivanov gestured at the fuming idiot.

"I'd like to point out that the bigger predators living deeper in the island haven't taken an interest in us yet," I added. "And if there are people here, we need to find them somehow. That means heading into the forest."

"Fire! We'll just light a fire, and they'll find us!" suggested someone not particularly bright.

"Or they'll think a powerful fire-attributed monster lives here," Angelina smirked.

"If you seriously believe that someone's going to fight their way through the monsters in the forest just to check out some smoke, then you're an idiot," Ivanov added. "And even if there are people on this island, there's no guarantee they'll be friendly. What if they're savages? Or cannibals?" The group's mood immediately plummeted.

"And now we decide," Ivanov said again, this time much louder. "Anyone willing to work for the common good, step over to that palm tree. Those who want to go solo, stay where you are. But keep in mind — once you join us, there's no backing out. No complaining. No refusing to do your part, whether you like the work or not."

In the end, almost everyone moved toward the tree, except for a group of about thirty — mostly guys. "We're not going to follow your orders, Ivanov, or your lackeys. We can take care of ourselves," said a muscular, bald brute.

"We're not forcing anyone to stay," Ivanov replied calmly. "If you want to die, that's your choice. And when we get out of here, everyone here will remember that." He waved them off. Looking at us with anger, the outcasts stalked off east along the shore — probably heading to another beach.

"Now, let's assign tasks!"

We split into groups — guards, hunters, gatherers, craftsmen, camp workers, and dependents. The last category included those who were practically useless. Take Polina, for example. She was small, weak, and didn't have any useful skills. Maybe she could help with small tasks, but for the most part, she was dead weight.

Each worker could take a dependent under their care, guards could take two, and hunters could take three. It took us nearly two hours to sort out who belonged where. And then we celebrated with food!

Thankfully, we had ice mages who could chill and freeze supplies. We even carved out a cave to use as a fridge. There would be more caves to come, it was just safer that way.

And me? I was heading into the forest. If I could raise some puppets, I'd be able to protect our settlement. My monsters would make sure nothing from the woods could get close. I wondered if I'd find people out there.

CHAPTER 18

"YOU SURE ABOUT THIS?" Ivanov asked as he walked me to the wall. It was a little battered, but it had held strong against all attacks.

"I'm sure. If anything happens, I'll just blind the creatures and run." I raised my hand, making it glow faintly.

"Maybe I should come with you?" Angelina offered. She and the other girls were seeing me off too.

"And go blind along with the monsters?"

"Got it. Alright, just come back with good news." She sighed and waved. I nodded in return.

I slipped through a gap in the wall and found myself in a ravine leading upward. There were traces of blood, burnt fur, and other remnants left behind by the monsters that had tried to attack the settlement. In the end, though, all the creatures had fled. But they could always come back...

That was a problem for later. First, I needed to find a sacrifice. And decide what to do with the skeleton. If I summoned him here, he would leave traces of himself everywhere, not to mention the slaughtered beasts. Someone was bound to notice the remains.

On the other hand, if I found people in this place, even hostile ones, it would be a decent excuse. For now, I decided I'd improvise.

I walked through the ravine, suffering from a severe cake deficiency. A rock wall loomed to my left, the same on my right. In some places, tree roots stuck out, and in others, small trees were growing straight from the stone — tiny but resilient, just like me these days.

No caves, no monsters. I didn't activate my death aura, I didn't see the point. The monsters would just run away, and I didn't need them to run. How else was I supposed to eat them?

Man, if only I could find a gate and stock up on crystals. Maybe even some weapons for the girls. Right now, those troublemakers had almost no protection.

The incline started getting steeper, but it was still a gentle climb. After a while, I reached the top and stepped into a tropical forest. First, though, I headed south toward the shore. I wanted to get a better look at my surroundings.

"Rr-r-r-r..." A tiger suddenly lunged at me from a bush! A massive one, too. How the hell did it hide behind that tiny bush without me noticing?!

The striped beast, complete with a pair of bull horns, pounced out of nowhere. But just before it slammed into me, my entire body lit up with a brilliant glow.

The roaring creature crashed into me, nearly knocking the wind out of my lungs. And, as luck would have it, the damn thing had a barrier! Channeling divine energy into my hands, I slammed my fists into its head while it sat on my stomach. It let out a pained snarl, trying to shake off the blindness and stand up.

A few moments later, the tiger regained its bearings, fixed its gaze on me, and opened its mouth. A very smelly mouth, I might add, perfectly capable of biting my head off.

The beast lunged forward, and I yanked myself back just in time. Its massive teeth snapped shut a quarter of an inch from my nose! In retaliation, I bit it right on its pink nose.

That seemed to stun the creature for a moment, making it recoil in surprise. I sprang to my feet and immediately kicked it in the face, planting 5 DE straight onto its snout. Its legs buckled from the impact. But the tiger didn't have to suffer for long.

I slammed both palms onto its skull, smashing its head into the ground, then leaped over its neck, landing on its back. Without wasting a second, I dug my fingers into its throat — the barrier was already gone. The tiger roared, thrashing around in an attempt to throw me off, but it didn't last five seconds.

"Phew... Rank C, huh? That was dangerous..." A crystal dropped into my hand. But where was I supposed to put it? I summoned the tiger puppet first, then found a leaf, folded it into a pouch, and tied it to my leaf skirt.

And then, I hurried back to the ravine. I was sure that tiger's roar had thrown everyone into a panic. And yeah, Anna was doing her best to stop the women from rushing outside to come and "rescue" me. Winters knew exactly what I was capable of and was certain I'd handle it.

"And where do you all think you're going?" I shouted, stepping onto the edge of the cliff, right above the wall below.

"He's alive!" Why was Angelina so happy about that? Hopefully, she wasn't planning on becoming the next Anna. No thanks, I didn't need that in my life.

"Alive and well. There are tigers lying in ambush out here, so don't come out until I've cleared the area." With that, I tossed a pouch to Anna. She didn't disappoint. Well, her poltergeist didn't. The moment she pulled out the contents, Ivanov turned pale.

"Rank C..." The others went pale too.

"So focus on keeping things safe over there. I'm heading out." But first, I checked out the shoreline, scanning as far in the distance as I could see. Nothing too interesting, but at least now I had a better idea of our surroundings.

It seemed my kitty was in trouble. I ran over to settle the matter. Three zebra-hyenas had gotten way too cocky, thinking that since my cat was in-jured, it was weak. Yeah, right!

I made it just in time, and together, we took them down without my feline taking any major damage. She didn't have a barrier, after all, while the enemies did. Now, I had four puppets, and we continued along the cliffside — me collecting crys-tals, my puppets growing in numbers. No duck puppets, though.

"Hey! On duty!" I shouted as I returned to the wall. "Catch!"

The guys stood there, dumbfounded, as the carcasses of giant ducks came flying at them. Someone even got pinned under one duck, which was understandable, since these things were the size of wild boars, with more feathers than meat, unfortunately. Speaking of feathers — I wanted a pillow!

"Oh, crap! Aghhh—" Oops. Got distracted and tossed the fourth duck a bit awkwardly. My bad... Oh well, there were medics, and the sisters would help. It was time for me to head deeper into the island.

I had left my puppets to hunt and gather car-casses while I activated my aura and wandered aimlessly. And I found bananas!

The palm trees by the shore were fruitless, but here, there was plenty of food. I climbed up a tree, plucked a banana, and took a bite. But just my luck, it wasn't ripe yet.

Then I saw a mountain. Was it a volcano? Vol-canoes erupt sometimes. Lava flows down, destroying everything in its path. I wondered what would happen to a gate if it got flooded with lava. Obviously, there'd be a mana explosion.

Of course, I headed toward the mountain, but I kept getting sidetracked. Coconut trees here, bananas there, and delicious mangoes! I could eat mangoes forever. Imagine a mango cake... Just thinking about it made my mouth water.

I had an idea... So I climbed up a palm tree and got comfortable. Since I had my cursed land, I could — Oh, damn! There was a whole group of people over there! Church folk.

Thanks to the Dominion and Territory runes, I could control my cursed land from the island. But it cost a ton of energy. I figured I better to set up an altar. Then the connection would be cheaper, if not free.

The question was, where? I couldn't let anyone find it. That would lead to some uncomfortable questions I'd rather not answer.

"Kraa!" A massive mutant parrot swooped down. How the hell did it sneak up on me?!

The only thing I had time to do was grab two ripe mangoes before its talons sank into my shoulders. Being picked up by birds was starting to feel familiar.

The parrot's eye view was great, there was no longer a need to climb the mountain. To the northeast, there was a lake. Not a huge one, but decent-sized. And to the northwest — a swamp. A massive one. And there were ruins! That's where I needed to go. I just had to figure out how to make my "taxi" fly me there.

But then, I needed to eat first. The mangoes were so sweet and ripe. I thought I should bring some back for the girls. They were a handful, sure, but they'd always helped me without hesitation.

I also needed to recharge their blessings — the charge had dropped to less than a third. They must have avoided a lot of trouble with it. I thought I should bless that sweet couple too — Basel and Polina. They were really useful, and Basel had fed me more than once. Kindness should be repaid with kindness.

I'd eaten, but now I was a sticky mess, covered in mango juice. My hands were uncomfortably tacky. Oh well, I'd wash up in the swamp. But first...

A black blade appeared in my hand, worth ten DE. One swing, and a deep gash opened across the giant parrot's neck. I grabbed its talons and struck with divine energy to weaken its grip — it had really dug in.

The bird didn't die immediately, not that it mattered much. At least it didn't have a barrier. So, while the monster was still in its death throes, we plummeted toward the ground at high speed. For a moment, I thought this was going to hurt, but the beast died, I revived it, and it started flapping its wings again.

I barely managed to pull my legs up in time to avoid crashing into the tree canopy. Not that it did me much good. We'd only flown a couple of miles before we apparently entered the territory of some other birds.

A flock of relatively small creatures — only about the size of a goat — swooped in, their beaks shaped like swords. They attacked swiftly and just as swiftly tore my parrot to shreds. Fortunately, I had already descended far enough that my fall into the tree didn't end with broken bones.

Well, not for me, at least. The tree, however, didn't fare as well. Why were the branches so fragile?

"Because someone eats too much and is way too heavy," came the parasite's perpetually grumpy voice.

"I don't think I'm fat enough to be that heavy," I said calmly as I got up and looked around. There were no enemies in sight.

"I'd recommend weighing yourself when you get the chance…"

Now that was intriguing. How much did I actually weigh? I needed to ask the information system.

Report on Alexander Scully

Age: 20
Height: 5.6
Weight: 187
State of development: 7

Negative conditions discovered:

Magical parasite
Hormonal imbalance
Magic exhaustion

THE COMING OF GOD OF DEATH

Poisonous leech on the back

I had grown taller by a whole inch. But why was I so heavy?

"With transformation and bodily enhancement, your muscle density increases, your bones become stronger, and highly concentrated reserves of nutrients are stored for emergency release in critical situations."

"I see... So the more you store, the heavier I get. Got it, I'll keep that in mind. But what's this 'exhaustion' about?"

"I suspect you have too much divine energy, and it's affecting your muscles through the Body rune. Your body is struggling to keep up with the load. You need more physical training!"

"Alright, alright... Wait, what the hell is that leech?" I reached for my back and hissed in pain as I yanked off a massive, ten-inch-long leech. It was bloated and heavy, with a sucker full of teeth on its belly. "And it's even... pois-son...ous..."

My head started spinning, but just before my legs gave out, I managed to crush the leech in my grip. It burst like a watermelon, spraying my own blood in all directions.

"Looks like paralysis," the parasite noted in a calm voice. I just stared at the clear sky and the occasional drifting cloud. The damn sun was shining straight into my eyes.

"Heal me already."

"Five minutes and thirty seconds. The venom is magical..."

As the poison was being purged from my body, I turned my attention to my cursed lands. I felt what was happening there.

The church's paladins were inspecting the ruins, the remnants of the lich's castle and, of course, my obelisk. Looked like they wanted to replicate it. Ha! No chance.

I spotted a monster's corpse. I could raise it and set it on the churchmen, but was there any need? Probably not. But I could use it as my eyes!

So, I raised the snake-like creature and sent it toward the lumber mill. On my own territory, where my Dominion ruled, I could raise puppets, summon guardians, cast curses, devour souls, and more.

The snake, which the paladins had slain, slipped into the forest unnoticed, heading exactly where I commanded. And while I was busy with that, some genius decided to try and eat me. The scent of blood had overpowered its fear of my aura.

It was something between a wolverine and a cockroach. It crept toward me cautiously, but the moment I flared my light, it howled and bolted. However, a larger beast lunged out of the bushes, grabbed the cockroach-thing, and vanished into the forest. What a fun forest it was. So much interesting stuff going on over there.

I figured it was time to get up. My body was starting to respond again, so I began healing myself by speeding up my metabolism.

"Reminder: your hormonal balance is still unstable. Either mate with females or engage in intense physical exertion!"

"What, you want me to lift rocks up and down?" I laughed, pushing myself to my feet.

"Would you like me to release a pheromone that will make every creature within a three-mile radius see you as a desirable female? Running is great exercise," the parasite declared in a tone of absolute scientific seriousness. "Ah... my apologies..."

I had to jab it with my energy to make sure it wouldn't actually follow through on that threat. A desirable female, seriously? No, thanks. As soon as I extracted this thing, I'd shove it into a zombie's body and sic a bunch of males on it.

"No, no... I was just joking..."

"Oh, we'll both be laughing soon," I said with a wicked grin, but then another roar distracted me. It sounded like the thing that ate the cockroach had just been eaten itself.

I decided to take a look and saw a massive bear! A hulking brute, armored, with a slightly elongated snout. No barrier, though. Its back looked like it'd be a comfortable ride.

A black shield appeared in my right hand, while my sword transformed into a spear, wreathed in darkness. I observed the fight, and the moment the monster turned its back to me, I sprinted out of the bushes. If I could get onto its back, I could kill it in one strike.

Suddenly, stone spikes erupted from the ground. I barely dodged the first two before another ten shot up! I had to leap backward twice.

This bastard was strong, and the sheer magic in those spikes told me that if they hit, it would hurt. Was it rank B? Probably. What a lovely island... I wondered if the entire beach's combined strength would even be enough to take this thing down.

"Graaaah!" the bear roared, trying to intimidate me.

In response, I slashed a black crescent straight at its face. The bastard reacted in time, and I only managed to slice off an ear, which really pissed the bear off.

It charged, and I backed off, straight into the trees. Good call. With a single strike, its stone-reinforced claws felled a tree as thick as I was.

I kept throwing crescents while dodging its spikes. But then, suddenly a pit opened up behind me! I flooded myself with divine energy, forming a barrier, and shattered all the sharp spikes at the bottom with my back. A second later, the beast shoved its enormous head into the pit. My shield was waiting for it.

I shifted my spear into a dagger and started stabbing relentlessly, pouring the power of death into its body.

"Give me your soul and die, spawn of fallen gods!" I spat, and just as I was about to strike again, the dagger elongated, piercing straight into the beast's skull.

A large crystal landed on my forehead. My shield, having absorbed too much damage, crumbled to dust. And my back... oh, my back hurt!

THE COMING OF GOD OF DEATH

I lay there for a while, trying to come back to life. Everything ached. My right arm was practically falling off thanks to the side effects of using five DE per attack. And I'd attacked a lot! I was running a complete deficit now.

"You still at it?"

"At my limit..." The parasite's voice sounded utterly drained.

Eventually, I started feeling better and raised the bear. Then I climbed out of the pit myself. My body was covered in bruises from the stone spikes, and I had a few cuts on my back. It was time to heal. I did so while riding my bear's back. It carried me toward the swamp.

On the way, I contacted the kikimora. She passed along some information and relayed a few questions from Tatiana. I answered what I could, and she'd pass my answers on to Tatiana, who would tell the others. In the process, I learned why we had ended up here in the first place. I'd have to explain it to everyone in the evening.

For now, there was the swamp, the ruins, and leeches. A lot of leeches. I thought I should just burn this place to the ground. But never mind that. "My bear, I believe in you! Go on! Swim!"

The swamp was all inky-black water and rotten earth. The vegetation wasn't much better. And I could feel cursed power in the air. Looked like there was something up ahead that a god of death and the underworld could really sink his teeth into.

Perched on my puppet's back, I speared the

leeches trying to climb onto it. Six DE per kill! Not bad, considering how many there were and how weak they were.

But as we progressed, my bear started slowing down and growing thinner. The bloodsucking bastards were draining it dry from its legs and its belly. I couldn't reach there with my spear.

Thankfully, there was an islet nearby. But the creatures kept coming! I had to climb onto my bear's head, because I couldn't kill them fast enough.

I could've used some fire... but then I had a better idea! The moment my bear reached the islet with the ruins, I jumped off, and the beast collapsed onto its belly, instantly crushing countless leeches. A flood of notifications about gained divine energy filled my vision.

Then the bear started rolling around on the ground, while I darted through the area, finishing off the remaining parasites. There was so much energy!

After wiping out about sixty of them, I sent my bear back into the water — again and again! The poor thing was down to skin and bones, but 1,500 DE was 1,500 DE. I could've gotten even more, but the leeches ran out. What a shame.

The bear was drenched in blood, and I wasn't too keen on sitting on it, so we continued to the ruins on foot. This place looked like it had once been a small town, but I couldn't tell who it had belonged to.

The buildings were ancient stone structures,

with most of them submerged underwater. Not that it mattered. What mattered was the presence of powerful, malevolent spirits.

A moment later, my skeletal warrior emerged from a black sludge beside me.

"Good... to see you... my Lord," the warrior knelt before me, and I gave him a nod.

"Guard me while I," I scanned the ruins and spotted a strange stone cube embedded in the ground, "build an altar."

Why not? I didn't care what it looked like. I wouldn't be drawing power from this land anyway. I just needed a relay, a way to connect with my other altars and my servants.

So, I sat on the cube, placed my hands on it, and began pouring in my energy. But then, zombies began to rise from the swamp! Bloated, green bodies of drowned corpses. Horrific faces, grotesque mutations, and a few massive, hulking figures.

Oh, right! I hadn't summoned my big guy yet! And just like that, a giant zombie brute spilled out from a massive pool of black sludge.

It was enormous — at least ten feet tall — with arms as thick as tree trunks. But it looked better than before. Not impressive exactly, just less decayed. Sleeping in the underworld must've done it good.

Hundreds of zombies kept swarming in from all sides. And they refused to submit, controlled by some sinister force. A poltergeist, maybe? Or an ancient, evil spirit?

BOOK THREE

"Hhhhhhaa!" My bear tried to roar, but it came out as little more than a rasp. It lunged at a group of zombies emerging from the water to the south and sliced off three heads in a single swing.

Three souls immediately shot toward me, finally finding peace. On the other side, my skeletal warrior engaged a group of advanced zombies — strong, fast, and armed. Their weapons were rotten, but weapons nonetheless.

"Gkh!" One of the zombies, a broad-shouldered brute with a curved sword, rasped as it struck my skeleton, forcing him to stagger. But my warrior blocked the blow with his shield.

The zombie dodged my skeleton's counterattack and drove its sword straight into his ribs! But it was just a skeleton, so that didn't do anything to him. The sword was stuck, though, which was good.

The skeleton took full advantage of that and smashed the weapon apart with his shield, then lunged forward and impaled the undead.

But there were too many of them. My brute was faring much better than the warrior. It simply swung its massive hands, sending zombies flying in all directions. Many of them landed right back in the swamp. For the record, the leeches weren't touching the zombies.

Unfortunately, this battle didn't last long. A group of clawed zombies crept up behind my brute, attacking its legs and forcing it to its knees. Then they piled onto its back, pinning it down.

They tore into its tough flesh and bones without hesitation. My bear in the south had already been ripped to shreds. Though even in pieces, it was still putting up a fight. Not that it mattered. The undead were swarming toward me now.

"You're too late," I said as a clawed zombie approached me from behind. In that moment, two runes on the altar flared to life, and the zombie behind me collapsed, its soul ripped from its body.

One by one, the other zombies dropped as well. Hundreds of souls soared toward me, finally finding the peace they had long awaited. None remained in the underworld. A few even departed for reincarnation, and I received a ton of energy for those.

"Forgive me..." the battered brute rasped.

"Don't worry, I was just testing your capabilities. And I'm satisfied. You need proper support, and you'll accomplish great things." I focused my energy on healing the injured zombie, and it bowed low, expressing its loyalty.

A few moments later, the skeleton approached. He had taken far more damage, but none of his enemies had managed to reach me. Good job.

Now, what else was there? I wondered if I should raise the zombies.

"Y-you... human... you will pay for this!" A crushing wave of cursed power suddenly bore down on me! And then, they appeared. Three ordinary black sludges, one in the shape of a woman.

Looked like the rulers of these lands had arrived. I wondered how much divine energy they'd give me. Heh. It was time to find out!

CHAPTER 19

The Academy
Sometime later

FAR MORE PEOPLE HAD GATHERED at the second meeting dedicated to the teleportation incident, so it was held in a large hall.

"Thus, the island is an extremely dangerous place," Tatiana concluded after recounting the latest events, including the attacks and the strength of the monsters.

She stood before a crowd of people seated in rows of chairs. Behind her was a large screen (currently inactive), and off to the side, several armchairs occupied by officials.

"They did the right thing by fortifying themselves on the shore," the governor said as he rose from his seat. "We are already preparing a rescue expedition, but the magical storm is only growing stronger. All teleportation systems in the region have been shut down. Therefore, the expedition will either have to guard the students after locating them, waiting for the storm to pass, or transport them by water."

"Searching that many islands will be difficult," someone pointed out.

"What choice do we have?" The governor scanned the hall. "That's why every noble house must contribute whatever it can. The more resources we have, the faster and more effective the search will be. We need rare artifacts, in particular." His gaze swept across the room, but no one seemed eager to part with their valuables.

"Of course, this is only temporary. Once the operation is complete, everything will be returned. In the event of the squad's death or the artifact's loss, the Empire will compensate for the damages."

The room immediately became more alive, though no one openly stated what they were willing to offer — too many potential enemies were present. Even those who remained neutral toward each other still harbored caution. Who knew when peace would turn into war?

"What about the group that split off?" someone asked Tatiana.

"All I know is that their leader is described as a 'tall, bald brute covered in muscle.' That's a direct quote."

"Buller... Where's that degenerate's father?" one of the furious patriarchs barked.

"He isn't here. That's not his heir — it's only

his third son. That's why he didn't bother attending," someone from the crowd responded.

"Or maybe the Bullers are behind all of this."

* * *

The swamp
Gauss

"P-please... have mercy... I don't want to vanish... I beg you..." pleaded the woman made of darkness. Her voice was eerie and terrifying. Maybe she could have scared someone under different circumstances. But not when she was sprawled on the ground beneath me. Yes, I was sitting on top of her to keep her from running away, while three semi-transparent male silhouettes lay nearby.

"I should just crush you and absorb you..." I grumbled.

And why wouldn't I? These bastards had forced me to reveal my true form, which cost me too much divine energy. On top of that, I'd be dead meat that night. Lying flat on the floor, too drained to move.

Damn, now I wanted meat. With some good sauce and some mashed potatoes.

"N-no, please! We can be useful... I don't want oblivion... I want to exist... I don't want to be forgotten!" The last word came out as a scream.

"You don't want to, huh? Then earn back the energy I spent on subduing you!"

"U-understood..." The woman struggled to free

herself, so I got up, allowing her to get up and stand in front of me.

And then, her black silhouette began to shift into something more solid. Was she a dark elf?!

"If I have a physical form, I will do everything in my power to repay you for what you spent on taming us." The gray-skinned woman's black dress dissolved, revealing a body that was undeniably beautiful.

I wasn't stupid, I knew exactly how she planned to repay me. "Nope." I held up a hand and shook my head. "You have two options. You can be sealed inside an artifact and guard my home, or you can become an undead with the potential to evolve."

"I... as a zombie...?" The naked elf grimaced.

"S-sister..." One of the male figures rose and also took the form of a dark elf. "Zombies have physical bodies..."

"But they're ugly! They stink! And their consciousness is limited! I don't want my mind to fade away!" The elf woman started crying — it seemed like losing her mind was her worst fear.

"The more advanced a zombie is, the higher its intelligence," another male voice chimed in.

"It's still a zombie..."

"Well, then, go into my artifacts." Honestly, it didn't matter to me which option they chose.

If they became zombies, I would gain four potentially powerful undead. If they guarded my home, I'd get strong spirits for defense. Of course, I'd have to suppress their will significantly so they wouldn't manifest in the material world. Otherwise, who would want to live in a mansion haunted by ghosts? And ultimately, they'd just be sitting in artifacts, waiting for an enemy to show up.

"Zombie! I choose zombie!" the elf woman nearly shouted, staring at me in horror... Wait. She couldn't read my mind — not while I was in this form. Could she read my expressions? She wasn't simple, that was for sure.

"Well, then, pick your bodies. Just keep in mind, you'll all start as rank-zero undead. I'll give you enough power to break through to the first rank, but when I leave this island, you'll have to abandon your bodies and follow me."

"They're all so ugly..." the elf muttered as she looked around.

"Sister, cover yourself." The second male stepped up beside her, summoning a cloak of darkness and draping it over her. Though, he did it rather reluctantly. Were they sibling lovers?

It was none of my business. Among dark elves, blood relations were a common thing. That's just how dark elves were. I'd explain later. Right now, I couldn't decide on what I should do. I was still overflowing with energy, I needed to use it somewhere.

"I'll take this one. It's less ugly, and it looks like a woman. It is a woman, right?" The elf crouched beside one of the bodies. She hadn't accepted the cloak. I wondered if she was trying to seduce me.

Actually, she was seducing her brothers. I almost felt bad for them. The way they were staring at her...

"Pick whatever you want. It'll turn into you anyway," I waved a hand dismissively. All the elves immediately turned to look at me.

"What do you mean?"

"Who do you think I am?" I stood up to my full height, unleashing a wave of death aura in all directions. "I am the God of Death and the Underworld! Don't compare my servants to mere undead. Every one of my followers carries a fragment of divine power."

"I understand. But how does it become me?" The look she gave me was shockingly devoid of intelligence. Or maybe that was just my imagination.

Sighing, I began explaining how it worked, and judging by the elf woman's expression, the idea of becoming a zombie was starting to appeal to her more and more. And why did I care? The swamp! There were so many leeches there! Was I not a genius? I'd let this quartet hunt the leeches.

"And one more thing — where's the nearest gate?"

"Gate? Oh, it's in that flooded tower over there. That's where the leeches are coming from," she said, pointing north to a leaning stone tower. "But I don't know what's inside."

"Good. Now do me a favor and put on some clothes."

"Hmm? Why? Don't you like what you see?" She spun around, showing off her undeniably stunning figure. She wasn't thick, but she wasn't a twig either.

"It's distracting. Get dressed," I ordered, giving her a firm look. In an instant, she was clad in a black dress.

"As you wish. I thought you liked looking at me," she shrugged, while her three brothers looked utterly disappointed.

"Now tell me about this place."

"Mmmm... Well, we lived here, fought off monsters, and then something happened and we all died. That's all I remember. Sorry."

"I see. Even souls this strong have lost their memories after centuries, maybe even thousands of years. Fine. Maybe serving me will help restore them. Now pick your bodies," I said with a wave of my hand. More expenses...

Spending ten DE per body, I infused their souls into them. That was enough for them to become advanced zombies. But their development would take the entire day. So, I led them into one of the houses to wait it out. They could find weapons for themselves — there were plenty lying around, though it mostly junk.

After that, I left the brute to help the elves while I took the skeleton to the swamp. If you don't have blood, the leeches can't suck it! Though they weren't a threat to me, either.

You've absorbed your enemy's power and get +6 divine energy.

You've absorbed your enemy's power and get +6 divine energy. [...]

THE COMING OF GOD OF DEATH

The moment I stepped into the water, the leeches swarmed me, but as soon as they touched flesh infused with divine energy, they died. Though, of course, that meant my divine energy was being consumed as well.

So, I hurried into the building, where I found the gate partially submerged in water. Except, it wasn't really a gate anymore; it was a dungeon. And judging by the state of things, this dungeon was what had created the swamp.

The shard was only rank D, which was strange — it should have evolved by now. I stepped inside and, surprise-surprise, there was a swamp. It looked almost exactly like the one outside, except there were more islets, and more trees growing on them.

Immediately, leeches latched onto my legs, which were submerged up to my knees, and the IS bombarded me with notifications. The skeleton started hacking at the water with his sword, and I got more notifications.

Together, we made our way to the nearest islet, which was about five yards across. There were bushes with berries growing on it, but I thought they might be poisonous. The leeches were, after all.

"Put one in your mouth but don't swallow. I'll check it," came the parasite's voice.

I did as he asked. The berry was big, red, and looked a lot like a strawberry.

"Eat it! Eat every single berry on this island!"

I burst out laughing. This was the first time

he'd ever told me to eat *everything*. Usually, he just whined and complained.

"Reason?"

"Pure mana! Massive concentration. It will help you develop!" I could hear the hope in his voice — he wanted me to grow even stronger than I was.

Sending the skeleton off to slaughter leeches, I settled onto the grass and started munching on the berries. They were delicious and the mana rush was intense. Nearly all of it was being absorbed, and whatever excess remained, the parasite devoured.

"Can I take these bushes out of the shard?"

"You can, but I doubt they'll survive or bear fruit. Also, these berries are poisonous."

"So I can't feed them to anyone else? And I won't die from them, right?" I asked, still eating. They were just too good.

"I've already developed a special compound, which neutralizes the poison the moment it enters your body. Besides, the poison doesn't kill, it just paralyzes."

"These berries are a trap," I realized. Clever. Eat a berry, pass out, and wait for the leeches to feast on you.

"Exactly. But you can feed them to others, if you share your bodily fluid to neutralize the poison."

"Saliva or blood?"

"Yes. Also urine."

"No thanks, I doubt they'd be willing to drink

that... Blood is too valuable. But saliva... I can spit in some water and have them drink it. That'll work, right?"

"I believe so."

"Great. I'll treat the sisters, Polina, and Basel. They need to get stronger."

"And what about your beloved?"

"Who's that?" I asked, genuinely confused.

"Anna."

"Well, she needs undead to develop — ghosts, evil spirits, that sort of thing. Anyway, these berries are gone." I sighed and moved on to another islet.

More notifications flooded in, but it didn't matter. I could channel some of the acquired DE into my body. It would leave me miserable later, but these berries were just too good.

Only when I put one in my mouth did my mind snap back into focus. The berries were addictive, dangerous, and... How easy it was to manipulate a human body. Just a minute without the berry, and I was already shaking in withdrawals.

"Parasite, can you do something about this?"

"I haven't identified the cause yet. I'm searching for solutions," he sounded just as puzzled as I was. I figured for now, I'd just be a berry addict.

BOOK THREE

* * *

Same place
Who knows how long after

"Master..." The skeleton approached me, smoke literally rising from his body. "Please... let me return... one hour..."

"Hm? Oh! Finally!" I couldn't hide my excitement. With a wave of my hand, a black sludge appeared behind the skeleton, swallowing him whole, and just like that, I was left without a guard. And the leeches felt it!

Immediately, they started swarming out of the swamp. I had to summon a spear and stab at them while using my other hand to gather and eat the berries. It was incredibly inconvenient, but what could I do? Letting the leeches die by touching me would be far more expensive in terms of energy.

So, I sat there, eating, until I moved on to the next islet. But as soon as I swallowed a single berry, the mana in my seal practically exploded, and warmth flooded my body.

I had reached rank eight. That was fast, considering I had only recently broken through to the seventh. Everyone was going to be so surprised. Should I move on to the ninth rank right away?

"I don't recommend eating any more. You just advanced."

"Yeah, I figured. I feel sick now," I muttered, spitting out a half-chewed berry and wiping my mouth. And to think, just a second ago, I couldn't stop eating them.

Fine. I'd pick all the berries and bring them back to my people as planned. But how was I supposed to carry them? I thought the leech boss's hide looked sturdy enough.

A short distance ahead, I spotted a small islet with a pedestal, and a leech the size of a bull. I decided to kill the creature and skin it, but the moment I approached, it spat poison at me! The saliva splashed into the water, turning it into a sickly green stain. A second shot followed. Then a third! What the hell, was this thing a machine gun?!

I created a full-body shield, but immediately regretted it. The poison was burning through my energy! It was like acid corroding metal, eating away at the shield.

I poured more energy into the barrier and rushed in to attack. But my spear slammed into another barrier. Seriously?! I was in my true form, overflowing with power, my spear was charged with divine energy... and the shield still held?!

"Piiiiiiiii!" The boss screeched, shifting into an ultrasonic frequency.

The parasite instantly blocked my ears — they literally sealed shut, as if pressed closed by invisible hands. That only helped so much, and the attack still rattled me.

This thing was powerful. No way it was a rank D! It should have been at least B-rank. Whatever. I was still just going to kill it.

The parasite helped me recover quickly, and I

charged, relentlessly hammering at the barrier. The leech, meanwhile, kept spewing poison like a high-pressure hose. But my shield absorbed everything, even as it drained my energy at an insane rate.

In the end, the leech's barrier failed before my strength did. It could no longer dodge or run, it just sat there while I circled around it, striking again and again.

"P...pi..." The creature, having lost an enormous amount of blood and filled with the power of death, finally collapsed.

But the barrier over the pedestal didn't disappear. Which meant I had to kill every leech in the swamp. How the hell was I supposed to find them all? This was a nightmare.

I had to make sacrifices, or rather, step into the water. I just walked through the swamp, maintaining my true form, letting the leeches kill themselves on contact with me.

By the time it was over, I'd burned through a good chunk of the energy I had earned.

Suddenly, my foot hit something metal. I curled my toes around the object and pulled it up. It turned out to be a metal staff, light blue in color, with a large red pearl set at its tip.

The pearl was wrapped in delicate metal leaves, which made it look elegant and luxury. It was definitely expensive.

Staff of the Blazing Gzyu
Rank: A

THE COMING OF GOD OF DEATH

Description: The Blazing Gzyu was a legendary mage of the southern continent and his staff was custom forged by the greatest dwarven smiths. Its knob holds a dragon's pearl — an extraordinary treasure that generates and stores pure mana.

"Here it is! The source of mana! That's why the berries are so saturated with it!" the parasite pointed out, though I had already figured it out myself. Mana was practically pouring from the staff.

The mana burned unpleasantly against my skin. Though at night, this staff could make for an excellent heater — no need for a campfire. What a great find!

"But this is an A-rank artifact... using it for warmth..." The parasite clearly didn't share my genius idea. What did it know? It just sat inside me, cozy and comfortable.

I kept wandering through the swamp, now much more enthusiastic. Who knew what else I might find?

Some time later, the skeletal warrior rejoined me. No, wait — not a warrior. He was finally a knight, fully clad in black plate armor! His weapons remained the same — a shield and sword. His helmet was completely sealed, without a single opening. In fact, his entire armor set looked way cool. It was exactly what I wanted.

"I am grateful, my Lord," the skeleton's voice sounded much more human now, which was a pleasant surprise. Though where was the voice even coming from? It didn't matter much.

We continued our hunt, and I lost track of time. But eventually, the dome fell, and I immediately destroyed the core, while mentally asking the pedestal for a good helmet! That's where I'd store the berries. Except...

Leech cloak
Rank: D
Description: A cloak made of leech hides. Poisonous if bitten.

It looked absolutely disgusting. Made from black leech hide, it was slimy and unpleasant to the touch. But that was just the outer layer. Inside, it was surprisingly soft, and quite comfortable to wear. And it could be used to carry berries!

I immediately got to work gathering as many of those miraculous berries as I could. I didn't leave a single one behind, and the skeleton helped. Though, in the end, we collected far fewer than I had eaten.

When I stepped outside, I was a little surprised to see that it was night already.

"Master..." a raspy, eerie voice called out, and then I saw the zombie.

She had almost completely taken on the form of a dark elf. Her skin was pale and ghastly, with traces of decay still lingering. Seeing something like that at night would cause nightmares for years in most people. But I wasn't human.

"Biologically, you are human," the parasite

corrected me. Annoying know-it-all.

"I see everything's going well for you. Good job," I nodded at them.

"Do... ing... our... best..." The elf bowed. She was naked again and looking rather gross.

I had allowed them to take half of the DE they earned. It helped them heal and evolve.

"Oh... right, I forgot." I waved a hand, and the four zombies were instantly clad in armor.

"Th... an... k... you!" The voice carried a hint of resentment, as if chastising me for not doing that earlier. Forgetting happens to the best of us!

We headed home. The brute stayed behind, while the skeleton escorted me for a bit. But after realizing that in my Great Form, my aura worked far more effectively, I sent him back to the swamp.

I reached the beach without any trouble. The moment I dispelled my divine body, I nearly howled in pain. The last few hundred yards were rough, I was limping the whole way. Good thing I had the staff to use as a cane. As I approached the wall, I heard shouting. Loud, angry voices. Had they really lost me?

BOOK THREE

* * *

Wall in front of the ravine
Several minutes ago
The sisters and others

"You idiots! Where do you think you're going?! If he's alive and not stupid, he'll stay put for the night!" Ivanov snapped at the four determined women.

"That's exactly the problem — it's already dark! He might need medical attention!" Katie shouted back.

"Alex has returned home exhausted more than once. When he's this drained, even standing is difficult for him!" Lena added. The sisters' eyes burned with intensity, their fists clenched.

"Don't be fools! You'll get yourselves killed and achieve nothing!" Ivanov didn't back down.

"He's right. I'm sure Alex decided to wait out the night, and all you'll do is make things worse for him," Basel interjected, and Polina nodded in agreement.

"We're stronger than you think," Angelina's hair blazed with fire, she looked ready to charge through sheer force.

"Think this through!" Ivanov practically pleaded, afraid of losing their medics, and their strongest fighter.

"He's dead! There were C-rank beasts out there!" a man shouted, but the moment the four women turned to look at him, he quickly retreated.

"Who's dead now?" I finally showed up, poking my head through a hole in the wall, only to find my entire crew of troublemakers gathered there.

"Alex!!!" They all screamed. Not three, not four — everyone yelled at once, nearly deafening me. And why did Ivanov look so happy to see me? I really hoped he wasn't one of those. You know, the strange ones. I thought I should probably be careful around him.

"Yes, yes, it's me. Help me out," I muttered, disappearing behind the wall as I started climbing over, then down the other side. Not an easy task in my current state.

"Why are you blushing?" Anna asked Angelina in a displeased tone.

"You always have to know everything, don't you?" Angelina growled back, her eyes fixed on my bare ass. What the hell was she staring at? Did a leech get stuck there or something?

Soon, I handed Basel the folded cloak and told him to be careful with it. The staff, I simply tossed down.

"You cleared a shard?" Ivanov stared at me in disbelief.

"How could I just walk past it? Got held up a bit — the thing inside was tricky."

"A bit?! We all nearly lost our minds! You're our medic and the only one who can contact the Empire!" Ivanov was getting angry, and so was everyone else, looking at me like they were personally offended that I was still alive.

"By the way, I got in touch with home again. A search team has been dispatched from the capital. But we'll go over the details later. First, food and something important," I said, pointing at Basel and Polina, then at the sisters and Anna. "You and you, come with me."

Leaving Ivanov to stew in confusion, I rushed to my place. First, we needed to eat the berries before they spoiled. Everything else could wait.

Once inside, the room felt cramped. Mostly because of Basel. And what was Angelina doing there? I only called the sisters and Anna. Whatever…

"Listen up," I said, unfolding the bundle from my cloak.

"Berries!" Angelina grabbed one but stopped just before popping it into her mouth when she heard me.

"They're poisonous. Eat one, and you'll be paralyzed."

"Then why do you have them?" Angelina put the berry back, staring at me. She had covered herself with leaves, though rather clumsily, and a nipple was still peeking through. The others had done a better job at it.

"They're packed with pure mana. Thanks to them, I broke through to the eighth rank." Judging by their faces, that caught them off guard.

"But how? They're poisonous!"

"How? By getting used to the poison," I shrugged, my hands glowing with energy. Though I conveniently left out the part where it only took me five minutes. "Now, my bodily fluids should work as an antidote."

"A-a-a kiss?!" Polina instantly pressed herself against Basel, who gave me a rather hostile look.

"H-h-heck..." Katie turned red, lowering her head.

"Alright," Lena nodded. Angelina licked her lips, while Anna looked furious.

"Kisses? Gross. I'll just spit in some water, and you can drink it," I said, the very thought of kissing them making me recoil. As for Basel, I'd rather spit directly into his mouth than kiss him.

"That's disgusting!" Angelina wrinkled her nose, and the others nodded.

"Am I... agreeing to this?" Polina muttered, glancing at Basel. He clearly wasn't thrilled, but after a moment, he nodded.

"A kiss!" Angelina insisted.

"No way, but I can offer blood instead."

"Blood? Well, that's not as gross," she said with a shrug, and the others nodded in agreement.

"Wow... women really are bloodthirsty. My saliva is disgusting, but kisses are fine. And blood? Sure, in any form," I muttered, shaking my head.

After consulting the parasite, who was still awake, I diluted the necessary amount of blood with water. Then we divided the berries and got started.

"Oh my god, this is delicious!" Angelina moaned, and she wasn't the only one.

"Eat slower and drink more water!" I scolded, but they ignored me, stuffing their faces with berries.

"I can't... stop..." Basel mumbled, showing no intention of sharing with Polina. Not that she was any better — she kept eating, barely remembering to breathe. But suddenly, she trembled and let out a relieved sigh.

"Fifth..." she murmured before continuing, though her body could no longer absorb mana. Her rank breakthrough had saturated her completely, so she handed the rest of her portion to Basel, surprising him. "You owe me a favor..." she whispered.

They kept eating — no, gorging — while I had to yell at them to drink more water.

"Mmm..." Katie hummed in delight, followed by Lena. Just as I expected, they were already on the verge of a breakthrough. Now both of them were at rank sixteen.

A little while later, Anna also broke through, surprising me. Apparently, she could develop through normal means as well. She was now at rank thirteen.

The remaining berries were split between Angelina and Basel — the two most problematic ones.

"Drink more water! You're absorbing too much poison!"

"Uuuuuuuh..." Basel groaned and stopped eating, handing the rest to Angelina. He clearly didn't want to — these berries were priceless — but I had warned them that they would spoil quickly. Soon, they'd be nothing but pure poison.

Basel had reached rank fourteen, but his arms went numb, and his whole body felt sluggish. Polina had to help him recover.

Angelina was the last one left. Her eyelashes, eyebrows, and hair burned with fire, and she looked completely strung out, unable to stop. But then, it happened.

First, she broke through. Then, she completely seized up. I told her to drink more water. But at least she looked happy. And she would for a while, until the paralysis wore off.

"We still have some berries left," Anna said.

"Polina, be a dear and go get Ivanov," I asked, and she reluctantly peeled herself off Basel and ran off. A short while later, Ivan Ivanov arrived, looking slightly bewildered at the scene before him.

Berries scattered across the cloak. People sprawled out like drug addicts. The scent of blood in the air.

"Eat the berries, and you might break through. But they're poisonous, so here's the antidote," I said, pouring my blood into a fresh jug and stirring it with a finger.

"Are you joking?"

"No... not joking... we... all... broke through," Basel barely managed to say, making Ivanov's eyes widen. He immediately dove for the berries, looking more desperate than anyone.

Just two were left when he suddenly groaned and took a deep breath.

"Holy... hell..." he muttered. "You got these

from a shard?"

"Yeah, and there won't be any more."

"Got it... people would start a war over these. Thanks for sharing! I won't forget it."

"Alright, now it's time to share what I've learned." I stood up and forced myself to swallow the last of the berries.

Ivanov nodded and left to gather the others. This was important information. I wanted to see how they react. But first, I needed to revive Angelina. She was just lying there, paralyzed, her leafy outfit failing to keep her chest covered.

CHAPTER 20

WHAT CAN I SAY about people? Being human feels like a prison sentence. And during the so-called 'survivors' meeting, I was reminded of that. For some reason, a lot of people assume everyone around them is stupid, so they see no point in listening to others' opinions. Others let emotions completely override reason and logic. And then there are just straight-up idiots, like the trio of guys I was looking at now.

"If this little guy could do it, then so can we!" A third-year student, who looked pretty sturdy, pointed at me while his two lackeys stood by, nodding along. I'd like to note that on our first day on the island, not one of them had even tried to fight the monsters.

"I see your death coming. And your buddy on the left too. The one on the right? He'll live. Probably ditch you both. And he'd be right to — you're just a couple of fools walking straight into death's arms," I cut in.

We were sitting in several circles around a ring of stones, with four small fires burning nearby. The trio stood in the middle. Apparently, we'd set up this 'platform' where anyone could speak their mind. But for what? There should be one leader making the important decisions. Everything else should go through assistants.

"You see death? What kind of crap are you talking about?"

"It's not crap! He warned me about the shark, and I survived!" a girl shouted from the crowd.

"He probably just saw it!"

"From over a hundred yards away? Are you an idiot?" she shot back. The guy's veins bulged. He clearly didn't take well to being insulted, especially by a girl.

"No point arguing. If you beat me, fine — go wherever you want," I said. Was I just too lazy to deal with this? Yeah, probably. But I wasn't lying about their deaths. I could see the black smoke rising from them. Might as well take advantage of a couple of fools.

"Hah! You said it yourself!" The guys grinned, thrilled at the chance. I stepped into the circle and took a look around. The entire crowd was watching us, and the whole scene... I don't know, it felt more like savagery than anything else.

A lot of the girls were still naked. Sure, some covered themselves, but others had already given up on the effort. There weren't even any leaves left to make clothes.

Some had started covering themselves with clay and small leaves, while others, like Angelina, had fashioned something to cover their lower half. Clay and leaves. And I noticed a few were even trying to sew together clothing from animal hides.

The guys, though, were filthy, despite the ocean being right there. And, of course, completely bare-assed. Not surprising, since every last leaf had been claimed by the girls. I also noticed the crowd had settled down enough that some guys had stopped hiding their admiration for the women.

Then again, without pants, it was kind of hard to hide anything. Just a bunch of savages. But I'm getting distracted. Right now, everyone was watching us, hungry for a show. I could see it in their eyes.

So here I was, standing across from these three. A classic trio — one fat, one skinny, and one average. The average one was the ringleader.

"Fight!" Ivanov's voice rang out, and all three Adepts [10-19] lunged at me. My hands lit up. They were light on the surface, darkness underneath.

The fat one charged straight at me. The middle one came from the left. The skinny one from the right. The fat guy crackled with electricity, the skinny one was trying to form a wind barrier, and the leader — an obvious fire mage — was procuring a fireball.

Thought they had me surrounded? Ha! It was time to show them what short people can do!

I sprinted toward the fat one and slid underneath him, passing right between his legs. The moment I was behind him, I popped back up and kicked him right in the tailbone. My magic-enhanced kick sent him flying straight into the fire mage. Cue the shouting and swearing. The poor skinny guy froze for a second in shock, which cost him.

I jumped at him and slammed my palm into his gut, breaking his weak little barrier in one hit. He collapsed onto his knees, coughing and clutching his stomach. Some fighters they were. But whatever, I wasn't there to actually hurt them. Let them stand guard at night or something.

I didn't even bother waiting for them to get up. Just gave them a few well-placed kicks to keep them down while they struggled to stand.

"Bastard!" the fire mage spat and hurled his fireball at me.

I had one quick thought — what if that thing hit the crowd? Luckily, Basel was on it. He stepped forward and took the hit himself. Didn't even flinch. As for me? Of course, I dodged. The fireball was slow. The mage was clearly running on empty — his concentration was crap. And this guy thought he was ready for the forest? What an idiot.

I closed the distance in a flash and hit him twice in the stomach. He doubled over instantly. That's when the fat one went for me again, this time unleashing a lightning attack. I twitched — it was unpleasant, but bearable.

"I-I-I surrender," he stammered, raising his hands when he realized I was still standing just fine.

"I'm not even an Adept, and I beat you easily," I said loudly, shaking my head. "If you're so eager to prove yourselves, guard the beach. Maybe you'll actually take down a monster."

At that moment, the IS notified me that my divine energy balance had increased. I turned and walked back to my spot, where five pairs of admiring eyes were waiting. The fifth? Polina. Though she was admiring Basel, not me.

After the fight, Ivanov stepped into the circle. "Well, since there are no more questions or complaints, I suggest we wrap up and get some rest. Tomorrow is our first expedition, so I recommend getting plenty of sleep."

Most of the crowd immediately started dispersing. But just then, one guy ran up to me.

"Please, wait a moment!" he called.

He was tall — probably six-three, maybe taller. Thin as a rail, almost elf-like. I recognized him immediately. He was the one I saved from drowning when we got transported here. And he was also one of my believers, giving me 0.5 DE. I'd kind of forgotten about that.

"Hey," I nodded and shook his hand. He looked a little surprised but quickly covered it up.

"Allow me to introduce myself. Leo Izimov, heir to the family. You saved my life, and I want to thank you." Thin as a twig, but his eyes were sharp.

"I'm a light mage. Helping people is in my blood," I shrugged.

"Still, I'm grateful!" He took a step back before bowing, careful not to knock me over with his forehead. He really was long.

"I also looked into you and found out that you manufacture furniture. My family owns a small business specializing in paint and varnish production. We can supply you with materials at a good price."

"Oh? That's a solid offer. I'll pass your proposal to your father during my next communication session," I said, pleased.

We'd been having trouble sourcing the right kind of lacquer and paint for our furniture. Not just any kind would do, and the locals weren't selling to us. We had to order from other cities.

"Thank you. I'm sure this partnership will be beneficial for both families."

We chatted a bit longer before parting ways. On my way home, I took note of the shelters. Some people were already living in tiny caves. Others had built makeshift huts. And a few brave souls were just sleeping under the trees, lying on animal hides.

People made barrels for clean water, built toilets, and set up campfires along the entire shore. I also noticed makeshift spears crafted from wood and sharp monster bones. Stone doesn't conduct mana as well as monster bones, so that was the right call.

"Ahh... y-yes... harder..." We heard moans echoing from one of the caves as we were inspecting the site. Looked like someone had decided to enjoy themselves. The girls walking with me didn't react at all. Well, except for Polina, who turned bright red and clutched Basel's arm even tighter.

"So... you're staying with us again?" I looked at Angelina who walked into our "house" with us.

"Most of my people already have homes. Some joined groups or shacked up with guys. Now I'm alone," she shrugged and flopped onto a fur, turning her back to me.

If my entire body wasn't aching, maybe it would've been hard to ignore that beautiful figure and round ass. But right now, I didn't care. Even fighting that trio had taken a toll on me. The only silver lining was that breaking through to the eighth rank had significantly reduced the side effects of prolonged divine body use back in the swamp.

I just needed some sleep, and I'd be fine. That's why I picked a spot against the stone wall, where no one would roll over, smother, or grab me in the middle of the night. The girls all decided to sleep far away from me. Even Anna, which was perfect.

I had my cloak under my head, and it was nice and soft. I did offer it to the girls, but they found it disgusting, which was fine by me. If they didn't want it, I'd enjoy the comfort.

Everyone was exhausted, so they knocked out quickly. However, it didn't take long before voices broke the silence. Damn it... I didn't think this through when I suggested Basel build his house so close.

"Are you sure?" Basel's whisper wasn't exactly quiet.

"If you don't, I'll rape you myself!" That was Polina. And she sounded pissed.

"We can all hear you—" I started, but Lena clamped a hand over my mouth.

"This is interesting! Don't ruin it," she whispered, eyes practically glowing with excitement. I looked at Anna, and she nodded.

"Polina's full of surprises. I never thought she'd be so bold," she whispered back.

I groaned in frustration and wrapped myself in my cloak, trying to block everything out and sleep.

"Basel, I liked you from the start. You're incredible. Handsome, strong, and you have such a great personality," Polina's voice came through, interrupted only by kisses.

I cringed. Guess romance wasn't my thing. The sisters, on the other hand, were way too into it, practically squealing. Why were they so invested in someone else's love life? Gross.

"And you... so delicate, so gentle... makes me want to protect you and love you," Basel's deep voice rumbled.

Why was this happening to me? I suddenly wanted to smash my head against the wall and pass out. But no, they just kept talking and kissing, for a solid half an hour. Just as I was finally getting used to the noise and my eyes started closing, the sisters decided to chime in.

"Anna, what do you think? Will they even be able to...? Polina's tiny, and Basel... well, you know..." Lena mused.

"Honestly? No idea," Anna shook her head. "I don't think they'll manage. Or Polina's going to need urgent healing. We should be ready just in case."

"I wonder if she's a virgin?" Katie asked quietly.

"With how determined she is? Probably not," Angelina answered. Judging by the rustling sound, she had sat up. "What about you? I'm a virgin."

"We are too," Lena answered for both herself and Anna, who just nodded. I'd already figured that out, but it was still kind of surprising. I always thought club girls only went out looking for one-night stands. Turns out, they just wanted to dance and unwind.

"Wow! That's rare. How do you deal with hormones and stress? I tease guys and fight — it really helps me blow off steam," Angelina admitted. She really was the worst kind of opponent for a proper mage. How could anyone focus on casting spells with that kind of distraction running at them, bare-chested and confident?

"Shopping, dancing, and dressing up! That's what really calms us down," Lena said.

Huh. So they were all virgins. That was unexpected. Or maybe I had known and just forgotten? Whatever. If I didn't remember, it never happened.

"I have someone I like to torture. It brings me

the greatest pleasure and really helps relieve stress," Anna said with a wicked grin. For some reason, everyone turned to look at me.

"Ouch, ouch, ouch!" Polina's voice suddenly cut through the conversation, making the girls freeze.

"You okay?"

"Keep going!"

Okay, that's it. I was ready to cover my ears. I was not going to listen to this nightmare. Too bad the parasite was asleep. Otherwise, I'd have made it shut off my hearing entirely.

And then... moans. Gasps. More moans. Yeah, despite the girls' earlier doubts, it seemed like those two managed just fine. And honestly? I had no idea how. Not that I cared. The only problem was that the noises kept getting louder. Even with my hands over my ears, I could still hear them.

Tomorrow, I'd force them to move to a cave. Or better yet, make Basel dig me one. At least then I'd have decent soundproofing.

And then, the chain reaction started. I was sure most of these people weren't even dating. It was practically sleeping with the first person they saw. How did that even happen?! Gross.

Wait... Was I any different? Zhanna and I hooked up the first day we met. No, wait! That was the parasite's fault. It flooded me with pheromones, and that's why everything escalated so fast. So no, I'm not like them. Humans are all animals, I'm not.

"This is so embarrassing..." Katie mumbled.

"I'm so turned on! If you don't hold myself back, I will rape your boyfriend," Angelina panted. That was dangerous. My whole body ached — how was I supposed to fight back?

"He's not our boyfriend!" Katie shot back. "We can marry whomever we want."

"Ohhh, I see. Saving yourselves for 'the one,'" Angelina nodded. "Respectable. I'm strong, so I get to choose my future husband too. But if he's weaker than me, the family will take him. Not that I like weak men anyway. Which is why I've never..."

"Alex and I are getting married after we're done with the Academy," Anna announced.

"Yeah, I got that," Angelina laughed. "You follow him around like Cerberus, guarding him from competition."

"Yes! Yes! Yes!" Polina screamed.

"God, why is she so loud and intense?" Anna groaned, looking at the blushing sisters. "That's it! I can't take this anymore. Tonight, I'm losing my virginity!"

"Ow! Let go of me, you idiots!"

The sisters tackled the redhead. What happened next? I have no clue. My eyes finally closed on their own. At last... sleep.

BOOK THREE

* * *

"There are ten men on guard outside. Another two are staying inside," reported a man in black, positioned on the roof of a house opposite the mansion.

"These guys don't sleep or eat at all! Are they even human?!" someone on the radio complained.

"Their armor is probably modified with a life-support system. Stay focused. Assault team, are you ready?" asked another man on the roof.

"We've been ready. All forty men are in position."

"Excellent. Third squad, do you copy?"

"Loud and clear. We're ready."

"Begin the diversionary operations. Buy us twenty minutes."

"Yes, sir!"

At that moment, raids erupted across the city, targeting various aristocratic properties, including the Scullies' furniture factory.

"Move out! Burn it to the ground," barked a leader as a sixty-man squad burst from black vans, charging onto the factory grounds.

They were clad in old but reliable armor, meant to pass them off as bandits or mercenaries. Leading them was a mage in light armor, gripping a staff.

"But there are workers inside. They run two shifts."

"Who cares?!"

"Kill! Kill! Kill!" Bloodlust fueled their charge. Gunfire erupted, and the first patrolmen — guards in white armor bearing the Scullies' emblem — collapsed, dead.

"Weaklings! Ha! Where the hell are they even shooting? Look at these amateurs!" the attackers laughed openly. The guards fired back again and again, but their shots barely landed. Meanwhile, every return shot dropped a factory guard instantly to the ground. But as soon as the raiders reached the factory doors, more figures emerged from inside.

These were men in black suits, hoods over their heads, wielding axes. Right behind them, factory workers in blue coveralls, also armed with axes, some even jumping out the windows.

"They're insane! Just completely insane!" the raiders shouted, unloading their weapons into the charging lunatics. But then... "What the hell?! Why won't they die?!"

"We're under attack from behind!"

"What the fuck?! We killed them all!"

The fallen guards suddenly stood up and opened fire again. Their aim was still pitiful, but some bullets found their marks. And once their ammo ran out, the zombies — and it was them — discarded their guns, drew their axes, and charged.

Screams, gunfire, and chaos ruled at the factory. The raiders were seasoned fighters, but their enemies refused to die. Shoot them, stab them in the heart, even sever their heads — they still got back up!

"Cursed bastards! Are you undead?! How?! How the hell do light mages have the undead?! In the middle of the city?!" the enemy mage shrieked. He flung water-attribute spells, but what could he from under a pile of dead bodies? He was a Junior Mage [20-29], about six times stronger than an average human. But these zombies, encased in armor, were heavy.

The screams continued as the mage was stripped of his staff and hacked apart with axes until his barrier collapsed. Per orders, they avoided damaging the armor and equipment, which was why they inflicted so many wounds instead of finishing him outright. By the end, the entire factory yard was littered with corpses.

And the zombies who had been "killed"? They simply played dead. Others, who hadn't even been touched, quietly gathered bodies. Just in time for the arrival of the security forces. A full battle unit, about two hundred strong.

"This is horrifying," the unit commander muttered, scanning the carnage as he approached the factory manager, who, surprisingly, looked completely unshaken.

"That's putting it mildly. They didn't spare a single soul. Looks like they had orders for a full sweep," his assistant added. Then the commander spoke again.

"But this... this is a massacre. Why did they decapitate the factory workers? And how many bullets did they use? A hundred per person? And most importantly, why did they lose?"

"Maybe reinforcements arrived?"

"Maybe... Alright, we'll—" The commander's phone suddenly rang. "Shit! Another attack on the other side of the city! Handle things here."

He sprinted toward his vehicle, taking most of his forces with him. And he wasn't wrong to rush — the city was on the brink of an all-out war.

The most brutal battle raged at the Scullies' mansion.

"Why the fuck won't they die?!" a soldier in black armor cursed. He hid behind a massive military shield, firing at a white-armored guard.

The raiders had already breached the estate and were engaged in combat. But despite their numbers, just ten guards put up a fierce fight!

And then, the mansion doors burst open, and a woman stormed out, dressed only in a see-through nightgown. "I'll kill you!" she roared as water armor enveloped her. Massive clawed limbs coated her legs, while her arms bore gauntlets with razor-sharp water blades. The armor itself resembled a beast.

"There she is! Kill her!" A voice echoed through the raiders' intercoms. Two soldiers charged at the woman. One wielded an electric whip; the other transformed into a twenty-foot-tall stone giant.

"Fool!" Tatiana laughed, taking the whip's strike on her left arm. "Pure water doesn't conduct electricity!"

"Oh, fuck..." the attacker swore. He hadn't expected his opponent to purify her water so thoroughly — especially in a city, where the air was filled with countless elements.

A massive stone warrior blocked Tatiana's path. She easily dodged his enormous fist, her claws scraping against the rock, but they didn't cut deep.

At that moment, the mage with the whip dissipated his weapon and attacked from behind, throwing punches. Tatiana got distracted, and paid for it. The stone warrior's fist slammed into her, sending her flying backward through a window.

But she immediately jumped to her feet, and from the shattered window, a barrage of water bullets rained down, hitting both mages and any foot soldiers caught in their path.

Meanwhile, the advanced zombies were pushing the enemy back with relentless force. Among them, one warrior stood out — a close-combat specialist wearing armored gauntlets over his gear. He fought three opponents at once!

The central fighter attempted a downward slash, but the warrior deflected the blade with the back of his hand, knocking it off course. In the same motion, he drove his fist into the enemy's throat, which was protected by armor, but the impact was enough to knock the man unconscious.

His two comrades took the advantage of the warrior being distracted and plunged their swords into him, piercing his armor. Their blades got stuck in his body, but the man didn't die! With a wide swing of both arms, he grabbed them by the necks. Then, pulling the swords out of his chest, he executed them with their own weapons.

At that moment, Tatiana came crashing through the air, slamming into the mansion's wall. The impact broke her concentration, her water armor splashing into a puddle, and blood trickled from the corner of her mouth — she had internal injuries.

"That bitch! We wasted so much time and energy just on her!" the whip-wielding mage growled, battered and bruised. The stone warrior wasn't in great shape either.

"It's those damn tits! She left them exposed on purpose to break our concentration," the stone mage grumbled.

"She's hot as hell, and her tits are divine, but we need to put her down," the whip mage sneered and swung his weapon, only to be blindsided from the left by the gauntleted warrior.

But the mage was no weakling. With a single kick, he sent the warrior flying. After all, he was a Battle Mage [30-39] at his peak.

"Out of my way, weakling," he smirked.

"She's getting up," the stone warrior pointed at Tatiana. Her nightgown was in tatters, exposing everything for the enjoyment of the onlookers. Her eyes burned with fury, and her teeth clenched in rage.

"I'll kill you!" she roared again, charging forward, forming new water gauntlets.

But before she could reach them, a skeleton warrior in black armor burst out of the mansion. His heavy footfalls rattled the ground, drawing everyone's attention.

"What the he—" The stone guy never finished his sentence, because the black knight rammed him with his shield, sending him sprawling.

"Raaahhhh!" Tatiana howled like a wild beast, seizing the moment. As the whip mage was distracted, she coated herself in a thin layer of water and tackled him, twisting his limbs into a painful hold.

It wasn't just any hold — his arms and legs were locked in a way that made any movement excruciating. Worse yet, his head was trapped between her massive breasts!

The man struggled, thrashing violently. He tried to break free but couldn't. He even unleashed electric shocks, but pure water didn't conduct electricity, and Tatiana's water completely sealed off any air pockets. He couldn't breathe, not even a sliver of oxygen reached him.

He fought with all his might, but nothing worked. His air ran out fast, and death was near. And would be a humiliating death. Even after his demise, people would mock him suffocated by boobs. The worst part? Tatiana was much weaker than either of the two mages.

"What the hell are you?" the stone mage muttered in disbelief. He kept striking the black knight, but the warrior simply wouldn't die. And there was no barrier protecting him, no magic. But somehow, the knight's sword, shrouded in black smoke, was shredding his stone armor and barrier!

"Aaaaaahhh!" Suddenly, one of the raiders was lifted into the air, impaled by dozens of glass shards. His lifeless body was then hurled into another attacker.

The mansion's guardian spirits were now actively joining the fight, and only now did the stone mage realize that almost all of their men had already been defeated!

"How... how is this happening...?"

"You are nothing... compared to... the power of my master..." The giant skeleton's eerie voice sent shivers down the mage's spine, even through his stone armor. He wanted to run, but who was going to let him? And besides, his energy was nearly depleted.

"I surrender! I surre—" He never finished. A synchronized barrage of gunfire tore into his back, depleting the last of his magical reserves. His barrier shattered completely. As his stone armor crumbled away, the skeleton swung his blade and beheaded the man.

Only the undead saw what happened next. The stone mage's soul separated from his body and raced toward the altar hidden in the mansion's basement.

"Thank you... whoever you are..." Tatiana murmured, covering her chest with one arm as she approached the skeleton. The undead knight knelt before her.

"I am merely a guardian of your patriarch, my lady. The artifact summoned me, but rest assured, I will always protect your home."

"I see... Thank you so much," Tatiana said, a deep blush spreading across her face as she flashed a bright, grateful smile.

* * *

Home sweet home
Morning
Gauss larva that will never become a butterfly

I woke up feeling like I was dying from the heat. But when I opened my eyes, I saw a tunnel with a light at the end. No, I wasn't dead, my nose was way too itchy for that. My arms, however, wouldn't move, even though I could feel them. What the hell was going on? And why did it feel so heavy? Like a damn hippo was lying on top of me!

I tried shifting from side to side — it was difficult, but it worked. Then suddenly, something rolled off, followed by: "Ow!.. Ugh, that hurt..." I heard Katie's voice, and suddenly, things felt much lighter. I kept going. "Ah!"

"Oof..." First one down, then another, but something was still on top of me. No matter how much I wiggled, I couldn't shake it off. It was clinging on like a cat with its claws sunk in. Fine. Time for a different approach.

I rolled to the left, trying to untangle myself.

There was another "Ouch!" from someone as they hit the ground. But that was enough. I could finally move my arms and legs! I crawled forward, toward the light, and realized I was wrapped in a zebra-hyena pelt and my cloak.

"What exactly were you doing last night?" I shot the sisters and Anna a confused look. They looked worn out and sleep-deprived.

"Protecting you from Angelina," Lena laughed. I noted that her small chest was still covered with leaves, as well as everything below the waist.

"Great. Another headache for me," I muttered, freeing myself. Angelina was outside, sprawled on top of the mess of fur, clutching tightly onto it, fast asleep. Then I turned back to the girls. "Wait... did you stay up all night?"

"Like anyone could sleep through that..." Katie blushed and turned away.

"We spent the first half of the night keeping her under control. Eventually, we just decided to wrap you up in fur. Then, during the second half... well, everyone around was moaning, and then monsters showed up because of all the noise. We had to fight and heal the wounded," Lena sighed.

"I see. Come here, I'll give you a boost," I said, genuinely grateful. They protected my sleep and let me get some proper rest. They deserved some thanks.

Ten minutes later, all three of them were practically glowing with energy. Though the sisters reacted way too much to my touch. Just an observation, but their skin was incredibly soft and smooth. So much so, that I felt like I needed to meditate again.

Once I was done with the girls, I stepped outside. It was still early morning, and the camp looked dead. Only a couple dozen people were up and moving about. I spotted Ivanov and headed his way. He looked exhausted, so I took care of that.

"Thanks! That really helped. What a night!" he shook his head.

"Monsters?"

"If only!" he said. "The whole camp turned into a fuckfest! Some idiots even lost their minds and decided they wanted women without asking first. That turned into an all-out brawl. Luckily, no one got killed or raped. And then, after that, the monsters showed up. Weak ones, though."

"Well, I cleared out the area, so things should stay quiet for now," I noted.

"Yeah, well, the small fry just came to scavenge the bodies. It was bound to happen. Anyway, let's eat. We've already started cooking." Ivanov led me to the dining area. Stone tables, stone chairs, stone pots, and clay plates. The food? Fish. I was surprised. I didn't even know they'd gone fishing. I had to admit, it was really good. A bit bony, but that wasn't a big deal.

As we ate, the camp slowly came to life, more people making their way to the dining area. Nearby, hides were drying in the sun. I had no idea if they'd turn out well. I passed along what Alexander knew about treating hides to Ivanov, but it wasn't much. We really needed a skilled water mage. They'd make the whole process so much easier.

"Morning, everyone," a familiar voice called out. Enter the happy couple.

Polina looked absolutely radiant, though she was limping badly. Basel, on the other hand, looked completely drained, but his face held the most disgustingly smug smile I'd ever seen.

"Morning," the girls stared at Polina, making her blush.

"Sorry... I'm loud."

"Oh yeah... loud," Katie muttered.

"I'm pretty sure half the island heard how many times you came," Lena giggled, making Polina hide her face in her hands. "Need any medical help?"

"Wouldn't say no... Basel's a giant. In every sense..." She shot her boyfriend a flustered glance, but he just kept grinning like an idiot.

"Then come see us after breakfast."

"Uh-huh..."

As we ate, we went over the upcoming expedition. My puppets were monitoring the area, but there were still small creatures hiding out there. We needed to gather fruit, leaves — so the women could finally cover themselves — vines, roots, and wood, lots of wood to build a barrier separating us from the beach. And plenty of other things. There was a mountain of work to do.

Wait. The mansion was attacked last night? Those sons of bitches. Alright then, they asked for it.

CHAPTER 21

"SHA...KER..." murmured the gray blotch of a soul floating before me.

Of course, it only spoke in my mind. The soul was fresh but weak. Hell had torn it apart badly. Still, I managed to extract the most important piece of information: hatred. Pure, seething hatred toward the one who had ordered the attack on my family.

As a result, he and his men were dead. Some were now in my Hell, the rest in the afterlife. That's what happens when you die on my turf. You get exactly what you deserve.

And I did get quite a few souls out of it. Too bad there was no altar at the factory, I could have gotten even more. I might have even been able to empower my zombies.

Despite their struggles, they managed to fend

off the attack. But I realized it wasn't enough. I needed more fighters. Ones that were stronger and more resilient. Most importantly, ones indistinguishable from regular humans.

"Caw! Caw!" The raven called out, but only in my mind. I could feel it, even from a distance. All thanks to the altar in the swamps. It was far, sure, but nowhere near as distant as Blaga. Because of that, I could contact the kikimora and the others whenever I wanted. But that could wait. I had more pressing matters to handle.

"Caw!"

I let the soul I had been interrogating pass on, I had promised as much. Then, through the raven's eyes, I surveyed the factory's interior. My poor zombies! They had been gutted and torn apart. Twenty bodies lay in two neat rows, their limbs and guts scattered beside them.

But then, darkness surged from the raven, enveloping the corpses, and the other wounded zombies inside the building. Many of them had been working despite their injuries.

"You fought well. My power is running low, but you two," I focused on a pair who had been reduced to little more than scraps. Nearby zombies were already gathering their pieces. "You were the most persistent. You will be rewarded."

As the zombies reassembled their bodies, my power surged through them, and their limbs fused back together within seconds. I wondered, if I covered my brute in metal, would people believe he was a combat mech? Then again, what would be the point? He'd be just as bad a shot as the rest of my zombies.

I had already inspected the battlefield, and it was a mess. Though, the more advanced zombies at the mansion had fired far more accurately. The problem was, the enemy didn't let them fire at all, luring them in to close combat almost immediately.

I also questioned the skeleton and was surprised by Tatiana. She fought like a furious berserker, used her beauty to her advantage, and took down an opponent much stronger than her. I would need to reward her. After all, she had defended both the house and the altar.

As I pondered, the zombies finished pulling themselves together. They needed to wash off the blood, change clothes, and get back in order. Their armor also needed repairs, and not just theirs — we had looted a good amount of enemy gear.

The only downside was that I had to hand the raiders' corpses over to the imperial authorities. Otherwise, I could have immediately raised a hundred new zombies. Even though I hadn't kept the souls of those fighters and soldiers, their bodies would still have been useful. Ordinary souls would have sufficed for basic undead troops.

"You did well. Continue protecting the mansion and Tatiana. You may stay outside, but do not leave the grounds."

"Thank you, my Lord. It is an honor to defend your home."

"Hm? I can tell you're holding something

back…"

"Your mother… she is a beautiful woman. I think my wife looked like her. Or was it my daughter? Or my mother…? Forgive me, I don't remember."

"Well, maybe if you grow stronger, you'll recover part of your memory. But don't count on it too much. Some things can't be fixed, least of all a soul."

"Even so, thank you for the hope," he said. If skeletons could smile, I was sure he would have. Now he stood outside, stationed at the gates — a massive, imposing guardian in full armor.

Then I moved on to the factory again. Some windows were shattered, the ground was drenched in blood, and bullet casings were scattered everywhere. And then there was the pile of loot.

I had already sent word through the raven to Zhanna to have everything repaired. And, of course, repainted. We also needed to stock up on ammunition.

And one more thing — my little monster, the brand-new logging truck, had made it through unharmed. That was a relief. I had been really worried about it. We had just finished fixing it!

I was done at the factory. Soon, everything would be cleaned up, the windows replaced, so I sent the raven flying toward the logging base. My puppet had already arrived there, and from what I could see, my Chinese workers had taken a serious beating. They needed repairs.

Now, one more matter to handle. I needed to

track down this Shaker and bless him with a little curse of my own. Speaking of that — what was Talster up to?

*   *   *

One of the best restaurants in town
Private VIP room
Same time

"You look terrible," noted the thin man with long black hair and ink-black teeth. He sat at a table overflowing with food and alcohol, surrounded by plush sofas.

"Looks like Scully cursed me," sighed the tall, overweight man. A large bump stood out on his forehead, and a bruise darkened his eye.

Sure, he could have asked his healer to take care of it, but the poor guy was already exhausted. His master made him work overtime.

"So it's not a rumor?" the third man at the table asked. He was a white-haired man in his fifties, dressed as always in a strict black suit.

"No, I..."

At that moment, the thin man's hand twitched, and under the pressure of his knife, the plate cracked, sending a sharp shard flying straight at Talster's neck. But an artifact activated just in time, blocking the attack.

"Something like that," Talster sighed, picking up the broken piece of the plate. He poked at it with his finger and nearly pricked himself. And he was a strong mage, with a body far tougher than most.

"No wonder you haven't been showing up in public," the white-haired man nodded. "Any idea how they cursed you?"

"Yes." Talster pulled out a shattered phone. He dropped it often, but it still worked. On the cracked screen, a video played. "I looked into it. That bird belongs to Scully's assistant."

"So it flew over while you were screwing one of your debt slaves, cursed you, and then just flew off?" the black-haired man looked at Talster, but he didn't respond. The video made everything clear.

"I hope you're not going to act rashly. The night raid proved that the Scullies have a lot of tricks up their sleeve," the white-haired man remained perfectly calm. Yes, they had suffered a loss, but this was just the beginning of the game, a warm-up.

"Yeah, that was a complete disaster," the black-haired man muttered. "Maybe I should just kill that bitch myself?"

"Haven't you been punished by the Emperor enough?" The white-haired man's eyes narrowed, and the black-haired one flinched.

"No... I've had more than enough for a lifetime. You're right, I'm sorry, I won't suggest anything that stupid again. My entire family is already being held on a tight leash after what happened with the Academy training and the hospital."

"Exactly," the white-haired man said, then

turned back to Talster. "Proceed carefully."

"Of course."

"And one more thing. About our missing people. Unfortunately, Scully didn't die. It's a shame, it would have been a gift from fate. But there's a bigger issue. Every single artifact and piece of gear our people had with them was destroyed."

"You think he took them with him?" Talster asked. He took a sip of wine, but suddenly, the glass shattered, spilling wine all over him. He barely reacted — he was already drinking from a second glass using a straw.

"No idea. But if I were him, I'd keep anything important on me at all times."

"I see... that's unfortunate." Talster started eating a cutlet, then suddenly began choking.

The black-haired man immediately rushed over, transforming his hand into black smoke and shoving it into Talster's mouth. A second later, he pulled out a bone.

"Thanks..." muttered Talster after his coughing spell was over.

"That curse is strong," the white-haired man grimaced. "You should hurry up and get rid of both the bird and the woman. No games, no twisted amusements. Just kill them, burn the bodies, and drown the ashes in holy water."

"I'll start preparing right away," Talster hissed through clenched teeth.

He had nearly died an utterly pathetic death — choking on a bone in a cutlet. Where the hell did it even come from?

That would be investigated soon enough. And whoever was responsible would either be sold into sex slavery or executed. That would depend on their gender and looks.

* * *

Home temporary home
Gauss

"Alex, are you coming or what?" I heard Katie's grumbling voice from outside. I was taking a while. Grabbing my staff, I stepped out. I decided not to take my cloak, in case there was a chance it'd get damaged. Outside, the whole team was waiting.

"Here, temporary loan." I handed the staff to Angelina. She gave me a look that screamed, 'What kind of crap is this?'

"That's actually an A-rank artifact."

"A? Are you out of your mind? Where the hell did you find it? And don't tell me you cleared an A-rank gate!" That wasn't Angelina, but one of the people joining the expedition.

Turned out everyone was waiting for me, so the whole group had gathered in front of my house — thirty people in total, including us. Not a small number. Most were armed with spears and stone axes.

"Found it in a D-rank gate," I shrugged, and all eyes turned to Angelina.

"I don't know how to use a staff..."

"Then give it to me!" A guy stepped out from

the crowd, reaching for it.

"Yeah, keep dreaming!" Angelina pointed the staff at the sky and focused. A second later, a powerful burst of flame shot out like a small dragon's breath.

"Holy crap! It has a mana battery," she muttered.

"It really is A-rank! That kind of power..." Ivanov murmured, while a few people eyed the staff with greed. "It only works for fire mages?"

"Yeah," I nodded. "The staff generates pure fire mana, so no one else can use it. Unless you just want to swing it like a club. It seems sturdy enough."

"A club... an A-rank staff..." Ivanov looked like he was about to faint. I just shrugged, not seeing the problem.

We let Angelina play around with the staff a little before heading to the wall. The lower part was now reinforced with stone, featuring a passageway and strong wooden gates.

It was good to have earth mages. Though they worked the hardest, which was why they spent most of their time lying around like seals, recovering mana.

My puppets had already moved further out, so we had to be careful. Who knew what kind of creatures had wandered in? Not that it mattered, everyone was already trembling with fear. The group barely moved. But...

"Women, you really picked the perfect time," I muttered as both my arms were suddenly hijacked.

Anna clung to one, looking a bit embarrassed — it was still skin-to-skin contact, after all. Well, technically, hand-to-chest contact, since the leaves she used for cover didn't do a great job.

Angelina was hanging on my other arm, and the two girls were glaring daggers at each other.

"Leave them be. It's better than letting them dwell on our situation and lose focus," Ivanov chimed in, walking nearby.

"What situation? What's so bad about our situation?" I looked at him like he was an idiot, and he seemed genuinely surprised.

"Well, you know... the island, the monsters..."

"So what? Rescue teams are already searching for us, we have a secure shelter, food, water, and a roof over our heads. We even have healers. Several healers, in fact."

I looked back at the sisters. They had gotten noticeably stronger over the past few days. Somehow, their healing had become more effective. And it wasn't about their ranks increasing — this was something else entirely. I needed to figure out what.

"We're putting our lives at risk every day. What if a strong monster shows up? Or a pack of monsters? The guards might not make it through the night." Ivanov was definitely a pessimist.

"You just described the life of an average commoner in our city," I laughed.

Zhanna and the others lived with the constant fear that a trip to the store might end with them being eaten by creatures from the gates. People had simply gotten used to it. My words made Ivanov think.

"Let's build a network of tunnels in the rock," Lena suggested.

"You're right! That way, we wouldn't have to defend the entire beach, just the cave entrances," Katie added.

"Oh! And we should limit the number of entrances and seal off the rest!" Lena looked at her sister, who pondered the idea before adding, "We'll need ventilation. Also, we need to figure out the toilet situation. And one more thing — we shouldn't store meat in the living caves, or we'll all freeze."

"We can just make a cellar. Cold air sinks, so I don't think it'll be a problem," Lena grinned.

Ivanov looked at them as if orcs had just gotten PhDs. Not that I blamed him. Aristocrats were usually pampered weaklings who couldn't do anything themselves. Alexander had a maid dress him, and I'd even heard of nobles who couldn't bathe or brush their teeth without a servant's help.

Then again, to be fair, aristocrats devoted most of their lives to magic and combat. That kind of lifestyle let them get away with being completely useless in day-to-day life.

"I really like the tunnel network idea," Ivanov finally spoke up. "Let's discuss it when we get back. For now, we've arrived."

We had exited the ravine. Everyone was on

edge, but they soon relaxed. First, we ventured deeper into the forest to a spot where I had seen banana palms. We picked a ton of bananas, and no one tried to eat us. Though, there were plenty of my puppets' tracks around, which had some people nearly pissing themselves.

After a few trips back to the ravine — where we left the bananas for the camp to collect — we headed to the cliffs. That's where we ran into our first enemy.

It was a dog-sized monster that looked like a dog, and even barked like a dog. So we killed a rank F dog. They say people make hotdogs out of them, so we took the body.

Then we moved on to chopping down trees and tossing them off the cliff. Below, people were waiting to drag the logs to the shore, strip the bark, and cut off the branches. Then, using earth mages, they drove the logs into the ground, reinforcing them to build a palisade, separating the camp from the water.

We also gathered leaves and bushes. The flexible branches would be useful for all sorts of things.

Once we confirmed the area was safe, we brought in more people. Things moved much faster after that. And everything was going great until...

"Ivan! A storm incoming!" someone shouted.

We ran to the guy who yelled that. He stood at the cliff's edge, staring into the distance. There, storm clouds loomed, stretching across the entire horizon, closing in on us.

"Perfect!" I declared. Everyone looked at me like I was an idiot. They were the idiots.

"What? I'll let my people a storm is heading our way. They'll use it to figure out our location. You should be happy."

"Scully's right!" someone said. Good. Not everyone was an idiot.

"I agree, but first, we need to survive this storm. I have a bad feeling about it. The wildlife has vanished, like the animals are afraid of it," Ivanov muttered.

He might be onto something. The animals really had disappeared. That meant we needed to hurry.

"Basel, Kire, Ignacio, Alexey — head down! We need deep caves. No way our houses will survive this storm," Ivanov commanded, and the guys immediately sprinted toward the ravine.

"Katie, Lena, and Anna, go help them. Make sure it's done right," I sent the girls along. They couldn't go without Anna anyway — if the poltergeist lost range, their "clothes" would vanish.

Everyone else doubled their efforts gathering wood. But the plan had changed. We needed a massive log house. Maybe several. And since I knew more about construction than the rest of them, I had to head down and show them how it was done.

It had to be a very sturdy house, too. Judging by the clouds growing darker and the sea getting rougher, we might be looking at a tsunami.

We also sent people to check on the "separatists", but they were gone. Left their beach without a trace. No one had any clue where they went.

I sent word about the storm through the kikimora. The response came two hours later. Apparently, we were somewhere between the Philippines, Indonesia, and Siam. That was good news and meant the search area had narrowed considerably.

The bad news? There were hundreds, if not thousands, of uninhabited islands out here. But whatever. It'd be figured out somehow.

We were building a sturdy single-story house. It was made of thick logs, as reliable as possible under the circumstances. I kept a close eye on the construction.

Every gap was sealed with clay, though we left ventilation, which could be closed if needed. The windows were tiny and could be plugged like bottle corks.

While we worked on our large, long house, the earth mages were carving out caves in the rock behind us. The caves had already been there, but they were small, so the mages expanded them.

All the excess stone had to be carried outside, which took a lot of people. Even the women were hauling rocks. Of course, that led to constant complaints.

"Ow! I dropped a rock on my foot!"

"Watch where you're going, you chicken!"

"H-help... I got pinned..."

And so on. Work was in full swing, but the

storm was getting closer by the minute.

The floor of the house was made of the stones from the caves. We built columns from stone, as well, and started on the roof. No, scratch that. We built the roof in a panic because we were running out of time.

And the women weren't helping. Some were dragging their belongings into the house, some were carrying stones and getting underfoot. One idiot got so distracted staring at a woman's chest that he fell off the roof and got crushed by a log.

"Alex, you've been working so long without a break. Here, have some water and something to eat," a sweet voice interrupted my focus on the roof beams. A young woman stood in front of me, holding smoked meat and a cup of water.

"Thanks." I took both, but given her height, I was practically talking to her breasts, which were right in my face. At least she was wearing a skirt made of leaves. The men were suffering and rejoicing at the same time.

And my hormones… yeah, still raging. I should have listened to the parasite and done some serious physical training. My body was overstrained from divine energy, and it was messing with me.

Alright. It was time to lift some logs, but first, I'd eat. Whoever smoked this meat did a terrible job. Then again, why would aristocrats know how to smoke meat? I sure didn't.

Some time later, the gatherers returned completely exhausted. But we didn't let them rest — we put them to work on the house.

The sky had already darkened, the wind had picked up, and it was getting cold. Really cold. That threw us off a bit. If only we had proper clothes...

The hides we had drying weren't fully dry yet because of the storm, so we couldn't wear them. We used them as rugs instead.

We lit fires, but the smoke was a problem. This wood created a lot of smoke, which was an issue both inside the house and the caves, especially with the wind blowing it right at us. Half an hour after lighting the fires, we were all choking on smoke, so we put them out. Now, fire mages were our heat source.

In the caves, warmth was somewhat contained. But in our unfinished house? Not so much.

We had to work even faster, making the final touches while the wind was strong enough to blow Anna away if she stepped outside.

Trees bent, the sea churned with mini-tsunamis, and the cold was biting. Some people were already shivering so hard their teeth clattered. Only the ice mages were fine, though that depended on their affinity. Ivanov, for example, was very cold, his nose running. He was an ice mage, but his affinity wasn't very strong.

With all the rushing, people got injured, and a couple of earth mages collapsed from mana exhaustion.

"We're done! Seal the windows!" Ivanov ordered as we finally finished the roof and patched up the last gaps.

Finding the leaks was easy, since the rain had already started. Water was pouring in from every crack that wasn't sealed well.

Once we closed everything, the wind was gone, and the air inside finally warmed up. People let out sighs of relief. But oh how the hides stank! Guess we hadn't processed them properly. Or we screwed up something else. I don't know. But stink was better than freezing to death.

"We just have to wait out the storm," Ivanov said. "Everything will be fine. And thanks to this weather, the Empire now knows where to look for us."

"Really? They'll find us?!" a girl's voice called out.

"Of course they will," another reassured her.

"Ow! Who's that?! I'll kill you!" Angelina yelled, suddenly lighting up the room with the staff's fire. "A-Alex? What are you doing?"

"You're warm," I noted, pressing against her. She was like a furnace. So nice... so warm...

"Anna! Where are you going?!"

"It's really warm..."

"We're in too..."

In the end, the four of us crowded around Angelina from all sides. I got the most comfortable and softest spot — right in front.

I buried my nose just below her breasts, with the breasts themselves resting on the top of my head. It was so warm that I started feeling drowsy from the comfort.

"Let's cover ourselves with the hide too," Lena

suggested.

I had to let go of my personal heater. We ended up spreading out the leech cloak to sit on and wrapping ourselves in the hide. But of course, we kept hugging Angelina.

"At least this chicken is good for something," Anna purred contentedly.

"Not only do you shamelessly use me, but you also insult me!"

"Basel, can we hug you?" The big guy was holding Polina close, and she looked as pleased as a cat. But some other girls were shivering from the cold, while Basel had a strong fire attribute and was naturally warm. In the end, six nearly naked girls ended up clinging to him from all sides.

By the way, the caves were warm, but there wasn't much space, so only the weakest were sent there — mostly second-years. Almost all of them were Apprentices [1-9]. Adepts [10-19] were much tougher, so they were sent to the house.

That said, the caves kept expanding since the earth mages were constantly working on them. And the combat squad was also stationed in the house in case of a monster attack.

For now, everything was calm. Well, as calm as it could be. At least no one was trying to kill us. Oh, wait, I lied! Nature was trying to do that. The house was sturdy, but we could hear trees falling and small rocks pelting the walls.

I sent one of my puppets to check what was going on. What it saw wasn't good. Not only had lightning struck the creature twice, but the beach was also flooding! Good thing we had sealed eve-rything up — no water was getting inside the house. Monsters, on the other hand, might.

Right before my puppet's eyes, a turtle-like monster washed up on the shore. Then, another bolt of lightning struck it. At least we had covered the roof in clay, so it wouldn't catch fire. Not that it would matter much, considering the storm would snuff out any flames instantly.

"Ah-choo!"

"Bless you!"

The temperature was dropping fast. Even my puppet was freezing, and then it rushed toward the ravine. At least the creature was big and heavy, and the wind wouldn't blow it away.

My tiger hippo bolted toward the shore, all be-cause of the fish-like monster that had washed up! And this thing had two arms, which it was using to crawl in our direction.

"Raaaahhh!"

"W-what was that?! Monsters?" someone pan-icked.

"The wind, just the wind. I'm sure of it," I re-assured them.

"Alright."

The monster screamed so loudly as my puppet devoured it alive that it drowned out the storm. I had to be more careful. Then again, how was I sup-posed to do that when three more of those fish things tumbled out of the sea?

I sent all my puppets to the beach, but one got torn apart by lightning. Another got blown away by the wind. In the end, only four made it, and together, they took down the fish.

That was a battle won, not the war. The monsters just kept spilling out of the waves. I had already poured a lot of my strength into my puppets, but just as we finished dealing with another batch, IT appeared.

"Roooooaaaar!" A beast the size of a ship. How exactly was I supposed to kill this thing? Oh well, I'd figure it out. And then we'd eat it.

CHAPTER 22

A MASSIVE TENTACLE SLAMMED into the beach, carving a trench about three yards long and over 3 feet wide. It wasn't just a regular tentacle. This was more like an appendage, a fingerless limb.

My hippo puppet rolled to the side like a sausage, dodging the strike with a loud clatter of black armor. Where did the armor come from? Turns out, I could equip my puppets. Though I nearly tore my guts apart from the strain of crafting armor for a hippo-like creature while making sure it didn't restrict movement. It was no easy task to design and forge armor for a beast like that while keeping it mobile.

The hippo kept rolling, and the tentacles kept striking! There were exactly five left. There had been six, but we had already torn one off.

After a short battle, I was down to just four

puppets: a striped hippo, a zebra-hyena, some ten-foot-tall baboon, and a tiger with bull horns. The baboon fought with swords like some kind of an ape-knight, while the others — armored freaks — looked ridiculous.

Boom! Another tentacle smashed into the sand, and the beast let out a deafening roar. Its enormous body was already covered in wounds, but they were healing fast, and the creature wasn't running out of strength. The monster itself looked like an overfed piranha — wider than it was long. It had a tail too, but getting near it was a terrible idea. That thing struck like a whip, which was why we were fighting it head-on.

After another missed strike, the monster changed tactics and slammed all its tentacles at the hippo at once. On my command, the hippo crouched low, and long spikes shot out from its armor.

The tentacle crushed the puppet down into the sand, but it survived. The arrow-shaped spikes buried deep into the monster's limb, which pissed it off.

The creature let out a furious roar and, lifting its appendage with the hippo still stuck to it, began smashing my puppet against the ground.

While the monster was distracted, the gorilla crept in close. Its swords darkened with a black haze as I poured divine energy into them.

A moment later, the gorilla leaped high and slashed both blades right at the base of the tentacle. A furious roar rang out, and the severed limb holding the hippo, crashed onto the sand.

Meanwhile, the zebra-hyena dug its spiked hooves into the creature's flesh, trying to claw its way up to the fish-monster's head. My tiger flanked the beast, keeping it occupied while desperately avoiding its thrashing tail.

Unfortunately, the tiger failed to draw the monster's attention, and a moment later, all the remaining tentacles came down on the zebra-hyena in a frenzied assault.

Armor crumpled, bones snapped and shattered, and the body turned into a mangled mess under the sheer force of the blow. But the hyena was too small, and two of the tentacles missed, slamming into the fish itself. Just like when you try to swat a mosquito on your forehead and end up smacking yourself at full force.

The gorilla seized the opportunity, and I had already infused its blades with more energy. Another tentacle hit the sand, severed clean. Then, the beast suddenly lunged forward...

The gorilla found itself beneath its massive maw. Teeth tore through the armor I had reinforced myself. I had poured so much energy into that armor, and it just bit right through, swallowing half the puppet in one gulp. Straight down to the waist...

The gorilla vanished into the monster's stomach, where powerful acids immediately began melting it and the armor away. Divine energy was draining at a ridiculous rate!

And no, I wasn't about to let the gorilla go.

Quite the opposite, everything depended on it. My puppet started hacking away with its swords, carving through the beast's stomach. The monster didn't like that one bit.

That gave my tiger an opening — it climbed onto the creature's back and bolted for its head, aiming to blind it.

At the same time, the hippo, back on its feet, charged forward, ramming its horn into the beast's side, making it stagger.

The zebra-hyena, its spine broken, dragged itself toward the monster and started gnawing on it. Tentacles hammered down on the zebra-hyena, but there wasn't much left to break.

"Rooooaaaaar!" the beast roared again, and suddenly, from deep in its throat, the upper half of the gorilla burst into view! It was clawing its way toward the brain. But that wasn't enough, and the gorilla's legs shot into the monster's mouth.

Where its waist had been, a black spike jutted out, and pushing off from the tongue, the gorilla dug into the creature's upper palate. The monster hated that. I hated the ridiculous amount of energy I was spending on all of this. Still, that was a problem for later. Hard to get mad when you're snuggled up against something soft and warm.

Holding Angelina close felt ridiculously nice. Outside, the cold was brutal, our breath turning to mist in the air, but the five of us were cozy and warm. Almost too warm.

Meanwhile, the monster was panicking, flailing around, thrashing in what could only be called a full-blown meltdown. Controlling my puppets was already hard, but keeping them coordinated was even harder.

Somehow, with the tiger's help, I managed to take out the creature's left eye, then the right. My beast was already digging into the eye socket when the last remaining tentacle grabbed it by the hind legs and yanked it out, hurling it toward the sea.

The tiger flew nearly one hundred yards before crashing into the water, where dozens of smaller fish were waiting. Not that their size made much difference. Any one of them was big enough to bite the tiger's head clean off. Which was exactly what they did.

But that didn't matter anymore — my gorilla halves had reached the monster's skull. No matter how strong it was, it was defenseless on the inside.

Slowly but surely, my beasts gnawed their way through, destroying the monster's brain completely and killing it for good. Now came the hardest part — getting out.

People were going to lose their minds when they saw two halves of a gorilla crawling out of a fish's skull. So, I quickly fused the gorilla back together and started making my way out.

Escaping was much harder than getting inside the monster's mouth... Whatever. Once I was out, I grabbed my zebra and tossed it into the water for disposal.

The rest of the broken puppets followed. With that done, the hippo and gorilla — the only ones still in decent shape — hurried into the forest.

The weather, I should mention, was an absolute nightmare. Any minute now, the rain was going to turn into snow, or worse, hail! Hopefully, no more fish would show up. Just in case, I stationed my puppets on a cliff.

They still had their armor, and it was heavy enough to keep them from being blown away. But just to be sure, the gorilla sprawled out on the rock while the hippo sat on top of it.

Huh, turns out the hippo was a girl, and the baboon-gorilla was a boy…

"Ah-choo!"

"Bless you!"

There was a lot of sneezing going on. Hardly anyone was sleeping, it was too cold and too unnerving. The storm was relentless, and people kept thinking they were hearing battle noises.

Ivanov was sitting in the freezing air, gripping his spear tightly, tense and ready for an attack. Meanwhile, Basel had other concerns. The girls surrounding him were shamelessly taking advantage of the situation, which was driving Polina mad. Their wandering hands were getting way too bold…

Time passed, but no one attacked us. Well, no one but nature. The hail and snow hadn't started yet, but it was already freezing. Angelina had begun using her staff for warmth, and the fire mages took turns helping out. Tonight, they were the real superheroes, even Zverinski. He had two busty brunettes nestled against his sides and some chubby guy pressed up against his back.

Hardly anyone was sitting alone. There weren't enough hides for everyone, so people huddled together for warmth. Occasionally, there were loud slaps and shouts of "Watch your hands!" Some had finally relaxed enough for their minds to wander in other directions.

"Well, stop playing hard to get! We'll warm up this way!" came a voice from the cave.

"You have a hand, don't you? Use it. What does that have to do with me?" a woman's voice shot back, followed by laughter.

"Don't get cocky. Your bloodline is nothing compared to mine," the insulted guy hissed.

"Oh yeah? Wanna compare dicks? Mine's way bigger," another woman's voice retorted, then burst out laughing. "Oh, wait! I'm a girl, I don't even have a dick. But neither do you! You think threatening a woman with your 'bloodline' is impressive, dumbass?"

The offended guy fell silent. But these kinds of exchanges were becoming more frequent. And then the building shook. Something had slammed into it.

Panic broke out! I had to shut it down fast.

"It's just a small tsunami," I said loudly, lifting my head from Angelina's stomach. "The house will hold, but I'd recommend the earth mages reinforce the walls. Just don't seal all the gaps, or we'll suffocate."

"Basel, Kire, Ignacio, and Alexey! You're on reinforcement duty. We'll need water mages too!" Ivanov shot to his feet, immediately taking charge.

He was a natural leader, lacking in personal power and influence, but that could come with time.

People scrambled into action. Rocks were hauled from the caves to reinforce the walls, while the water mages worked to keep the tsunami from reaching the house.

It was incredibly difficult to do without direct sight, so progress was slow. Meanwhile, the waves kept getting stronger. One nearly reached my puppets!

The ocean also swallowed up the dead fish bodies, even the giant one, wiping away all traces of the battle.

On the island itself, things were relatively calm. The brute reported that the swamp was holding up, and the hippo confirmed that the forest was still standing.

I was also keeping an eye on the situation in Blaga. The raven had already flown to the logging base, nearly dying a dozen times along the way before finally figuring out to fly low through the trees instead of up in the open sky.

Through it, I managed to patch up the Chinese. Their hunt had left them in rough shape. I granted them armor and weapons made from my power, though they would only last about four hours. Not wasting any time, they rushed off to continue hunting.

As for the raven, it was flying back to protect Zhanna. Just as I thought of her, I got a signal from the kikimora...

BOOK THREE

* * *

Blaga
Zhanna's flat
Night

Four men stood in front of a sturdy metal door while a fifth crouched down, picking the lock. All of them were dressed in black, with balaclavas covering their heads.

"Orders are to kill her, but have you seen those tits?" one of the assassins whispered, holding up his phone with a picture of the target. "She's not even a mage, just a regular person. Why don't we have some fun with her first?"

"Idiot, she has a bodyguard! Lives with her. If you can take out a professionally trained guard without making a sound, then do whatever you want with the target. If not, we kill them both and get the hell out," the biggest of them growled quietly, so no one outside could hear.

"She's fucked!" The first man grinned, pulling out a pistol with a silencer.

"The door's open. The bodyguard's on the right, the target's on the left," the lockpicker whispered, easing the door open as the men slipped inside.

They found themselves in a hallway. To the left was a corridor leading to the kitchen, with a bathroom and toilet nearby. A little further down, there were two rooms — one on the left, one on the right.

These were the bedroom and the living room. Straight ahead was a closet.

Two men headed for the bedroom, while three moved into the living room. Zhanna was in the bedroom, and since it was hot, she was sleeping without a blanket, wearing nothing but a nightgown. Though it concealed the mature woman's curves, the idea of "having fun first, killing later" suddenly seemed like a great plan to the intruders.

They crept toward her, silent and careful. One of them already had a gag ready to shove into her mouth, while the other prepared to grab her arms and legs. And then came the scream.

"Mo-mo-monster!"

"Raaaar!" A roar echoed through the apartment, followed by the grotesque sound of flesh being torn apart.

At that exact moment, Zhanna's eyes snapped open. Two men were standing in front of her, staring toward the living room in shock.

Her hand shot behind her head, reaching the gap between the mattress and the bed frame where she kept a semi-automatic pistol. A split second later, two shots rang out.

Both men collapsed, dead before they hit the floor. Zhanna sprang out of bed and rushed to the living room, only to find the battle was already over.

"I think it's time for you to move into the mansion," the kikimora remarked, shifting back into her human form.

Her face was splattered with human blood,

blood that had sprayed everywhere from the assassin whose throat she had torn open with her claws. The sight and smell disgusted her. She had wanted to atone by fighting monsters, but sometimes, humans were far worse than any beast.

"Zhanna!" The elderly neighbor-lady burst into the apartment, frying pan in hand. The intruders didn't bother locking the door when they came in. "Thank the goddess you're alive and safe! Are you hurt?"

"No, Miss Maria, I'm fine," Zhanna couldn't help but smile at the feisty old woman with a frying pan. The gunfire had woken the entire building.

"The burglars, though, don't seem so lucky... Hm, they had weapons? Guess they weren't your regular burglars."

"Guess not."

* * *

House by the cave
Same old island

I was beyond furious. It was time for war. A guerrilla war, to be precise. I asked Zhanna to do some digging and find out about all the property my enemies owned. The raven would handle the rest, flying around and burning it all to the ground.

I hadn't found Chaikin or Shaker yet, which meant I couldn't put a curse on them. Fine. Let their wallets suffer instead. Of course, plenty of people would lose their jobs, but there were solid compensation packages for situations like this. And I'd make sure those came straight from the owner's pockets.

The only issue was that the bird still hadn't returned. It had almost gotten eaten again. I told Zhanna to move into the mansion as soon as she was done dealing with the police and security.

I also sent word through the kikimora that we were fine. Freezing, but fine. In return, she gave me a pleasant update — the sale of the monsters I'd caught in the wildlands had brought in nearly sixty million! Most of it was from the A-rank creatures, though. Looked like we had taken down something really valuable. She also praised the new hires, saying they worked hard and well. Maxim was thrilled, though he did continue to pester Irina with his advances.

The blonde, big-breasted, and curvy woman had clearly caught his eye. But she wasn't too happy about the attention and had asked me to talk to him. Honestly, I might as well make him his own zombie maid. Does something like that exist?

I mean, someone who had been busty and beautiful in life and actually wanted to serve that old man? I had a feeling one day of work under him would feel like a month in the afterlife. Give it a week or two, and she'd have atoned for every sin she ever committed.

The factory windows had been repaired surprisingly fast, and I also passed along Leo's message about the varnish. Zhanna would speak with his father and arrange supply shipments. That would be a huge help since production was ramping up.

Maxim was training the zombies, and their work efficiency was steadily improving. Even now, the van could barely keep up with deliveries, and the money kept flowing in. We were moving on up!

I also asked Zhanna to look into the staff I'd found. After all, I had a diamond-tier account on the SCU website. Any information I needed was free. All I had to do was type in the staff's name, and bam! Instant details, including the price of the last one sold. Three hundred million! Even for an A-rank artifact, that was a lot.

"Why do you look so damn happy?" Katie muttered in irritation, eyeing my face. "Don't tell me you actually enjoy snuggling up to that goat?"

"You say that again, and I'll kick you so hard you won't know what hit you," Angelina growled, shooting Katie a death glare.

"I got in touch with home. Turns out, that staff is worth three hundred million."

"That's it? I thought it'd be at least four hundred," the rich girl said, genuinely surprised. I had no idea her family was so wealthy that three hundred million was considered low. "Can I buy it from you? Or rather, my family."

"Sure. I don't need it," I agreed, lifting my head slightly. I could see her face through the gap between the breasts resting on my head. She looked pleased with her purchase. And I was happy about the money. Honestly, I was just happy to be on this island in general.

Once I mastered teleporting between altars, I'd build my own kingdom here. No one would be able to reach me, and the surrounding islands would make for perfect hunting grounds.

"Scully!" Ivanov suddenly ran up to me. "You said you got in touch, right? Can you pass on a message?"

"Can it wait until morning? It's nighttime over there too."

"I suppose it can," he nodded, though I could see the hesitation in his eyes, and something else. Jealousy. He wanted to take my spot. Yeah, right! It was warm and cozy here. He could go find his own place to warm up. "I want to send a list of who's with us, along with some intel on the area."

"No problem," I nodded.

So Ivanov went off to supervise the mages. The waves kept battering us, and the sea level had risen so that soon it would start to flood us. The mages were already working to prevent that.

Those poor souls were working on the verge of complete exhaustion. There was no excuse to slack off on training. In my opinion, the level of preparation among the Academy students was extremely low. And it wasn't just my opinion — the Emperor himself was literally tearing and hurling things about, complicating the training. In short, it was good practice for them. Let them work!

"Hm?" I murmured as Angelina wrapped her arms around me, like batteries.

"What? You're allowed to hug me, but I'm not allowed to hug you?" she said, a trace of embarrassment in her voice. Anna was ready to pin the girl down.

"As you wish."

I closed my eyes and tried to fall asleep. It didn't work well because of the noise, but eventually I entered a state of half-slumber. In that state I managed to rest while still partially aware of what was happening.

The water level kept rising, and it began seeping in through the cracks. The mages did everything they could and, as they say, "busted their asses" just to avoid dying. And since I didn't see any black smoke, I knew that no one would die. Though I wouldn't tell them that.

My calmness reassured the girls, but sleep eluded them. They chatted quietly, asking Angelina questions, to which she replied and fired off counterquestions.

I ended up getting some good rest. The commotion had raised the air temperature, and people began to warm up. Sealing many of the cracks helped too.

Ventilation had to be installed in the caves. Basel attempted to make it at the very top of the caves, and it seemed to work. Although, water poured in from there. But then the air mages did their best. Magic is everything!

Closer to morning, the storm began to subside, and exhausted people collapsed into sleep without any strength. The temperature outside also started going up.

In the end, I got a good sleep and woke up

when everyone was still sleeping. I was hungry, but to break free from Angelina's grasps, I had to make an effort.

I walked through the house and unsealed all the windows, shattering the stones that had been installed to protect against water. Then I opened the door and stepped out onto the devastated beach. Many trees hadn't withstood the storm, but the palm trees proved resilient. They bent, but did not break.

"So... what should I eat?"

Here and there, one could spot marine life washed up on the beach. But then I decided to scout the area with the puppets. I was astonished by what I saw.

* * *

Almost an hour later
Gauss

Turns out, starting a fire without actual fire is pretty damn hard. But who's a genius? I'm a genius! I was sitting on a rock, roasting fish on a stick. And there was an entire bucket full of fish next to me.

"Man, some salt would be nice..." I grumbled, gnawing on the back of some unknown fish. Its back was meaty and delicious, but I didn't want to touch the belly. I also cleaned off the tail.

Each fish weighed about 14 ounces and kind of resembled a wolffish-smelt hybrid. This was my seventh one. I was also washing it down with canned stew and sweet, juicy corn. Didn't even know what was inside the can until I popped it open.

"Scully! Where the hell?!" Ivanov was awake. And not just him. With him shouting like that, he probably woke up the whole camp.

"What are you talking about?"

"The bucket! A metal one! And canned food? How?! Where did you get it?!" His voice had already drawn a crowd from the house — people were pouring out, staring in shock.

"Well, you know how the saying goes: 'early bird gets the worm,'" I shrugged and pointed to the left. I was sitting with my back to the sea.

Everyone turned their heads and saw... "A ship!" Ivanov was about to start stuttering at this rate. His nerves were really shot. He needed some rest or maybe some pills.

"A ship! It's a ship! We're saved!" someone shouted.

Yeah, no kidding, it's a ship. Where did they think I got all this fish from? The hold was packed with it. Still fresh, too.

It was a fishing vessel, not a huge one, definitely not big enough to carry everyone. But it could take the strongest of us, though first, it needed repairs.

"So, who here knows how to operate a ship?" I asked, and the crowd fell silent.

"What would you all do without me?" I shook my head and stood up.

"You know how to sail it?" Everyone stared at me, their eyes filled with desperate hope.

"No. But I can contact home and find out how."

You've changed the destiny of many people and get +712 divine energy, +10 believers.

End of Book Three

Want to be the first to know about our latest LitRPG, sci fi and fantasy titles from your favorite authors?

Subscribe to our **New Releases** newsletter:
http://eepurl.com/b7niIL

Thank you for reading *The Coming of God of Death!*

If you like what you've read, check out other sci fi, fantasy and LitRPG novels published by Magic Dome Books:

NEW RELEASES!

The Selected
A LitRPG Action Adventure Series
by Vasily Mahanenko & Yuri Vinokuroff

Nanomachines
A Progression Fantasy Adventure Series
by Nikolai Novikov

We Are Legion
A RealRPG Action Adventure Series
by Dmitry Dornichev & Evgeny Fox

The Dark Summoner
A Portal Progression Fantasy Series
by Andrei Tkachev

The Other Side
A Progression Fantasy Adventure Series
by Rodion Korablev

The Dark Healer
A Historical Progression Fantasy Series
by Alex Toxic & Nadya Lee

Me and My Demons
A Portal Progression Adventure Fantasy Series
by Oleg Sapphire & Alexey Kovtunov

The Village
A LitRPG Progression Fantasy Series
by Dmitry Dornichev & Alexey Kovtunov

Condemned (Lord Valevsky: Last of the Line)
A Progression Fantasy LitRPG Series
by Vasily Mahanenko

Living Ice
A Portal Progression Fantasy Series
by Dmitry Sheleg

Ghost in the System
An Apocalypse LitRPG Series
by Alexey Kovtunov

The Goldenblood Heir
A Portal Progression Fantasy Series
by Boris Romanovsky

Law of the Jungle
A Wuxia Progression Fantasy Adventure Series
by Vasily Mahanenko

Crossroads of Oblivion
A Portal Progression Fantasy Adventure Series
by Dem Mikhailov

The Healer's Way
A Portal Progression Fantasy Series
by Oleg Sapphire & Alexey Kovtunov

More books and series are coming out soon!

In order to have new books of the series translated faster, we need your help and support! Please consider leaving a review or spread the word by recommending *The Coming of God of Death* to your friends and posting the link on social media. The more people buy the book, the sooner we'll be able to make new translations available.

Thank you!

Till next time!